TILL FOREVER BEGINS

BOOK 1

TILL FOREVER SERIES

DONNA RICHARDS

Published: February 2026 by Chronos Publishing

ISBN: 978-1-917377-13-3 Paperback Edition
ISBN: 978-1-917377-14-0 Ebook

Editing by @pinpointediting
Book Cover by Jules Ripas
Illustrations (Chapter Art) by Matt Goldup

To all the people that haven't found their wings…
let the morally grey man be your butterfly.

ACKNOWLEDGEMENTS

Firstly, thank you for taking the time to buy and read my book. It really means the world to me that you wanted to. I really appreciate it, and I hope you stay along for the ride.

Taryn: Thank you so much for taking on the Till Forever Series. It really means a lot to me that you believe in it.

PinPointEditing: Thank you for being so kind and understanding with everything you do. You've helped me realise that I can do this and continue to grow with my writing. I don't just consider you my editor, but a friend. I hope you're prepared for more voice notes and messages along this journey.

EverAfter PR: Thank you so much for being there from day one and helping me through the world of social media. You've helped me learn and grow, and I consider you a friend.

To my family: Thank you for taking the time to ask how it was all going and for supporting me in my writing. You've always been there when I needed support, and I'm truly grateful for it.

K & K: You two wonderful ladies have been so supportive and kind since I've met you. Thank you for being there with all your help. I know we will forever be friends.

Shaylynn: You are such a stunning young woman who I've watched grow from a baby. You have been so excited and invested in my writing all the way through. I cannot wait for our road trips to the author events! You keep shining, girl! Love you!

Jodi: To think you've been stuck with me as a friend for 24 years! You poor soul! lol I'm sure I've bored you half to death with talking about my books and everything I'm going to do. Thank you for sticking with me all these years.

Kate, my mate: Thank you for letting me ramble on about my books and ideas. Also, thanks for letting me air you for periods of time because I was writing! haha I know you love me really. Thank you for being my friend and letting me do car karaoke every time we are in the car together.

To my beautiful daughter: You are such a kind, beautiful girl who I love wholeheartedly. Remember, no matter what, you can do anything you dream of.

To my little boy: You have been through a lot in the beginning, but you fought through it all, and I know that's what you'll continue to do in life. I love you both! Xx

Author's Note

Please note: This series is set in London and is written in British English.

County Lines: County Lines is a term used to describe gangs and organised crime rings that deal with illegal activities within the UK. This term is normally used in regards to trafficking drugs to and from different areas of the country. However, in the story, it refers to crime organisations that run 'counties' and deal with multiple illegal activities, not just drugs.

Please read the content warning on the next page.

Content/Trigger Warning

Readers are strongly advised to read the trigger warnings listed below. This book is intended for readers 18 and above, as it contains morally complex characters and dark themes.

Till Forever Begins includes but is not limited to the following:

Dubious consent scenarios, Mention of emotional abuse, Alcohol consumption, Blood and gore depiction, Dismemberment, Mention of death of a parent, Gun violence, Kidnapping, Organised crime, Mention of Domestic Violence, Mention of controlling behaviour, Mention of GBH with intent – Domestic Abuse, Mention of prisoner on remand, Attempted sexual assault (Not between MCs), Psychological manipulation – stalking and harassment (not between MCs), Drugging, Fighting, Physical GBH/Assault/Violence (Not between MCs), Sexual assault/rape (not mentioned but can be interpreted) (Not between MCs), Torture, Explicit sexual content.

Whilst I have tried to include all the warnings, it's important to remember that triggers are subjective and personal to each individual. If you feel a trigger needs to be added or to discuss, then please email me at donnarichards@donna-richards.com

1
ARIA

"Miss…? Miss…?" The taxi driver interrupted my thoughts. "Are you getting out?"

My hand was refusing to open the door. Was it trembling slightly, or was my mind playing tricks on me?

Truthfully, I didn't want to get out of the cab. Instead, I wanted to run home and hide from the world. Bracing myself, I took a deep, shuddering breath. Fumbling with the handle, I willed my body to work again. I reluctantly stepped out, and the taxi's engine thrummed as it drove off—my one escape gone.

I looked down, straightening my pencil skirt and smoothing my blouse. People rushed past in all directions, busy on their phones as they swerved around each other.

My knees were trembling so badly I felt that they were about to give out, so, I straightened my spine and focused on moving to the entrance of the tall, sleek building before me. Taking a deep breath, I walked through the lobby, my heels echoing off the white marble floor; every step a reminder that I was free, no longer under the control that once defined my life. This was where I would start being *me* again.

I reached the desk, and the receptionist glanced up politely. "Welcome to Luxe Corp. How may I help you today?"

I wondered how many times a day she had to say that. "Hi, I'm Aria Summers. I'm here for my induction and to do some paperwork," I said, trying not to sound as anxious as I felt. "I start Monday."

"Ah, yes; the new admin. Welcome to Luxe Corp."

I gave her an awkward smile. I guessed it was her job to know who was coming and going.

"This way," she said as she stepped out from behind the desk, her smile never leaving her face.

I followed her to the lift, not looking back but nervously observing my surroundings. Subtle tones of vanilla scented the air.

The receptionist opened the lift doors and pushed the button for the floor we needed, giving me a moment to compose myself.

The thirty-eighth floor was a complete contrast to the quiet space downstairs. The office buzzed with conversation, keyboards tapping in sync with one another. No one lingered, not a minute wasted. It was the type of place where every second cost money, and they all seemed to know it.

It was everything you'd expect from a high-end Canary Wharf office.

The hallway seemed to go on forever, with a few matte black door-frames set along the ivory coloured walls decorated with monochrome photography showing off the landmarks of London.

As I hurried to keep up with the receptionist, I could feel eyes burning into me.

She pointed as we walked. "There's a break room down there where you can get coffee. Please help yourself once you've completed onboarding with HR, and the bathrooms are further down the hall. This afternoon will be your induction."

Eventually, she pushed her way through a door to a small room. In the office beyond, a man was visible through the floor-to-ceiling windows, his back to me. He must have been the CEO. My new boss. I hadn't met him at my interview; that had been with the HR manager. I guessed people like him didn't need to worry about new starters. His arms were gesturing, suggesting he was talking on the phone, his broad shoulders stretching his suit jacket with each hand movement.

"This is Mr Knight's office—our CEO. Sometimes you'll have to take work to him," explained the receptionist.

Mr Knight? My heart jumped into my throat.

No, it couldn't be.

She started walking back through into the main office, and I hurried to keep up.

We stopped at a small desk near the back. It was modern and white, the stationery neatly arranged around it—a contrast to my head, which seemed to be an utter mess right now.

"This is your desk." I nervously glanced down, tugging at my sleeves. "There are details of how to log in to the laptop. Once on, it will prompt you to complete your recruitment documents for HR. If you have any issues, they will be able to help you." She smiled again and left. Nervously looking around at everyone, who no longer seemed at all interested that I was there, I sat down, turned the laptop on, and followed the instructions.

It hadn't taken long to complete and submit the HR forms, and now I was treating myself to a well-deserved coffee in the break room before I tackled the Health and Safety training online. The machine finished making my cappuccino, and I grabbed the cup, placed a lid on it, and turned around—bumping straight into someone. He grabbed my arms to steady me, and I froze at the familiar scent of citrus and spice, something I hadn't encountered since—

"Aria?" he whispered.

I didn't want to look up, but my eyes had other ideas.

That perfectly sculpted jawline showed his rugged side, a shadow of stubble defining its shape, and I saw the tattoos that were trying to escape the collar of his shirt. I took a step back, releasing my grip on his toned arms. I knew this face too well, knew the crystal-blue eyes that stared straight into my soul.

Sebastian Knight.

Of all people, it had to be him.

I'd escaped one past, only to be slammed back into another.

"What are you doing here?" he asked.

"I … I work here," I replied hesitantly.

His eyes widened briefly, a flicker of surprise passing

through his gaze.

"Small world, little sis," he said as he leaned casually against the wall.

"Don't call me that."

We were never related. Our parents met one summer and tied the knot, some whirlwind romance that turned into a nightmare. For the two years they were together, all they did was argue.

"Still as sassy as ever." He chuckled.

I ignored the jolt of pleasure that chuckle sent through me and asked, "What are you doing here?"

"I'm the CEO."

My eyes widened as my stomach dropped to my toes. "What?"

Sebastian was my … boss? My cheeks burned. Could he tell how flustered I was? I touched them to check, but they were ice cold—probably from shock.

"I've got training I need to do," I said abruptly.

He put his hand out, gesturing that I could go.

I swallowed hard.

The last time I'd seen Sebastian was the night he'd left me standing in the kitchen, four years ago.

ET LUX IN
TENEBRIS
LUCET

2

SEBASTIAN

I sat back in my chair, the black leather creaking, and stared absently into the untouched glass of whisky in my hand. It was only 11 a.m., but after seeing her, I felt the need for the burn of alcohol. My screen flashed with a meeting reminder. I absently noted it, my thoughts lingering on Aria Summers.

When I'd last seen her, she was an eighteen-year-old. That girl was a vibrant little soul. She'd notice the beauty in everything, full of empathy and compassion for others. Her presence had a calming effect on everyone around her. She was preparing to start uni to study social work, to pursue a dream of wanting to support people through their hardest times.

I was surprised to remember that she still smelled the same, that fresh green apple scent. I was never sure if it were her brand of shampoo, but it lingered whenever she was near.

Seeing her again stirred something in me. Something I hadn't felt in years. Was it hope or connection? I wasn't ready to admit it to myself.

Alongside that positive feeling was the opposite—guilt.

It had been four years since the night I'd left her, bright-eyed and full of sass. I was twenty-two, already consumed by a shadowy underground world my family knew nothing about. The hurt in her eyes had haunted me since I walked away.

I downed the drink, pushing those memories back down as far as they would go, then got up and made my way into the main office, reaching Aria's desk at the back.

"Let's get lunch."

Her eyes darted around at everyone, undoubtedly all looking at us, before they met mine. I couldn't care less that people were staring. None of them would dare say a word to me.

"I don't think that's a good idea. I don't even know when my lunch break is," she said quietly.

I held out my hand, and she stared at it, the conflict clear on her face. She hesitated for a second longer, sighed, but then took it and stood. Her touch was gentle, like it was when we were younger. Placing my hand on the small of her back, I guided her out of the office.

It wasn't long before we reached the restaurant and the waiter greeted me, taking us to my usual table. I pulled the chair out for Aria, and she sat with her hands in her lap, looking around, before sitting opposite her.

"Usual?" the waiter asked.

"Yes, and a cappuccino."

He gave us a curt nod and left. I looked over at Aria, who gave me a tight smile. Before I could speak, Hayden Lyons, my brother in all but name, strolled in, his coiled hair bouncing. I'd met Hayden ten years ago when I was sixteen, in the dark world of a crowded underground ring, both of us young, ready to take on a world that offered us more than the life above.

He was quick in the ring, but his comebacks were quicker.

He was my first fight, and he quickly became my brother—when I left that world, he stayed, but our friendship had remained solid.

His eyes widened as he realised who I was sitting with.

"Aria Summers. It's been too long." He smiled at her, and she got up, giving him a small hug.

"Hey, Hayden. What are you doing here?"

"Had a meeting with this guy." He whacked me on the shoulder. "Didn't realise you were back."

The waiter came over with our drinks and nodded at Hayden, wandering off again to get him his usual.

"I've only been back for a short while," she said as they both sat down.

"You didn't tell me." Hayden looked over at me as he sat at the table.

"I didn't know."

Confusion ran over his face.

"She started at Luxe Corp today. I had no idea."

Aria tucked her natural blonde hair behind her ears, then her hands fell to her lap again.

The waiter brought Hayden's rum, and he took a sip.

"We should go out for a drink tonight. Catch up," he suggested.

I swirled the amber liquid in my glass, then brought it to my lips, my eyes fixed on Aria.

"Oh, erm, I've got plans."

"C'mon, it'll be fun." He flashed his smile at her. "I'll bring Serfina. You remember her, don't you?"

Hayden's girlfriend loved a night out. Any chance she had to get dressed up and parade him around, she took.

She bit her lip, and my eyes dropped to it for a moment.

I rubbed the back of my neck. "You don't have to, if you've already got plans."

"Erm, sure …"

"Great." Hayden patted me on the chest. "Sebastian will pick you up."

A knock at the door sounded, and I looked up to Aria entering my office.

"HR said you wanted to see me?"

"Ah, yes. Sit down."

She did, and a silence fell over us for a few seconds.

"I'm in the market for a new PA."

She arched her brow, confusion in her eyes. "Ok …"

"So, go get your things, and bring them to the desk outside my office."

"What?"

"I'm making you my new PA."

"Sebastian, I'm not qualified to do that. I'm fine where I am."

I stood and leaned against the desk next to her.

"Aria, you know me better than anyone. You'll be fine, and anything you don't know, I can show you."

"But isn't there meant to be some kind of process—"

I cut her off, tilting her chin with a finger for her eyes to meet mine. "All the paperwork is done. You don't have to worry about anything."

"But I have my induction—"

"I've sorted it all. You don't need to do it. Just get your things, and I can go through some bits with you."

She chewed her lip, her fingers playing with her sleeves. I took hold of them.

"You'll be fine, I know you will," I reassured her.

She smiled, still a little unsure, but her grey eyes shimmered in the light. "Thank you." She gave me a tentative hug and quickly stepped back.

That was odd. She was a tactile girl. Over the years, I'd missed her spontaneous hugs and how we used to be. I'd never expected Aria to walk back into my life, but now that she was, I was going to keep her as close to me as possible. I'd do anything for this girl, and if making her my PA would put a smile on her face, then I'd take that and anything else that came with it. I wanted to know what had dimmed her exuberance for life and why she was taking an admin job when she'd always dreamed of being a social worker.

It wasn't long before she returned with all her things and sat at her new desk.

I leaned in behind as she logged on. Fuck. That damn apple smell of hers tingled all my senses at once. I placed my hand on top of hers that rested on the mouse. It felt soft and delicate, just like her.

My eyes flicked down her body, slowly trailing back up to meet her own for a few seconds, before locking onto the screen. "If you click over here into this program"—my hand moved the mouse, taking hers with me—"you can do it all from there."

My hand lingered on hers, and I turned to face her. Her cheeks were flushed, and she jerked her hand from underneath mine, placing it firmly in her lap as though my touch could cause her pain.

"Thanks," she mumbled, staring at her lap.

"If you need anything at all, you know where I am."

With that, I straightened and walked back into my office.

Of course, I sat there watching her out of the window. Whilst it was a view I was going to enjoy, Aria had just become a puzzle I needed to solve. Something was not as it should be with my girl.

I had business to do though, and I couldn't sit and pine like a schoolgirl, so I picked up my phone and scrolled through the contacts until I brought up Scott Langley's number.

"Sebastian Knight, what can I do for you?"

"I've got a business opportunity I thought you might be interested in."

"You know I'd never pass up a chance to work with your name."

"I thought you'd say that. My PA will set up a meeting next week."

"Looking forward to it."

With that, I hung up. The Langleys were a powerful, wealthy family. My father had done business with Scott's father before I had my dad removed from the company. The Langleys weren't in our league, but they weren't far off.

"Aria?" I called out as I opened the office door.

She turned to face me.

"I need you to set up a meeting for me."

"Ok." She smiled.

"Do you need me to go through how to do it with you?"

"I'm sure I can work it out," she replied, then turned to face her screen.

She probably could, but I was still going to watch her. Was this going to be a problem and could I keep the boundaries of being her boss?

3

ARIA

I threw my bag on the floor and sank into the sofa. What a day. I rubbed my forehead back and forth, then let out a yawn, brushing my hair back. I bit my lip, debating for a moment whether to simply not go back on Monday.

But, Sebastian was *here*, of all places, and now I was his PA. Four years and I still felt that excitement in my stomach when he was near.

He's your boss now. You need to forget the past and move forward.

At least I'd managed my first day without any hiccups. That was a small victory.

I looked around at the unpacked boxes scattered on the floor. It had been a few weeks since I'd moved from Leeds to Woolwich, yet I couldn't bring myself to fully trust that time was behind me. It wasn't the nicest place to live, but it was all I could afford right now. My intention was to find somewhere better with the money from this new job.

I took my phone out of my pocket, noticing a text from my mum.

Mum: *Hi darling, how was your first day? X*

Oh, it was great. I only bumped into my former stepbrother who I've had feelings for the whole time I've known him, and guess what? He's my boss.

No. I couldn't tell her that.

Aria: *Yeah, today was good. I was just getting settled really x*

Mum: *That's good to hear, darling. Hope I can see you soon. I miss you x*

Aria: *I miss you too x*

Laughter from the TV, a sitcom of some kind, startled me out of my reverie. I hated a quiet apartment, and I'd switched it on as soon as I'd walked in. I buried my face in my hands. Why did I agree to go out tonight?

Since moving back, my social life had been non-existent. The only time I saw my neighbours was when they were screaming at each other in the hall. Not that it was any better in Leeds. There was no point trying to make friends. It was easier that way—no one would ask questions that I couldn't and didn't want to answer.

There was only one person I had trusted, and he had paid me off and ordered me to leave. The last place I'd seen him had been in that hospital room.

Maybe I should let him know I was safe. I bit my lip as I scrolled through my phone, bringing his contact up. My thumb hovered over it, hesitating.

No. I should leave the past where it belonged.

A loud knock at the door startled me, fear crashing through my body. I took a deep breath, my heart racing as I made my way over.

"Who's there?"

"It's me." Sebastian's cool tones drifted through the door.

I gripped the handle and forced it down, palm sweaty against the cold brass.

Sebastian stood there, leaning casually against the frame with a Cheshire-cat grin.

"Why aren't you ready? Get dressed, Nyx."

My breath caught. *Nyx.* I hadn't heard that nickname for so long.

"How do you know where I live?" I questioned, folding my arms.

He brushed his raven hair back from his face, his smile widening. "You work for me. I have access to everything."

"That's a breach in company policy, you know."

"Well, you did agree to me picking you up. How else would I know where to come?" He laughed to himself, a sound as intoxicating as he was. Charm always did come naturally to Sebastian.

"You agreed to this, and I'm not leaving until you're ready. Now go." He winked.

I was in two minds. A night out sounded fun and exciting, something I hadn't had in a long time. But equally terrifying was the thought of leaving my comfort zone … I was so used to a safe routine that I'd forgotten what it was like to be twenty-two. Maybe I should have been out enjoying myself, but after everything I'd been through, I just didn't think I knew how to anymore.

I begrudgingly opened the door wider, letting him into my flat. He stepped in, looking around the living room.

"You should really unpack at some point."

I rolled my eyes at him as he sat on my sofa, his arm naturally hanging over it as he observed me.

"Off you go," he said, and without any more thought, I did.

It had been so long since I'd been anywhere. I looked through the clothes hanging up in my wardrobe, not sure what to wear. I pulled out a few options and slung them on the bed, contemplating for a few moments. I picked up a long red dress and held it against me, turning to look in the mirror before screwing up my face and throwing it back. I sighed, plonking myself on the bed. Maybe if I sat here long enough, he'd leave me in peace.

No chance. Sebastian was nothing if not persistent, and he always got what he wanted.

Sure enough, the bedroom door soon burst open to Sebastian standing there.

"Nyx, what's taking so long?"

My eyes widened, heart racing, as I stood from the bed. "Sebastian, you can't just burst into my room."

He soon closed the distance between us as he made his way over to me, glancing down at the clothes on my bed, then meeting my gaze. I swallowed hard.

"The black one," he said, picking it up from the pile and holding it out. My eyes flickered down to it in his hands.

"I don't think …"

He raised an eyebrow, effectively cutting my protests off.

He reached out slowly, tentatively, his fingers stroking across my jawline, and he tilted my head to meet his eyes.

"Ok," was all I managed to get out.

He leaned into my ear. "Good girl." His voice was barely a whisper.

My breath hitched, that raw sound of his voice vibrating through every nerve in my body, hitting me right at my core.

I shouldn't cross that line. Not again. Not now after everything I'd escaped. I couldn't go through any more pain, but Sebastian was my safety. Always had been.

I looked down at the dress and took it from his hand. He needed to leave this room before I started something that should never happen between us.

I took a deep breath as he lingered. "Do you need to watch me get dressed as well?" Trying for a confidence I didn't feel, I pushed him. "Get out."

He smiled, rubbing his fingers over his chin, his eyes flickering over me one last time before he made his way to the door.

I held up the tight black bodycon dress he had picked out. He'd always had good taste.

ET LUX IN
TENEBRIS
LUCET

4

SEBASTIAN

I reluctantly returned to the living room to wait for Aria to get dressed. I didn't think she needed me hovering over her, despite not wanting to let her out of my sight. She managed to make me feel the same way I did for her when she was eighteen.

My eyes drifted to a photo frame on the cabinet, and I found myself drawing closer. It was a picture of Aria with her mum in Margate. She must have only been around seventeen here. They looked happy—something I hadn't been often growing up.

I ran my thumb over the photo thoughtfully before placing it back on its shelf.

My eyes flickered to the different coloured glass butterflies that sat covered by a bell jar on the windowsill. She'd always loved butterflies. Her bedroom was full of them when we were younger, on the walls and pretty ornaments.

"I'm ready," Aria said softly from behind me.

I turned to face her and paused, my heart racing. The dress hugged her in all the right places, like I knew it would. Her blonde hair sat perfectly around her face; her eyes were dressed in soft, smoky shades of taupe and plum, accentuating them. She was beautiful—she had always been beautiful, but there was a more graceful beauty now that she was no longer a self-conscious teen.

Her grey eyes twinkled like the moon. That's why I called her Nyx—after the Greek goddess of the night. A light in the darkness I didn't deserve but couldn't look away from.

"Did you want a picture?" she asked, her brows raised. Had I been staring too long?

"Why would I need a picture when I'm stuck with you every day?"

I studied her face, expecting her to come back with something smart like she used to, but instead, her eyes lost that twinkle, the light I treasured so much extinguished with a single word.

What had happened to her?

"I mean, us working together and everything." I tried to smooth it over, but she only gave me a tight smile in return. I cleared my throat. "Shall we get going?"

The music from the stereo broke the awkward silence in the car. I glanced over at Aria; she was looking out the window. I opened my mouth to speak, but she beat me to it.

"Sebastian."

"Nyx."

Our eyes met for a split second as her warm smile returned.

"I didn't mean it the way it came out," I explained.

"Honestly, it's fine. Let's just have a good night." She placed her hand on mine, which was resting on my thigh.

I squeezed it, smiling back before turning my gaze to the road. Her hand was as warm and soft as I remembered. I probably held it a little longer than I should have, but I missed everything about her. She'd always managed to make me feel seen in a world that had only ever shown me pain. I just couldn't place what was so off about her.

It didn't take us long to arrive, and I pulled up in my usual spot outside the club. I looked over at Aria again; she was playing with the sleeve of her dress. Was the fearless girl I'd known nervous?

"We don't have to go in if you don't want to," I said softly.

"I want to." She let go of her sleeve and smiled at me.

I took her at her word and stepped out of the car. Music thudded against the club doors, spilling out onto the street. I adjusted the ID bracelet on my wrist before walking around to her side and opening the door. I took her hand, helping her out, and didn't let go. The queue was long, but I guided her straight to the front.

"Mr. Knight," the bouncer greeted me, nodding.

I acknowledged him as he removed the barrier to let us through. I kept a firm grip on Aria's hand as I guided her through the entrance to the main club area, looking back now and then to check she was ok. The music vibrated through me as I stopped to look back at her one last time. Our eyes met and she smiled at me again, reassuring me enough that I finally released her hand.

I scanned the room for Hayden and Serfina—they were by the bar, drinks already waiting.

I greeted Hayden with our usual bro handshake. He raised his eyebrows and glanced at Aria as we pulled apart. I rolled my eyes at him.

Hayden cleared his throat, his eyes meeting Aria's as she politely smiled.

"Good to see you again, Aria," Hayden said.

Serfina, on the other hand, was her usual excited self and pulled me straight in, squeezing tight.

"Sebastian, where have you been hiding?" she asked cheerfully.

"My usual spot. The office."

"Such an important businessman now."

"Something like that."

She turned to look at Aria. "Look how beautiful you are," she said, taking hold of her hands and admiring her.

A beauty she was, but I didn't want to let them know I thought that.

"Hey, Serfina. I'm really glad to see you again." Aria smiled at her.

"You must be the only one." I chuckled, gently placing my hand on the small of her back.

"Oh, hush you," Serfina said, playfully nudging me, then wasted no time pulling Aria into her orbit.

"Get this down you, girl," Serfina said, handing Aria a drink from their collection on the bar.

Aria stared at the drink for a few seconds, wariness replacing the smile, before downing it, causing her face to screw up with the aftertaste. Hayden and Serfina cheered for her. I, on the other hand, felt something else. Something I didn't want to put a name to.

"She's a keeper," Serfina whispered in my ear.

I smiled politely back at her, dismissing her comment, and she pouted at me in response, taking hold of Aria's hand. "Let's leave the boys to their grouchiness and go party."

Hayden tapped my chest, bringing my attention back to him, and I grabbed my drink from the bar.

"She seems … different," Hayden mused.

"She is. She's quieter. Something has happened to her. I don't know what." My eyes drifted back to Aria, who was watching Serfina down another shot, not taking one herself.

"It's been four years. People change." Hayden shrugged, taking a sip of his drink.

I looked back at him. "We both know this girl used to love a party."

"Maybe she's all partied out and manages to keep her shoes together now."

I laughed. The number of times Aria had called me drunk at some random house party, complaining she had lost a shoe. It was like Cinderella had met *Groundhog Day*.

"Imagine starting a job and finding out your previous stepbrother, who you haven't seen in four years, is now your boss. Of course you'd be adjusting to it all."

"Yeah, but she knows me."

"Correction. She knew you. Well, what you wanted her to see, anyway. I know you two had some weird 'connection' shit going on" he smirked at me before he continued "but just give her time."

I frowned at him. I'd never met anyone like Aria in my life. The second I saw her, I knew there was something special about her. I'd felt a need to protect her and keep her safe from the darkness of the world. She meant everything to me back then, this bright little spark who'd challenge me when I was being a dick and put me in my place.

"I'm going to check on her."

Hayden grabbed my arm before I could move. "She's fine with Serfina. Besides ..." Hayden raised his brows in the opposite direction of Aria, and I soon followed. "Looks like you've got an admirer."

I turned to glance over, my eyes greeted by a smiling brunette in the corner. She was the typical woman I would go for—someone who wouldn't expect more than one night. Someone like all the rest.

It was probably better that I left Aria; she didn't need me swarming her. She was my PA now, someone I shouldn't want. Completely off limits.

But forbidden fruits always tasted sweeter.

And I always got what I wanted, no matter the cost.

And right now, something was telling me I wanted Aria.

ET LUX IN TENEBRIS LUCET

5

SEBASTIAN

Four Years Ago

The only thing illuminating the hotel room was the moonlight.

It wasn't anything fancy, but all I needed was a bed.

Well, sometimes I didn't even need that.

"I saw you fighting earlier tonight." The brunette's voice was low and breathy. "I had to come and speak to you at the bar." Her fingers made their way to my belt buckle and unclipped it, releasing me. Her eyes flickered down, then met mine with a seductive look. She leaned into my ear. "I'm going to enjoy gagging on that," she whispered.

I hated it when they talked.

I grabbed the back of her head and pushed her to her knees. Her eyes met mine, her hand wrapping around my cock, and she started stroking. She licked the pre-cum off the tip, tingling every nerve in my body, then teased my cock with her tongue.

My phone screen lit up, vibrating violently on the side.

Whoever it was could wait.

I felt the brunette's lips start to slide up and down, making my cock wet with each motion. I slowly started to move my hips, helping her take it all.

My phone vibrated again, and this time my eyes flickered to the screen.

Aria.

It was 3:15 a.m.

Why was she calling so late?

I reached over and grabbed it, pressing the button to answer.

"Sebastian, I lost my shoe," she slurred, her voice lingering on the word "shoe" for way too long. "I can't find it. Can you help me, please?"

Was she drunk? There was music blaring in the background.

I pulled my body back, my cock falling from the woman's mouth. She looked up, surprised.

"Where are you?"

"Erm, I'm not sure."

I held the phone to my ear with my shoulder as I pulled my boxers and trousers back up, tucking my softening cock back in.

"Aria, can you send me your location?" I zipped my trousers back up and then clipped my buckle back together. The woman stood up and huffed as she sat on the bed. I ignored her.

My phone pinged in my ear, so I pulled it away, glancing at the screen.

What was she doing in Hackney?

"Did you get it?"

I put my phone back to my ear. "Yeah. Stay there, I'm coming to get you."

"Ok, Sebastian. Just don't be too long; I'm starving."

I couldn't help but huff out a laugh. "I'll take you to get some food. Just promise me you won't move from there, Nyx."

"I promise," she whispered.

I ended the call and slid my phone into my pocket.

"You're going to leave me for another woman? Just like that?" the brunette asked. I'd almost forgotten she was still here.

"I am. Stay if you want, the room is paid for."

No woman compared to Aria. If she needed me, I'd be there in a heartbeat, and I wasn't about to forget that for a woman who meant nothing to me.

"When can I see you again?" She leaned forward, crossing her legs.

"That's not going to happen."

There was no guilt on my part. These sorts of women were nothing more than objects to me. A way to release that tension. This one was no different, and they knew what they were getting when they approached me. I picked up my jacket, making sure I had everything, then made my way to the door.

I turned back for a second. "Help yourself to the minibar."

I pulled up to the curb outside the location Aria had given me. A few people were hanging around on the pavement outside the house. They were clearly drunk, and the party looked like it was still going, with the music blaring and lights flashing.

There was no sign of Aria, though.

I dialled her number, and she soon answered.

"Where are you? I told you to stay here."

A knock came at my window. "I'm here." She said it through the phone, but she had a huge smile on her face.

I ended the call and stepped outside the car. "Nyx, what are you doing at a place like this?"

Her long, blonde hair wasn't straight like she normally wore it; it was bouncy and full of loose curls. Her shimmering grey eyes were unfocused—clearly from the alcohol—and her arms were exposed to the cold air, goose bumps covering them. She stood there in bare feet, the shortest skirt, her top barely covering her stomach, and one stiletto heel in her hand. I unzipped my jacket and wrapped it around her to keep her warm. She may have been a month off eighteen, but she didn't need to dress like that.

"What happened to the other shoe?"

She threw her arms in the air. "That's why I called. I lost it."

"And you thought you'd call Prince Charming?"

She turned to face me and patted my chest. "You're just a diamond in the rough."

"Ok, no more Disney references for you tonight." I laughed as she linked her arm through mine.

"Help me find my shoe?" She looked up at me with a wide smile, her eyes gleaming.

"Fine."

Aria looked out the window as I drove through the city, making our way home. "Oh, that one's open!"

I pulled into a lay-by next to the chicken and chip shop, turned the ignition off, and then got out. Aria was already at the shop door.

"What can I get you, boss?" the man behind the counter asked me.

I looked down at Aria. "What do you want?"

She placed her finger on her lips and examined the board for a few moments.

"A chicken burger with loads of mayonnaise and chips," she said. "Oh, and a Strawberry Miranda."

"And you, boss?"

"I'm good."

He nodded and started preparing the food. Aria went and sat down at a plastic table, crossing her legs, then her foot started to swing slightly. She still had my jacket on, but if I had it my way, she'd be wearing a pair of my joggers from my car boot to cover her bare legs as well.

My eyes made their way to her feet. "You dragged me around that house party to find your shoe. You're still walking around barefoot?"

"My feet hurt. If you didn't have clown feet, I'd have stolen your trainers from the car."

I snorted. "Clown feet?"

"Yes, those big old size fourteens of yours."

The man came over and placed the food down on the table. I watched her pick up the chicken burger, admiring it for a few moments. But before she could take a bite, I snatched it from her and bit into it myself.

"You're such a loser." She laughed, throwing a chip at me, then rescued the burger from my hand.

"You love it really, Nyx." I grinned at her.

Her eyes met mine. "That's debatable."

6

ARIA

Present

Serfina held my hand as she towed me through the crowd of people, making our way to the dance floor. The place was filled with people moving and having a good time. The bass sent vibrations through the room, causing the floor to shake. We found a spot where there was room for us to slide in. After the last few years, I owed it to myself to relax and have fun. I had been locked away and caged like a bird, and I'd stopped drinking, preferring to keep my guard up at all times. But now, standing here on this pulsing dance floor, watching the crowd sway with the beat, I felt … different.

Was this what freedom felt like?

I didn't know how to act without the constraints I was so used to. I had lost so much of myself. I was trying, fighting to get it back, but those memories of hands tightly gripped around my neck, followed by controlling whispers in my ear, lingered in the back of my mind.

Not tonight.

Tonight, I was going to forget.

I watched Serfina dancing around, her hips moving in time with the beat. She took hold of my hand, shaking it to loosen me up and get me dancing. Her energy must have flowed through me as my feet started to awkwardly join her. I could feel my heart syncing with the beat as it flowed through me, and with each vibration, it felt like the chains were breaking free.

The strobe lights flashed on and off over the crowd, making everything move in slow motion. Heat poured out of those dancing, mixing into the sea of people, their chatter drowned out by the pounding music. The little alcohol I'd had now spread through my veins, warming up all my senses at once, my body starting to loosen. I took a deep breath and let the music move me forward as Serfina pulled me closer. My hips now naturally met each beat as I ran my hands up my body to the sky.

Lost to the sensations, I didn't realise Serfina had disappeared back to the bar until she shoved another shot under my nose.

"Have another," she giggled.

As I took it from her hand, my eyes searched out Sebastian and Hayden—I hadn't seen them since we'd hit the dance floor.

I clocked Hayden, casually leaning against the bar, drink in hand, and sure enough, Sebastian was a little farther along—with a woman. At first, it looked like she was whispering in his ear, but when I squinted, I saw it.

She was kissing his neck, her hand running through his hair.

But his eyes were locked on me.

A burning sensation filled my stomach, and my heart skipped a beat.

I downed the shot, unable to take my eyes off them.

Serfina must have followed my gaze, because she shouted over the music, “That’s our Sebastian for you! Don’t worry about it.”

I didn’t want to worry about it, but I had this sinking feeling in my stomach, something I couldn’t shake.

I grabbed Serfina’s hand and dragged her to the dance floor, determined to shake Sebastian from my thoughts.

Serfina looked at me, surprise on her face. “Damn, girl, you can really move.”

A few dances later, I pointed at the bar. “Do you want another drink? I need some water.”

She raised an eyebrow. “Water? I’m good, girl. I’ll get some for you, though.” She giggled, wiggling off.

We spent most of the night on the dance floor, laughing and moving to the beat, until my feet needed a rest and Serfina had to use the bathroom. I stood at the bar alone, recuperating and drinking a vodka and Coke. I was starting to feel more like myself and thought one more drink would be ok. I noticed a tall, attractive guy at the other end looking at me, his dirty blonde hair pulled back, a few strands falling over his face. His shirt hugged his muscles; the buttons looked like they were pulling around his chest. I smiled shyly at him but then heard a voice from the past. *“Who are you smiling at? You look at me and no one else."* I tried to ignore it, but as the guy made his way to me, I started to panic a little—it had been so long since I'd interacted with anyone at a place like this, let alone spoken to a stranger. There had been a point when I wasn't allowed to speak to men at all. I shook myself from the memories just as he reached me.

"I couldn't help but notice you throughout the night. You're stunning."

He handed me a shot, and I met his eyes as he smiled at me. What harm could it do? I downed it, screwing my face up, this one had a strange, metallic aftertaste. This guy clearly had terrible taste in alcohol. He leaned back into me. His woody-spiced cologne lingered in my nose, and my cheeks burned.

"I'm Max."

"Aria."

His hands gently rested on my hips so he could lean in to talk to me over the music. I tensed but went with it, not wanting to cause a scene, but I was uncomfortable having a man I didn't know touch me.

"I saw you dancing. I couldn't pass up the opportunity to talk to you," he said.

I met him with a smile. Then, he did something I was not expecting: he moved his hands down to my bum, squeezing it as he pulled me into him. Who did this guy think he was?

"Let go of me." I pushed at his chest.

"Don't play hard to get," he replied, tightening his grip on me.

I felt sick to my stomach as I used all my strength to push his arms off me, but it was no use. His hands ran up my back, reaching my neck and making my skin crawl. He pushed the back of my head, trying to kiss me, but before his lips could meet mine, he was yanked away.

Sebastian.

He had grabbed Max's shirt from behind. Sebastian now stood in front of me, his eyes darting around my face and body. His hands touched my shoulders and then settled on my cheeks, looking into my eyes.

"Are you ok? Did he hurt you?" he asked, concern running through his voice.

"I-I'm fine," I managed to get out. "Sebastian, behind—"

Before I could get the rest of my words out, Max smashed a glass bottle over the back of Sebastian's head, causing him to stumble into me. I grabbed his arms to steady him. He touched the back of his head before looking down at his hand.

There was blood on his fingers.

ET LUX IN TENEBRIS LUCET

7

SEBASTIAN

It wasn't the first time I'd been bottled, and it probably wouldn't be the last.

My eyes darted back to Aria. Her face was pale, her hand over her mouth as she looked at my bloodstained fingers. I shifted my stance, blocking her view, and turned around to face the man standing there with a smug look on his face.

He wouldn't find it funny in a minute.

"Do you know who I am?" I asked calmly.

"I don't give a shit who you are," he shot back.

A smirk curled on my lips as I pushed back my hair from my face. Then I swung, catching him clean on the jaw. He stumbled back, falling to the floor, before wiping the blood away from his lip.

"You'll pay for this!" he snarled from the floor, slowly getting up and wiping his lip again.

I felt someone tug at my arm, forcing me to turn around. Aria stood there, staring at me, fear flickering through her eyes.

Was she scared of *me*?

"Sebastian, I don't feel so good," she said, her voice strained.

She grabbed hold of my arms, her feet unsteady. I tilted her head up me. Her eyes were glazed, and the weight of her head rested on my fingers. That asshole must have spiked her drink.

I had to get her out of here. The guy had disappeared, probably aware I was about to ruin him. Gently placing Aria's head on my chest, I wrapped my arm around her waist, starting to make my way for the exit, when Sefina and Hayden rushed up to me.

"What happened?" Hayden questioned, looking at Aria.

Serfina was already there at her side, helping support her.

"That asshole spiked her drink," I replied tightly, trying to restrain my anger.

"Is he still here?" Hayden asked.

"I don't know, but I need to get her home."

I glanced down at Aria, who was now mumbling in between giggles to Serfina.

"I'll find him," Hayden said, squeezing my shoulder.

I nodded at him and turned to get Aria out of there.

I gently helped her into the passenger side of my car, lifting her legs in.

She pointed at me. "You, Sebastian, are a gentleman." Her words were slurred as she smiled at me.

If she'd known what I'd done in a previous life, I doubted she'd be saying that. I closed the door carefully, then made my way to the driver side and got in, starting the engine. Aria put her hand on the steering wheel and leaned in.

"Should you be driving?" she slurred, pointing her finger at me like a naughty school child.

I couldn't help but let out a silent laugh. Did she even know what she was saying?

"Safe to say I'm well within the limit," I reassured her, leaning over to put her seatbelt on. "You, on the other hand, are not."

I pulled the car away from the curb and started to drive, glancing over at her as she was mumbling to herself.

"Did I interrupt your date with the brunette?"

Was she asking because it bothered her to see me with someone else, or because she thought she had ruined the night?

Her head was now leaning on my arm as I drove. I tensed, my stomach doing backflips at her touch.

"Sebastian, I can't feel my body," she mumbled.

"You'll be fine, Nyx. We just need to get you home."

"I don't want to go home to an empty flat, all on my own."

There was an unfamiliar pang in my chest. The girl I used to know looked the same, smelled the same, but that fire that had burned in her seemed to have gone out.

I'd get it back, though.

"I'll stay with you," I said softly.

I pulled up outside her flat and turned the engine off. She was asleep, looking peaceful; I didn't want to disturb her. I softly brushed the hair from her face and tucked it behind her ear.

She jolted awake, grabbing my wrist. "Callum! Did I cause a scene?" I froze as her eyes refocused and she looked at me.

Who the fuck was Callum? "Sebastian? What are you doing? Where am I?" she questioned, looking around.

"You're home. I brought you home," I replied, trying to calm her.

She released the grip on my wrist, then looked out the window for a minute—she must have realised where we were, because her body relaxed.

"Let's get you upstairs."

I wrapped her arm around my neck and then one of mine around her waist to keep her steady. There weren't many steps; she was on the first floor. Yet, after several attempts, she was still struggling to get one foot in front of the other, so I opted to swoop her up in my arms instead.

"Put me down," she giggled. "When did you become so buff?" She squeezed my bicep.

I couldn't help but pull her in a little closer to feel her warmth in my arms, something I hadn't felt in a long time. She wouldn't remember this tomorrow, but I would.

I reached the door and opened it, glad that she'd not carried a handbag and given me her keys to look after.

"Are you staying for a nightcap?" She kicked her shoes off the minute we stepped in. I made my way to her room and gently laid her on the bed. "Taking me to bed already?" More giggles followed.

I pressed my lips together. The thought of even entertaining the idea of taking her to bed in this state was ludicrous. I was many things, but I was not that kind of man.

"That's not going to happen." I sat at the end of her bed. "Get up."

She grumbled at me, forcing her body to sit up.

My hands found the hem of her dress, and I hitched it up over her hips. "Put your arms up." She reluctantly lifted her arms, and I pulled her dress over her head.

She soon flopped back onto the bed. I glanced over her for a moment, then I leaned over, kissing her on the forehead.

"Eww." She wrinkled her nose.

I let out a little laugh and pulled the covers over her. That little spark of hers was still in there somewhere. Making my way over to the chair in the corner of the room, I sat down, resting back into it. There was no way I'd leave her alone like this. I'd sit here all night watching over her if I had to.

A few hours had passed, and the sun was on its way up. Apart from her talking in her sleep and shifting about in bed a lot, it seemed the drugs were out of her system and that she'd be ok. I didn't want to leave her, I never wanted to leave her, but she wouldn't remember asking me to stay, so I decided it was best to go.

8

ARIA

My eyes flickered open and closed, attempting to adjust to the bright light shining through my window. The sun was warm, kissing my skin with its radiant glow.

Why did my head hurt so much?

I buried it back in my pillow, not wanting to get up, but my phone had other ideas as it buzzed with a message. I shifted my body and reached over, grabbing it off my bedside table.

Serfina: *Girl, get ready.*

Serfina: *I'll be at your place in half an hour.*

I glanced at the time. 10:30 a.m. It felt too early for this. I was glad it was Saturday and I didn't have to worry about work, because there was no way I would be able to function after last night. Why couldn't I remember anything? My phone buzzed again.

Serfina: *You'd better be awake.*

I smiled.

Aria: *I am. Why do I need to get ready?*

Serfina: *There's only one place to go after a big night out.*

I smiled, knowing exactly what she meant. I could practically smell the bacon.

I reluctantly pulled the blanket off myself. I was in my underwear; I didn't know how I'd managed to get undressed.

It was the beginning of May, and the weather was warm, preparing itself for summer. As we sat in the café, Serfina's long, chestnut brown curls bounced about as she looked over the menu. Her eyes were a striking combination of auburn and brown, like autumn leaves. She always was stunning.

It was your typical London café: cosy, friendly, and welcoming, a few people scattered around, eating and chatting.

"I don't know why I look over the menu. I get the same thing every time," Serfina said, placing it back down. "How are you feeling after last night?" she asked carefully.

I rubbed my fingers over my forehead. "I don't understand; I thought I'd been sensible. Do not let me drink that much next time."

She raised her brow. "I don't think that was all alcohol."

I tilted my head, my brows furrowed. "What do you mean?"

"Some asshole spiked your drink. Sebastian took you home," she explained.

I leaned back in the chair, trying to recall last night, but it was blank. Knots tied in my stomach, a sick feeling started bubbling, and my hand rested on my mouth.

"I don't remember any of that."

"All that matters is that you're safe. Sebastian took care of it all," she reassured me.

What did she mean, Sebastian took care of it all? I sat there for a few minutes, trying to recall any detail, however small. I didn't want her to think I was interrogating her by asking her a hundred questions. She must have noticed I was preoccupied.

"Aria." She placed her hand on my arm. "Try not to worry about it. Nothing bad happened to you. Sebastian made sure of it."

Before I could say anything, the server came over.

"Are you ready to order?"

"Yes, I'll have number four, and Aria …" Serfina looked at me.

"Oh, the same, please."

"And two cappuccinos. This one needs some caffeine."

A few minutes later, the server returned with our coffees, and while we waited for the food, Serfina and I chatted about everything and anything, laughing along the way. It was nice to have someone to talk to. She had a genuine warmth about her, and we instantly clicked again, like we hadn't spent four years as strangers.

I knew we'd be friends for the long run—those older women who sat there giggling with each other. The minutes passed quickly, and before I knew it, the server was back with our breakfasts. I added mayonnaise to the plate, because why would you eat it with anything else? It smelt so good. The fried slice looked amazing and crispy, just how I liked it. I was about to take the best bite of my life when it was snatched out of my hand.

Sebastian sat down next to me, and I heard a crunch.

"Good choice," he said with his mouth full.

I frowned at him.

"Did you not grow up at all in four years?" I snatched it back, taking my own bite.

"Clearly not." He chuckled.

"He doesn't know how to grow up," Hayden said, appearing from behind.

He hit Sebastian on the back, then sat next to Serfina, who put her cheek out for him to plant a kiss on.

They were cute together. They had this couple-goals vibe going on, and you knew it would last just by looking at them. Hayden was a good man—a man who respected his woman and protected her, something I never felt in my last relationship. I glanced at my wrist and pulled my sleeve down.

Sebastian must have been watching me, because he leaned closer, his hair falling over his face. "Everything ok?"

It wasn't its usual combed-back style today; it was more natural. Messier. It suited him. It somehow managed to make him look more handsome, something I never thought possible. I met his eyes.

"I was until you ate my breakfast."

"Well, in that case …" Sebastian grabbed it from my hand again, taking another bite before holding it above his head.

"Give it back." I giggled, trying to reach it.

Serfina cleared her throat. "Have you lovebirds finished?"

My cheeks went bright red. Lovebirds we were not, but it felt like the connection we'd once had had never broken.

Sebastian nudged me, giving me back the remainder of my fried slice.

"Wait until I get my revenge," I teased.

He rested his hand on my thigh, and heat spread between us as if his touch had been forged in the depths of hell. My eyes flicked up. Hayden and Serfina were in deep conversation.

His citrus aftershave hit me instantly as he leaned into my ear. "Don't make promises you don't intend to keep," he whispered, voice smooth.

I met his eyes. "Oh, I intend to keep this one."

His eyes darkened.

I could feel my cheeks starting to burn again as I swallowed hard to try and wet my throat, which had dried. He traced his fingers up my thigh, which sent every nerve in my body into meltdown. It was like he'd thrown petrol onto a flame and was watching it burn.

I'd always felt this attraction to him when I knew I shouldn't, and somehow, those feelings had never left.

"Sebastian, do you want an espresso?" Hayden asked him.

He rubbed his fingers over his chin. "I think I'll have something sweet this time."

Then he winked at me and carried on talking to Hayden.

9

ARIA

Four Years Ago

I rested my head in one hand, and the other held up my spoon, watching the milk drip back into the bowl of cereal I hadn't touched.

"Aria, don't play with your food. You're not five anymore," my mum said, taking the bowl away and passing it to Cathrine, one of the kitchen staff.

I rolled my eyes at her, forcing my body out of the chair to toss the spoon in the sink. Then, I promptly slumped back down, laying my head on my arms on the table, letting out a heavy sigh.

"Morning." Sebastian strolled in, grabbing a breakfast muffin that Cathrine had just made, and sat next to me.

I watched as he covered it in butter and marmite. Gross.

"Morning Sebastian," Mum said, getting up from the table.

"What's up with her?" he asked her, nudging me, but I didn't move.

"She mumbled something about Mason, and that's all I got." She shrugged, heading out of the kitchen. "Right, I'm late for an appointment. Your father has already left for work."

I felt a tickling at the back of my neck, so I turned my face to Sebastian. His own head was now laying on the table, and he met my eyes with those bright blues of his.

"What did he do?"

Mason and I had been together for a few months. We were both studying A-levels in English and Sociology, and I'd met him in class. We got on really well and would study together. He'd asked me out, and I said yes.

"Nothing." I sighed.

"Don't lie to me, Nyx."

I peered over at Cathrine, who was pretending to clean the counters, but I knew she was eavesdropping, like she always did. I gestured with my head to the door, then stood, holding my hand out, which Sebastian took.

I led him into my room and shut the door behind us. Then I sat on my bed, back to the headboard, and he joined me, placing his arm around my shoulders.

"Why are you being so secretive?"

"Oh, please, we both know Cathrine tells my mum everything."

He raised his brows in agreement, then placed his hand over mine to stop me playing with my sleeve.

"Now, tell me."

I let out another deep sigh. "He tried to … you know," I said quietly, my eyes flickering to my hands that were still covered by Sebastian's.

I felt his body tense against mine, his arm pulling me closer to him.

"He what?" Anger thrummed in his voice.

"We were going to. But I changed my mind, and …" My voice trailed off.

He tilted my chin with his fingers to meet his eyes. "Did he force himself on you?" Blue flames ran through those eyes of his.

"No. Well, he tried, but I hit him real hard in the face."

"I'm going to kill him." His voice was laced with fury as he jumped off the bed.

I rose to my knees, grabbing his arm. "Please don't, Sebastian. Just leave it."

"Nyx, do you really think I'm going to let him get away with that?"

"Please, I've got two months left of college and then I never have to see him again."

"Nyx …"

"No, Sebastian." I took hold of both his hands, and I felt the tension leave him as I pulled him to sit back on the bed. "Besides, I'm pretty sure he'll have a black eye, and that's punishment enough."

He half smiled at me, placing his hands on my jaw. "Nyx, you're special. Don't give your heart to these boys who don't deserve you."

Butterflies appeared in my stomach, sending signals to all of my nerves at once. The heat from his touch spread to my cheeks, and they were probably bright red by now.

He didn't know it, but my heart belonged to him.

He wrapped his arms around me, pulling me in, and my head rested on his chest, that fresh citrus smell of his hitting me all at once. He stroked my hair, and I could hear his heartbeat getting faster, his breathing shallower.

"Promise me you won't give anything up until you're fully ready."

I'd give everything to him in a heartbeat, if only he saw me that way.

"Promise," I whispered.

"I'm taking you out," he said, pulling away to stand and holding his hand out for me.

A few hours later, we pulled up in the car park of Folkestone Beach. It had been a while since I'd been here. The salty air hit me as I stepped out of the car. It felt like home—like I hadn't spent two years in the smoggy clouds of London.

Sebastian stood next to me, and I swiped his sunglasses off him, putting them on. He rolled his eyes.

"They look better on me, anyway."

I linked my arm through his, and we started walking down onto the pebbles, getting halfway before I had to stop to empty the stones from my shoes.

"Just take them off."

"No, because then my feet will hurt."

"I can fix that."

Before I could protest, he'd tossed me over his shoulder.

"What are you doing?" I giggled.

"Fixing your issue."

He took the shoe in my hand and threw it, then removed the other one and tossed that as well, walking us to the water.

"My shoes!"

"Fuck your shoes, Nyx. I'll buy you new ones."

My heart was pounding, and I could feel the heat from his body seeping into me. That fresh, citrus smell of his was sending my senses into meltdown.

He stopped, gently placing me back on my feet, right on the edge of the tide. The warm water rushed over my feet. Sebastian took his own shoes off and rolled his joggers up. When the tide came rolling back, I kicked, splashing him.

"You'll pay for that."

I stuck my tongue out and splashed him again, turning to run, but he grabbed my waist from behind and lifted me.

"Sebastian, put me down." I laughed, wiggling my legs and trying to pull his arms off me.

He walked us farther into the water just as the tide came back, splashing all up the back of my legs and arse.

"You asshole." I giggled, pushing away from him.

He just stood there, laughing at me, as I walked back to the shallows.

"Aria Summers? Is that you?"

I turned, facing the voice.

Luke Hills.

Surprise ran through me. We'd gone to school together. He was part of the friendship circle I had down here. The last time I'd seen him was two years ago, before Mum and I moved to London.

"It is you," he said, leaning in and hugging me.

As I pulled away, Sebastian appeared at my side, his shoulder touching mine.

"Thought you left us for the fast life."

"Well, I'm still there."

"That's a shame. We miss you."

Sebastian cleared his throat, and Luke looked over to him.

"Sorry, Luke, this is my—"

Sebastian interrupted me before I could finish. "Her brother," he said coldly, his eyes burning into him.

Luke pressed his lips tightly together, raised his hand to say "bye," and jogged off back to his friends.

"What was that?"

"I told you, Nyx. Boys like that don't deserve you."

"So, you're going to scare them all off?"

"If I have to."

Damn this guy.

"You're such a loser," I said, rolling my eyes at him. "I don't need you being protective."

He chuckled to himself, then leaned into my ear. "Don't worry, little sis. Your big brother will always keep you safe."

I pushed him. "Urgh, don't call me that!"

ET LUX IN
TENEBRIS
LUCET

10

SEBASTIAN

Present

"Mr Knight?"

It felt weird for Aria to call me that. It reminded me of when we were younger, when she'd called my dad by that name. A man I'd rather forget.

"Mr. Langley is here for you."

"Send him in."

She nodded and disappeared for a few seconds before showing him in.

"Sebastian, good to see you," he said.

Scott Langley was the son of Rupert Langley, an old associate of my dad's. They were always together when I was growing up, which was how I met Scott. We ended up at the same private school and university.

However, Scott had actually wanted his family business. I didn't. A promise to my grandfather was how I ended up in this position at the ripe old age of twenty-six.

I rose from my desk and shook his hand, then we both sat. My eyes flickered to Aria.

She looked good in her pencil skirt, hugging her hips. And those heels …

“I’ll go get some coffee.” She smiled and left.

“New PA?” He arched his eyebrow at me.

“Yeah, the last one wasn’t up to standards.”

“Well, this one’s definitely a stunner. Might have to ask her out.”

My jaw tightened, and I shifted in my chair.

“She’s not that type of girl.”

He lightly chuckled. “They’re all that type of girl when you’ve got the money.”

I glared at him, leaning back in my chair, my fists clenching.

“Have you finished making comments about my PA? Can we talk business now, or do I need to show you the door?”

He held his hands up in surrender as Aria reappeared with coffee. My body tensed as Scott’s eyes wandered to her arse, this burning rage filling my stomach, and I cracked my knuckles.

“Aria. Leave,” I ordered her.

She furrowed her brows. “What?”

“I said, leave!” I roared.

She jumped, fear flickering in her eyes, but she stood there frozen, gripping her sleeves. I stormed over to her and gently wrapped my hand around her wrist, guiding her to the door and closing it behind her.

I marched over to Scott, grabbed him up off the chair by his collar, and pinned him against the wall, my chest heaving.

No one looked at her like that and got away with it. I didn't give a shit that I was in the office, and no one would dare say a thing to me about it. He needed me for business, and I was doing him a favour by calling him in, but after what he just did?

"Sebastian, what the fuck are you doing?"

I pulled my phone from my pocket, finding the number I needed, and dialled, looking him dead in the eyes.

"One call, Scott, and I can have your family ruined," I stated coldly. "Is that what you want?"

Scott stared at me, stunned, and shook his head.

"All you did was look at my PA, and I've threatened to ruin your name. Imagine what I'd do if you ever touched her."

"Sebastian, please, I'm sorry," he said. "I had no idea she was something to you."

"Now"—I loosened my grip, pushing him towards the door—"get the fuck out of my office."

My eyes burned into him as I watched him hurry to the door, rushing past Aria and into the main office.

Fucking asshole.

I straightened my cuffs and ran my hand through my hair.

My stomach sank. I'd lost control and scared Aria, something I'd never wanted to do.

I took a deep breath in and exhaled slowly, making my way out to her.

She didn't turn or move.

"Aria?" I crouched down beside her.

I pulled the chair for her to face me. Her head was down, eyes fixed on her sleeves.

I placed a finger under her chin and tilted her head up. "Look at me."

She blinked, and tears fell from her eyes. My heart sank again, and I could feel acid swirling in my stomach. I had made her cry.

"Nyx, I'm sorry," I whispered, wiping the warm tears from her cheeks.

"It's fine." Her voice was flat, the words almost a whisper.

I hesitated a beat. "Nyx … what happened to you?"

"Nothing happened," she snapped, wiping her face and turning the chair away from me.

"Nyx. Talk to me." I placed my hand on her shoulder.

She shrugged it off. "I need some time."

I let out a heavy breath and stood. "Fine."

A few hours had passed, and Aria still wasn't talking to me. I understood why. She'd seen something I'd never wanted her to see—a side she had never seen when we lived together.

I guessed I was more like my dad than I thought. He'd constantly argue with whatever number wife he was on, even my mum. She passed away when I was ten—probably couldn't take any more abuse from my fucking asshole of a father.

"Sebastian."

My eyes flickered up to Aria standing in front of my desk. I was so deep in thought that I hadn't noticed her come in.

"Can we talk?"

I got up, making my way around to her, leaning against my desk and folding my arms.

"Sure."

She fiddled with her sleeves, so I took hold of her hand to stop her. If she was anxious about something when we were younger, she'd be straight to those damn things, but the minute I took hold of her hand, she'd be back to her sassy self.

Her eyes flickered up to mine, shimmering brightly, spreading that light that she was to me.

"What was that earlier?"

I let out a deep breath. "It's nothing you need to worry about."

She dropped my hand. "Don't do that. I'm not some little girl you can palm off anymore. I've grown up. I've had to."

"Look, these wealthy businessmen think they can just take anything they want."

"Such as?"

"He was looking at you in ways he shouldn't have been, and I won't stand for that."

She bit her lip, a smile unfurling, and took a step closer, resting her hand on my chest, sending my pulse into overdrive.

I swallowed to clear the lump in my throat.

She met my eyes as I looked down at her. "Thank you," she whispered. "But I can take care of myself now. You don't need to do your big brother routine anymore."

Oh, this was far more than a big brother routine.

This was something else.

I wouldn't allow anyone to look at her in that way.

And if they dared touch her? Well, I'd fucking kill them.

11

ARIA

"How's your mum doing?" Sebastian asked.

"She's good. I miss her, though." I sighed, taking a sip of my vodka and Coke.

We had decided to get drinks after work, and Sebastian had taken us to some upscale bar in the West End where he had a private room.

It didn't even look like a bar from the outside.

You walked in and it felt like the hallway was leading you down into the basement, where all of a sudden, there was soft music playing in the background of a room filled with modern, stylish décor and a bar.

Everyone looked like they were part of the corporate world with their tailored suits. It somehow reminded me of the places I'd end up in back in Leeds—but there was nothing corporate about those.

"Do you not get to see her much?"

"She's in New York now. I haven't been able to visit since she left."

It wasn't by choice. I hadn't been allowed.

"I'm sure you'll get to see her soon, Nyx." He smiled, squeezing my hand.

"You remember when she saw you carrying me in through the front door? She looked like she was about to commit murder."

"Well, you were seventeen, completely wasted, draped all over me." He chuckled, then took a sip of his whisky.

"I was not all over you," I protested, nudging him with my arm.

I'd missed him. We'd had a connection back then that felt as easy as breathing.

"Well, your mum thought something was going on between us. She had words with me after, and I had to reassure her there wasn't. She was quite scary, actually." He leaned back on the black velvet sofa and rested his arm behind me. "Just admit it, Nyx. I was pretty irresistible. I'd completely understand why you were obsessed with me," he teased.

I rolled my eyes at him. "Clearly you've got a big head. You really aren't that good looking."

Who was I kidding? This man was pure perfection. He looked like he'd just walked off a supermodel shoot in Milan. I used to fantasise over him doing things to me that I should never have thought about.

I shifted, crossing my legs. His eyes flicked to them at the movement, then back to meet mine.

"Don't worry, little sis, I won't tell anyone you've got a thing for your big brother." He winked.

I wacked him in the chest, and he chuckled. "Stop calling me that! Our parents aren't even married anymore."

He smirked, resting his hand on my thigh, then leaned into my ear. "That's a shame. I like forbidden things," he whispered.

My breath caught, my heart skipping a beat, and that heat spread straight to my core, melting all my senses at once.

He squeezed my leg. "You're looking a little flustered there. Alcohol getting to you?"

My hands found my cheeks. They were burning hot. This guy had me weak for him with just a few words.

"Erm, yeah, probably." We'd been here for a few hours, and I had drunk more than I'd intended.

"Never could hold your liquor." He laughed, swirling the amber liquid in his glass before downing the remainder.

Sebastian gripped my waist as he guided me out of the main entrance. The cool May air hit me, sobering me up slightly.

"Let's go to Soho." I looked up, smiling at Sebastian. It was only around the corner.

"I don't think so."

I pouted at him. "Since when did you become an old man?"

He laughed to himself. "Fine, but don't go getting yourself into trouble."

A mischievous smile came across my face as we started walking, and we soon entered another bar. The staff seemed to know Sebastian, and drinks were brought over to our table. The vibrations of the music snaked through my veins, and the spotlights flickered a mix of blues and reds.

I sipped my vodka and Coke, ready to take on the dance floor.

I leaned in to Sebastian. “Come dance with me.”

“I don’t dance, Nyx.”

“First time for everything.” I smiled, pulling him up from the chair, and he rolled his eyes at me.

We made our way to the dance floor, and I wrapped my arms around his neck. His hands soon rested on my hips. I started swaying my hips to the beat, and Sebastian was right there in time with it all.

I turned, fitting my back against his body, resting one arm around his neck and the other by my side. He slid his hands around my waist, resting on my lower stomach. I moved my hips, and his body followed, staying glued to mine. My heart was racing, and the heat between us was electric. His citrus tones flooded my system, heightening everything at once. My breathing became shallow. I could feel his warm breath on my neck, his stubble rough, but his lips were smooth as they traced over my skin.

“Nyx,” he whispered in my ear, turning me to face him.

There was a man wearing a sharp, black suit standing next to Sebastian. He was around six foot, with dark eyes that almost looked black. His light brown hair was cut short, shaved at the sides, and tattoos covered his hands.

“I need to go deal with something. I’ll just be at the table if you need me.”

I nodded and watched as they disappeared through the crowd, my brow furrowed. Everyone around was still dancing and enjoying themselves, so I decided to do the same. I'd ask Sebastian about it later.

It wasn't long before arms wrapped around my waist again, but they felt different. I turned and pulled away, shaking my head to let him know I wasn't interested. Then the lights flickered over his face, fully revealing his identity.

A face I knew.

He grabbed my wrist, tugging me back. My eyes darted around at everyone laughing and dancing with each other. Acid swirled in my stomach, and my breathing became heavier with each deep breath. That sick feeling was rising as I swallowed to try and keep the burn down.

"Get off!" I shouted, struggling to free my wrist. My heart was pounding, and the adrenaline took over, so I pushed him with all the force I could muster.

"You always were a little cunt," he hissed, backhanding me across the face.

I gasped, the sting taking my breath away, and touched the side of my lip. My fingers came away with spots of red on them. My heart was racing, getting quicker with each breath I tried to suck in. The room was spinning, and I couldn't focus on a single point to try and steady it.

Then I saw those familiar blue eyes looking straight at me.

Sebastian.

His mouth was moving, but I couldn't hear a word he was saying. I squinted, and then all of a sudden, everything was loud again.

"Nyx, what happened?" His fingers took hold of my chin as his eyes fixed on my lip.

His touched grounded me as I saw flickers of primal rage run through his eyes. Mine darted to the guy Sebastian had gone off with; two other men now stood behind him.

"Who did this to you?"

I couldn't get my words out, so I just pointed at the man backing away into the crowd.

Sebastian gestured to the two men, and they rushed in the man's direction. Sebastian's eyes met mine again. They were filled with burning rage, almost primal.

Knots formed in my stomach, and I grabbed his tense arm.

"Sebastian, please," I begged. "Leave it." This was all my fault; I should have moved away from the dance floor. I shouldn't be causing a scene.

He cupped my cheeks, and I felt the tension leave his body as he gazed into my eyes. "Not a chance," he said and dropped his hands.

I watched in horror as Sebastian stormed over, the bloke already pinned by the two others. Sebastian swung, knocking him to the floor, then grabbed him by his collar, pulled him up slightly, and went for him, one punch after another, crimson droplets spraying across the floor.

I felt frozen, rooted in place. I couldn't move, didn't know what to do, fear curling tight in my chest.

I felt hands on my arms, and I turned to see the first guy Sebastian had been with. He gently pulled me away from the scene, until I couldn't see Sebastian anymore, couldn't hear the crunch of bone.

The cold air hit my tears. I hadn't even realised I'd been crying. I took a deep breath, but the air was harsh, piercing my lungs, goose bumps crawling over my skin.

"It's Aria, isn't it?" the man said, turning me to face him.

I nodded.

"I'm Logan. I work for Sebastian."

I fixed my eyes on the door, praying to see Sebastian.

"Aria ..." I felt Logan's hands touch my shoulder, and I glanced back. "Everything will be fine. I promise you."

Somehow, I could see in his eyes he was telling the truth.

It felt like a lifetime before Sebastian finally came out.

The moment I saw him, my heart lurched, then slowly began to settle. I hadn't realised how tightly I'd been holding myself together until my breathing finally evened out. He stopped when he reached me, his expression unreadable for a second before he closed the distance.

I didn't think. I just stepped forward and wrapped my arms around him, clinging to the solid warmth of him as if it were an anchor.

Back when our parents were together, Sebastian would come home with cuts and bruises more often than not, and I'd fix them up for him. It had always felt normal back then, the two of us quietly taking care of each other.

It wasn't Sebastian who frightened me now. It was the memories I'd buried deep, clawing their way back to the surface.

When I finally lifted my head and met his gaze, all I saw in those blue eyes was steadiness. Protection. Safety.

He tilted my chin, looking at my lip. "It's split." His eyes then met mine. "Are you hurt anywhere else?"

I shook my head.

"Let me take you home."

"I'm fine. I was worried about you," I said quietly.

I pulled away, taking his hands. A few grazes covered his knuckles, but they looked superficial.

"I'd never let anyone hurt you." He pulled me back into him and pressed a kiss to my forehead.

ET LUX IN
TENEBRIS
LUCET

12

SEBASTIAN

I took a long drag of the cigarette before releasing the smoke into the air.

"She's got hidden trauma, you know," Logan said.

"What do you mean?" I leaned over the table, pouring the whisky into my glass, swirling it before taking a sip.

"The way she froze, completely shut down. I've seen it a thousand times."

Logan had once been my right-hand man. When I left the Organisation, he became more of a bodyguard, hiding in the shadows until he was needed. He was ex-special forces.

He never missed a mark.

"Did you know that guy?" I asked Logan.

He paused. "I don't think so. He was probably just trying his luck with Aria."

I rubbed my stubble. Maybe he was right.

I looked up, taking another drag on my cigarette before putting it out as Connor walked in.

"All sorted?"

"You did a number on that guy," he said, sitting down at the table. "But yes, not a trace."

"When have you ever seen Sebastian do half a job?" Logan chuckled.

"True." Connor shrugged, pouring himself a glass.

Connor was a pristine high-end barrister who had connections to everyone in that circle. He was fucking good at what he did. He'd get you off anything, no matter the evidence. He worked with judges, officers, and anyone law related to keep them out of the Organisation's business.

"Did I hear right? Has Sebastian been making trouble again?" Hayden said, waltzing in and joining us. "Thought you were done with this life."

"I am."

I didn't want to be, though. It was a constant struggle to stay away. These guys were the family I never had. I felt like I belonged here—not in the corporate world I despised.

I was trying to be as above board as I could for my granddad's sake, but every day was getting harder.

Then there was Aria. That light in the darkness that calmed my chaos with a single touch. She hadn't long come back into my life, and I wanted to be someone who deserved her, but the man I used to be was still in there, and he'd come out if need be to protect her.

Like last night.

"Hmm." Hayden patted me on the back. "Serfina's taken Aria out today."

"Where?"

"She said after your mess, Aria probably needed some retail therapy."

"Tell Serfina to charge it to my accounts. Anything Aria wants."

Hayden nodded, grabbing his phone.

"Logan, can you keep an eye on her?"

"Sebastian, Aria will be fine. Have you forgotten the family Serfina grew up in?" Hayden said.

Serfina's dad was once part of the Russian mafia before they were forced out. He ended up in London and met her mother.

Serfina was five when they moved next door to me. Her dad still had connections and was extremely wealthy. He raised his daughters to be fighters, and Serfina was a fiery one.

Logan leaned forward on the table. "Do you want me to go?"

"No, Hayden's right. She'll be fine."

"I've got to get going, I've got court in a few hours," Connor said, standing and then shaking everyone's hands before leaving.

"I've got to go see Soran. You coming?" Hayden asked.

"Yeah, but I'm driving."

The headlights from the passing cars flickered in and out of my windows as I drove down Edgware Road. It was always busy. The traffic. The streets. It was a vibrant place full of Middle Eastern restaurants and shisha bars that came alive at night. Hayden sat back in the passenger seat, fiddling with the positioning. He hated it when someone else sat there. I laughed under my breath, but it must have been loud enough for him to hear, because he frowned at me.

"Who have you had in this? It's dead straight," he grumbled, trying to get it just right. I rolled my eyes.

He must have got the seat just how he liked it, because he finally stopped playing with it. I could see him out of the corner of my eye, grinning to himself.

"You're officially Prince Charming now. Whatever will you do?" Hayden joked.

I glanced at him. *Prince Charming?* More like chaos in a tailored suit.

"Don't go there," I warned him.

"Oh, c'mon. It's clear you like her," he replied dryly, like he'd been waiting to say it.

He was right.

I did like her.

I liked her more than I should or wanted to admit to anyone.

Everything on my part had always been about protecting the light that she was.

Then things naturally started shifting between us just before she started uni. It became more than just a brother wanting to keep his sister safe.

And this time, I wasn't going to leave her.

The smell of freshly baked bread always hit me when I walked into Soran's restaurant. Hayden and I made our way through the busy space to the counter. The waitress's eyes darted uneasily to Hayden and then to me.

"Is Soran about?" I asked.

She glanced us over again before disappearing out the back. I casually leaned my elbow on the counter to face Hayden. Within a few minutes, a familiar voice came from behind.

"Sebastian, Hayden. Always a pleasure to see you," Soran said. You could tell he had a smile on his face just from his tone.

I turned to meet him. His thick black hair was in its usual style, slightly parted at the side and combed back. His beard looked fuller than the last time I'd seen him. I grabbed his hand and pulled him into a bro hug. He then proceeded to greet Hayden the same way.

"Come. Sit." Soran gestured towards the table. He turned to the waitress. "Dayi, bro."

She hurried out to the kitchen.

I'd picked up a few words of Kurdish here and there from time spent around Soran. He would tell us stories about his homeland and how he was named after the region he was born in. He'd tell us his bloodline was older than the streets of London. He was proud of his ancestry.

Like me and Hayden, we'd also met in the underground fight scene and hit it off quickly. We later allied, forming the Organisation with a few others.

With his background, it was only logical he'd step into this niche role. He had legitimate businesses, such as this restaurant, but he offered another service.

You needed someone to disappear? Soran was your man.

A few minutes later, the waitress came out with bowls of soup. The smell of earthy spices with a hint of sweetness hit me, followed by that of freshly cooked bread, like flour meeting fire.

Hayden wasted no time in tucking in.

"You know, your food is almost as good as my nan's jerk chicken," he joked.

Soran raised his eyebrows. "Don't tell my wife that."

I chuckled to myself. Soran's restaurant was by far the best; it was always full of people enjoying themselves. The server soon brought out an array of Kurdish cuisine until the table was filled with everything you could imagine, from lamb kuzi and kuba, to my favourite, the dolma.

I didn't know how he expected us to eat it all.

"No business until after we've feasted," Soran said firmly.

We joked and laughed as we ate, reminiscing about our time together like it was yesterday. I missed it. It was nothing like the rigid corporate world that only saw black and white. The world of pretence. No one was loyal to anyone. They'd soon stab you in the back just to be on top.

The underworld was different; we worked together in our own way. Everyone had a role to play, but when the time came, we blended into one.

The restaurant soon closed, leaving only us in there. Trails of steam rose from the Kurdish chai in the glasses in front of us.

"You got what I asked for?" Soran asked eventually, stirring in his sugar.

"All here," Hayden replied, pulling a USB drive from his inside pocket and sliding it across the table.

Soran was looking for someone, and Hayden was the guy who could track anyone or anything down. If he hadn't ended up down the illegal route, he'd be working for the one of the government's intelligence organisations. He could memorise complex codes and encrypted patterns, and once he'd seen a government server, he could visualise every weakness to it.

It was fascinatingly odd.

You needed information on people, and Hayden could hack any system without getting caught.

We sat sipping the tea in silence for a few more minutes before Soran stood up.

"Always a pleasure, Hayden," he said, extending his hand.

Hayden and I followed.

"Sebastian—the door is still open. We want you back," Soran said.

I shook my head. "You know I have other commitments."

"It's called a woman," Hayden interjected.

I shot him a glare.

Soran chuckled. "Always a pleasure."

I didn't know how long I had been sitting outside Aria's.

I peered at the time: 2 a.m.

I had dropped Hayden back home and somehow found myself outside, as if I couldn't resist the pull of her.

Her light was still on.

Our connection was still rooted deep between us. I could feel it, and I knew she could, too.

She appeared at the window, and my breath hitched. I took her in: that messy bun of hers she'd always have before going to sleep, with those little loose bits that fell over her face. And those eyes. It had always been those shimmering moon eyes—the way the light would touch the darkness of my soul.

Then she closed the curtain, shutting me out of her world.

I started the engine and slowly pulled away.

ET LUX IN TENEBRIS LUCET

13

SEBASTIAN

Six Years Ago

The cloud of smoke floated through the room as I exhaled, before taking another drag on the cigarette. Everyone sat around the table, quietly discussing what we had just done and what to do next to secure the turf we'd just taken over.

There was just one loose end, and he was currently tied up behind the door in the other room.

Still, I was torn, the memory of my granddad tugging at me not to cross that line. He'd passed not long ago, and ever since, I'd found myself being drawn deeper into the fires of hell.

I knew full well I was nothing he'd be proud of right now.

Before I could speak, Nicholas strolled through the door. He wasn't my first choice for what I needed, but I knew he'd eventually agree.

"Nice house, rich boy. Did your mummy buy it for you?"

I jolted up, the chair going flying behind me. Hayden grabbed my arm, shaking his head at me—a warning not to start anything.

Nicholas and I had never seen eye to eye. He'd grown up in this world, learned its rules the hard way, and believed that counted for more than anything else. To him, men like me didn't belong here. It didn't help that I'd stepped into his territory and beaten him in the ring, taking a position he'd always assumed would be his.

Since then, he'd made it his mission to undermine me at every opportunity, mistaking recklessness for strength and intimidation for leadership. He wanted what I had, and he hated me for having it.

As much as it grated to have him here, Nicholas knew money laundering inside and out. He'd survived by making it his speciality.

He laughed, pointing at me. "That's right—you and your mummy issues."

Fire raged through me, my fists clenching, my jaw tightening.

I went for him.

But before I got there, Valon, Soran, and Hayden had grabbed me, trying to hold me back.

"Sebastian, he's just trying to wind you up," Soran said. "Leave him." He squeezed my shoulder, and they released me once my body loosened.

"What did you call me here for, anyway?" Nicholas asked as he lit a cigarette.

"As much as I'd rather not work with you, you need us, like we need you."

"And how do I need you again?" He unbuttoned his jacket, then pulled out a chair and sat down, resting his legs on the table as if he owned the place. I gritted my teeth.

"You want to get out from under your brother's shadows, and we need someone who knows money laundering. I'll front the costs for you, everything in your name."

Nicholas flicked his cigarette on the floor. "You think you're some sort of leader just because you've taken over a tiny turf of no consequence whatsoever? You don't know the streets. I was born and raised in these back alleys."

"Yeah, we've heard it all before. Thing is, no one respects you."

His nostrils flared, and he swung his feet back to plant them on the floor, leaning forwards in his chair.

"What did you do with Alex?"

I made my way to the door, stepping into the room for a few seconds and dragging Alex out by his collar. His mouth was taped, hands and feet bound together. His face was red, covered with sweat and splatters of crimson from the earlier punches I'd given him.

I threw him down in the middle of the room. His breathing was heavy against the silver tape, his eyes darting around.

Nicholas let out a low whistle. "I'm impressed, rich boy."

That was something I never thought I'd hear him say.

"Everything is set up for us. Valon with products, Hassan sorting his routes. Hayden will deal with all the tech—"

Nicholas cut me off. "And the law?"

"Sorted. My barrister wants in."

He rolled his eyes. "Of course you have a barrister."

"Well, what do you say? Do you want to join us, or carry on being nothing more than a shadow in this life?"

He rubbed his chin, looking around at everyone before meeting my eyes again. "I'm in."

I took a deep breath, pulling my Glock from behind my back.

I knew this was what I needed to do from the moment we decided to start the Organisation, but my granddad's voice was niggling in the back of my mind, telling me not to do it, to be the good man he'd raised.

I pulled the trigger anyway.

14

ARIA

I had settled into my new role the last few weeks and was surprised at how well I was doing.

I knew I was capable; I just had this bad habit of not believing in myself these days.

I'd given up uni because I'd had to and was forced into a life I wouldn't have chosen for myself. Behind the lavish parties and wealthy lifestyles hid a world of shadows and broken promises. It had left me fragile, but I'd got through it, and I was free of those chains now, after leaving Leeds behind.

Sometimes I just had to remind myself of that.

I tugged at my sleeve, shaking the past from my body as I went back to typing the minutes from an earlier meeting.

My phone started buzzing rapidly on my desk. I glanced down at it: **Unknown caller**. I frowned.

"Hello?"

Silence.

"Hello?" I tried again.

The silence turned into a few muffled noises before the line went dead.

A faint uneasiness crept into the back of my mind, but I shrugged it off, focusing back on my work until a low whisper in my ear broke through my thoughts.

"What are you doing?"

My heart skipped a beat as I jumped back in my chair, turning my head to meet the voice. Sebastian stood there with his hands in his pockets, leaning towards me.

"Don't do that. You scared me," I said, my voice a little shaky.

He let out a soft chuckle by my ear, which sent vibrations through me. This guy smelt like heaven and hell all mixed into one. It was probably something like Roja Dove, knowing him. He liked his designer brands; I supposed that was a perk of being a rich kid—you had the money for things like that.

His scent lingered as he straightened himself, allowing me to move my chair around to face him. I looked up at his eyes, which were a brighter blue today, reminding me of a crystal sea. They were hypnotising.

"Coffee?" he asked.

"Sorry, what?" I questioned, removing myself from my trance.

"Do you want to get coffee?" he asked again.

"Oh, erm, sure," I accepted, standing.

"Good, because I don't think it would be socially acceptable to drink at this time of day," he joked.

"That kind of morning?" I probed.

"Something like that, Nyx." He pulled his sleeves down and straightened his suit. "Shall we?"

We walked through, making our way to the staff room, and Sebastian brought coffee over to the table I sat down at. I sat forward on the armchair, hugging my cappuccino with my hands, watching the steam rise from it. Sebastian leaned back on the other armchair, his arm casually draped over it as he sipped his espresso.

He looked like he had a lot on his mind, and I didn't want to push.

He soon broke the silence. "I need you to attend a business function tonight."

I slowly placed my cup down. "A business function? No, Sebastian, you don't need me for that."

"It's something I haven't attended in a while. This year, I'm needed."

"But—"

He cut me off. "Aria, as the CEO's PA, you are expected to attend, no arguments. Now, it's not the type of people I would normally associate with, but it's an important networking opportunity for their businesses," he explained.

I didn't quite understand what he meant by "their businesses." I know his company was one of the elites and had pristine clientele, but who were "they?"

He pulled a credit card from inside his suit pocket. "Take this," he said, handing it to me. "Get yourself a dress for tonight."

"I don't need your money," I insisted, pushing it away.

"It's the company credit card. It's a business transaction."

I sheepishly took the card. Was I just a business transaction to him now? He quickly stood up, buttoning his suit jacket.

"Take the rest of the afternoon off. Make sure your dress is midnight blue. I'll pick you up at 7 p.m."

"Why midnight blue?"

"Nyx, just be a good girl and listen for once."

I looked up at the five-star hotel as Sebastian handed the valet his car keys.

He leaned into my ear. "You look beautiful. The colour brings out your eyes."

The hairs on the back of my neck stood at the feel of his breath on my skin.

He placed his hand on my lower back, smiling. His touch felt warm, safe. Something I wasn't used to.

As we walked through the lobby, there were a few people scattered around, drinks in hand, talking quietly to each other. Sebastian guided me, his hand still on my back as we entered the main hall. The place was beautiful, from the crystal chandelier sparkling like a star in the room, to the elegance of everyone in their business formal attire. I felt Sebastian's hand leave my back, but its warmth lingered.

"I'll get us something to drink."

I nodded as he made his way over to the bar. I stood there awkwardly, feeling out of place. This type of event was something I had endured back in Leeds but never enjoyed. Even when our parents had been married, I'd avoided these types of social settings as much as possible. Sebastian soon came back with a glass of champagne, handing it to me. "Duty calls," he said, nodding at a group of older men in suits across the room.

With that, he left me stranded. Great. Was this how this evening was going to go? Me standing awkwardly by myself all night? I slowly made my way to the bar, avoiding eye contact and glancing at people as I walked past. With my back to the bar, I watched everyone mingling, spotting Sebastian over the other side of the room. He looked like he was in deep conversation.

"They're like wolves in sheep's clothing out there," a man next to me said quietly.

I jumped nervously, not having been aware of him so close, and turned to him as he casually took a sip of his drink. His olive skin was the first thing I noticed against his burgundy suit.

He turned his head slowly, making eye contact. His smile had a charm about it but no real depth. His jet-black hair sat perfectly slicked back, and his eyes … well, you could get lost in their darkness. He was a lot taller than me, and slim, but his tailored suit showed he was well-sculpted underneath. It was like looking at a masterpiece.

"I'm Nicholas Rossi." He held his hand out, bringing me back to the room.

"Aria," I said, shaking his hand. I didn't like the contact, but I knew I had to be professionally polite.

He arched a brow, his eyes wandering over my body, "What brings you here, Aria? I don't think I've ever seen you before."

"Oh, my boss." I pointed to Sebastian, who had his back turned.

Nicholas followed my finger.

"Sebastian Knight," he said flatly.

Confusion ran across my face. "You know each other?"

He leaned into me. "Oh yeah. We go way back."

ET LUX IN TENEBRIS LUCET

15

SEBASTIAN

I'd lost track of how long I had been stuck making small talk with these people, laughing politely at the correct time and adding invaluable information to their conversations.

They reminded me of my granddad, who used to bring me along to show me the business world that our family had built. Yet now, these events were tedious; they sucked the life out of me.

I hadn't had a chance to check on Aria since I got stuck here. I knew she hated these things, but in the past, she'd demonstrated she could always handle herself. I scanned the room, and my eyes locked on her at the bar. She was laughing and talking to someone.

Nicholas Rossi.

My jaw clenched. I knew there was a possibility of him being here with the type of businesses he operated. His eyes drifted to me, meeting my intense glare, a smug smile on his face. He looked back at Aria and lightly touched her arm. That was it—my breaking point. No one should be touching her but me.

As I reached the bar, I protectively placed my hand on Aria's lower back, my eyes fixed on Nicholas. What was he playing at? He stood there, casually sipping his drink, but there was nothing casual about him; those eyes told me he was up to something.

Something sinister.

I broke my glare and looked down at Aria.

"I think it's time we go." I tried to keep my tone calm; I didn't want her to pick up on the tension.

"What's the rush, Knight? We were just getting to know each other," Nicholas said.

I could feel the blood leave the fist I'd been clenching tightly by my side. My body tightened, causing me to add pressure to Aria's back. She shifted in response, taking a small step towards me.

"It's been a while since we shared a drink, Sebastian," he said, tilting his glass to me.

I took a deep breath. I needed to hold it together. He wanted me to react in front of Aria, to tempt the old Sebastian out, the one he knew. The one who so easily lost control. But I was trying not to be that man anymore, and I needed to keep it together in this place.

I felt the blood rush back to my hand as I released it from its clench. I eased the tightness in my body, smiling back at him.

"Not long enough."

I knew I shouldn't have said it, but I wasn't going to let Nicholas's smug face see me back down.

He slammed his glass down on the bar, taking a step closer to me.

I stood in front of Aria, shielding her.

"You don't want to do this here, Nicholas." I dusted his shoulder off, then tightly squeezed it.

"What's the matter, Sebastian? Keeping secrets?" he taunted.

"Don't push me, Nicholas," I warned him.

His smirk turned into a small, vindictive laugh as he took a step back. He picked his glass back up, taking a sip as he leaned back against the bar again. That was the thing about Nicholas; he could switch at any time.

"It was lovely to meet you, Aria. I'm sure we'll see each other again soon."

I took hold of her hand; it was trembling. There was no way he would be seeing her again if I had anything to do with it.

"I'll be seeing you, Knight," he warned, his eyes fixed on me.

I nodded at him, acknowledging the warning, and squeezed Aria's hand, turning for us to leave.

The lights of the city flickered in and out of the car as I sped through the streets, overtaking anyone who wasn't going at the speed I needed in that moment.

Nicholas Rossi. I knew my dislike of him ran deeper than it should have, but there was a reason for it. Something about him never sat right with me. I couldn't explain it, only that I trusted him about as far as I could throw him. He'd been looking for a way to get one over on me for a long time. And the fact he'd set his sights on Aria made my skin crawl.

His name just added more fuel to the fire, to the burning frustration I had inside of me. He had always been reckless. What was he playing at tonight?

My thoughts drifted to Aria as I stole a glance at her. She was watching the city speed past the window. I couldn't take it anymore; I needed to breathe. I swerved into the nearest lay-by, ignoring the horns blaring as I did so.

I turned the engine off, bashing my hand against the steering wheel, causing Aria to jump. It forced her to face me, but I didn't say a word. Instead, I stepped out of the car, slamming the door behind me.

I stepped out onto Westminster Bridge, striding to the edge of it. I stopped, gripping the cool rails tightly in my hands. "Fuck."

I must have said it a little too loud, as I got an odd look from the person walking past. I stared out across the Thames, the parliament lights shimmering on the water. I ran my hand through my hair, slightly pulling at it, before rubbing my face. What was wrong with me? Why had I let Nicholas affect me so much?

I didn't know how long I'd been standing there before I turned my head to see Aria cautiously walking towards me. I could feel her warmth from a distance, and my body eased. She stood next to me, her arm brushing against mine, my skin tingling from her touch. The water rippled from the warm June breeze. We stood there for a few minutes, just looking out, before she broke the silence.

"What was that back there?" she asked.

"Nothing you need to worry about, Nyx," I said quietly.

She frowned at me.

"Then why did you invite me tonight?" she asked. "I barely saw you."

I looked back out over the water. "I wanted you there," I said. "I just didn't realise how hard it would be."

Maybe I should tell her. Get it all out in the open and pray she'd accept the man I am.

Maybe then she'd understand why I left her years ago.

Instead, she let it go.

"I never knew how beautiful the view was from here," she said.

I looked down at her. She was far more beautiful than that. The way her hair fell softly around her face … she was truly breathtaking. I brushed a loose strand of hair from her face, my fingers lingering on her cheek. My pulse started to race, a tight tension pulling at my lower stomach. I swallowed hard.

All I could see was her.

All I wanted was her.

Fuck it.

My hand found her waist, her heart beating fast against mine. Our eyes met, neither of us able to look away. Her breath was warm, inviting, and my eyes soon dropped to those lips before I met them with mine. I didn't need air; she was all the oxygen I could ever want. How I'd longed to kiss her again, to feel that undeniable connection between us. Her hands slid up my jacket, resting on my chest, and I soon found myself wanting more. The kiss got deeper, my thumbs grazing her cheeks as my hands rested on her neck. It was like dynamite had just exploded in my core, filling my veins, wrapping its fire around my soul. Her tongue brushed against mine, teasing, as mine got desperate, needy. That spark had just set off a chain reaction.

I needed to stop.

But those lips …

I pulled myself away, our foreheads touching. “I shouldn’t be doing this,” I whispered, trying to catch my breath. “I’m no good for you.”

“Sebastian, I want you. I always have,” she whispered back breathlessly.

My heart skipped a beat. She had no idea how long I’d waited for her to say that. But I shouldn’t go there. Not again.

“No. You’re my PA. My stepsister once. We can’t.”

I pulled myself away from her, turning my back as I walked a few steps up the bridge. I had to put some space between us, because if I didn’t, I would take all of her, and she deserved someone better.

Someone who wouldn’t lie to her.

“Let’s get you home.”

ET LUX IN TENEBRIS LUCET

16

SEBASTIAN

Four Years Ago

The air was cold and damp. Drizzle fell from the night sky as a full moon illuminated the path for me. The cold air hit my lungs a little too sharply, causing me to grab my ribs. I climbed over the gated fence, landing clumsily on the garden lawn. Clive, the groundsman, had said he'd leave the kitchen patio doors unlocked for me.

I didn't want Aria to see me. I didn't want her to know I was leaving. But I had to.

The dried blood on my cracked knuckles caught my eye in the soft moonlight. If Hayden hadn't pulled me off him, I would have killed Nicholas tonight.

He would have deserved it.

He'd challenged me to a fight, and I'd welcomed it.

He soon backed down when he realised the only reason he was alive was because of Hayden.

I fumbled with the patio door, quietly pulling it open as I crept inside, closing it gently behind me. The moonlight shone into the room as I unbuttoned my shirt, pulling it down over my shoulders.

"Why are you always creeping about in the dead of night?"

I looked up, startled to see Aria standing there with her arms folded, tapping her foot on the floor.

"Fuck, Nyx. What are you even doing up at this time?" I shrugged my shirt back over my shoulders, starting to button it back up.

She didn't need to see the cuts and bruises under it.

"I couldn't sleep, so I came down to get a drink. Then I saw you stumble across the patio."

"Haven't you got uni tomorrow?" I said, leaning against the counter.

She needed to go so she didn't realise I was leaving. I knew it would hurt her.

She was the one thing I'd miss.

My light in the darkness.

She furrowed her brows at me. "Why are you acting so suspicious?" She took a step closer. "What are you up to?"

"Hayden's waiting for me."

"What happened to your eye?"

Her fingers gently grazed over my eyebrow, and I held in a hiss. Her eyes drifted down to my shirt, and she started to unbutton it.

"What are you doing?"

She gently pushed it off my shoulders, and it fell to the floor. "Sebastian, why are you covered in marks? You told me you weren't going to fight again." Her eyes met mine.

She traced over them lightly, tingling every nerve in my body all at once, sending out signals to light every part of me up. This was wrong on so many levels. I could feel the connection we had built shifting, going to places it had never been.

I gently took hold of her wrist, and her fingers stopped moving, but her eyes fixed on mine. "It's fine, Nyx. Nothing you need to worry about." My voice was soft and low.

"Let me get the first aid kit." She smiled and disappeared from the kitchen. A few moments later, she returned, setting the box on the counter next to me and taking a wipe out. I sucked a breath in through my teeth as it made contact with the cut above my eye.

"Oh God, I'm so sorry." She removed the wipe, placing it on the counter.

My fingers found hers. "You could never hurt me." I brushed the loose bits of her hair that had fallen over her face from her bun behind her ear.

"Sebastian." Her voice was lower than a whisper.

"Yeah."

Before I knew it, her lips had landed on mine. My heart had just managed to break free from its cage. My arms just dangled at my side; I was unsure if I should kiss her back.

No, I shouldn't. I took hold of her arms, pushing her back gently.

She looked at me for a split second, her cheeks bright red, before her eyes made their way to the floor.

"I'm so sorry," she whispered.

She turned to run away, but I grabbed her wrist to stop her, forcing her to meet my gaze again.

"Nyx, wait."

"Just forget it."

I didn't know what made me stop her from leaving. All I knew was my heart felt like it would suffocate without her.

My fingers traced down the side of her cheek, and my palm rested on her jaw, our eyes fixed on each other. This girl was beautiful.

She was more than that; she was stunning.

My hands soon found her hips, and I lifted her, turning us and sitting her on the edge of the counter. Her legs naturally opened, allowing my body to meet hers.

"Nyx," I whispered.

"Shhh." She placed her finger over my lips.

My gaze dropped to her pink lips, and I hesitated momentarily. My eyes found hers again, silently asking for permission. She nodded. My hands ran up her neck, resting on her cheeks. I leaned in, my lips softly meeting hers. They were warm and tasted sweet like cotton candy.

That one touch awakened every single part of my body. It reached my soul—something that never happened with women. The kiss became harder, more desperate, as I slid my tongue into her mouth. I wanted to taste every bit of her. Hers met mine, and her hands locked into the back of my hair. Her chest pressed against me as she tightly wrapped her arms around my neck, pushing our bodies closer. She lightly ground against my cock that was already begging to be inside her. My hands found their way to her arse, squeezing it tight.

My body wanted all of her. It wanted her on this counter, right now.

Her fingers found my belt buckle, and she started to unclip it. My hand reached for hers, stopping her before she could fully get it open.

"Nyx, are you sure?" I asked her breathlessly.

She nodded. "Yes. I want you to be my first," she whispered, her eyes shimmering at me.

Fuck.

I brushed her hair back again, resting my hands on her cheeks. "I'll be gentle, I promise." She nodded at me, and our lips met again, but this time more slowly.

My lips brushed across her cheek, and she tilted her head to the side, exposing more of her neck for me. I slowly kissed it, making my way down. Her breathing became heavier as I pushed her tank top strap down her shoulder.

Wait.

I shouldn't be doing this.

She was my stepsister, someone I had promised to protect and keep safe. I was letting temptation cloud my judgment. She was pure perfection—an innocence I didn't want to ruin. I was the complete opposite—dark chaos that broke everything it touched.

I needed to stop this.

My lips pressed onto hers, hard, raw and desperate, because I knew it was going to be the last time I kissed her.

I wrapped my hands around her waist and pulled her off the counter.

I pressed my lips to her forehead. "I'm sorry, Nyx." It was barely a whisper.

She watched as I rushed to grab my shirt from the floor, then made my way to the patio, flinging the door open. I looked back at her standing there for a few seconds, confusion running through her face and such hurt in those eyes of hers.

Then, I stepped into the garden, closing the door behind me.

I jogged through the grounds and pulled myself back over the gate.

I ran my hand through my hair, gripping it tight before letting go. What the fuck was wrong with me? All these feelings were rushing around my body that shouldn't be there.

It was better that I left. What could I ever give her? Darkness and pain?

No, she was better off without me and my shady world, dragging that light of hers down until it eventually went out.

17

ARIA

Present

I sat on the sofa, staring blankly at a page in the book I was reading. No matter how many times I read it, the words wouldn't go in—even though I'd read them a thousand times before. *Romeo and Juliet* was my favourite, but right now, all I could think about was Sebastian.

He hadn't been at work all week; his diary said he had a business trip, but I was sure it hadn't been there last week.

Was he avoiding me after our kiss? That was a ridiculous thought; he was a grown man, for goodness' sake, and the CEO. I needed to get over myself.

The kiss had sent a spark through me though, igniting all my senses at once. I had never felt such burning passion before—not in my last relationship. Not since the kitchen, four years ago. I ran my finger over my lips, wondering what it would have felt like if it had gone further.

I quickly stood up, trying to shake off that feeling. I shouldn't go there; I wasn't ready to go there, and he was my boss—not to mention my ex-stepbrother.

Even if he was an ex-stepbrother I'd once had a silly crush on.

A knock on my door interrupted my thoughts and I jumped, my heart pounding. I hesitated for a few seconds before creeping over and opening it. A bouquet of roses sat there. I glanced down the hall to catch a glimpse of anyone, but it was empty. I picked them up and closed the door behind me, placing them on the table before searching for a note. There it was—a little envelope tucked behind the thorns.

Even though I'm not here, I haven't stopped thinking about you.

I flipped the note over to see if there was anything else on it, but it was blank. Were they from Sebastian? I liked roses, just not red ones; they reminded me of something dark and sinister. Sebastian had known that once, but maybe he had forgotten. He was also one of the few people who knew where I lived.

I couldn't quite get rid of this small feeling of dread in the bottom of my stomach—the possibility that it could be *him* made me feel nauseous. But no, it couldn't be. He was on remand and wasn't allowed contact. I pushed the thought to the back of my mind and jumped as my phone buzzed with a text.

Serfina: *Hey girl, we need some retail therapy!*

I smiled to myself; Serfina was such a vibrant, beautiful soul. I was glad for her company.

Aria: *When do I need to be ready?*

Serfina: *I'll be by in about an hour! See you soon! X*

I needed this—to get out of these four walls and enjoy myself for the day. Then maybe my mind wouldn't keep wandering to Sebastian.

I spent most of the afternoon on Bond Street with Serfina. It was a vast contrast to the café we were in the other week, but Serfina could afford to shop here. There was everything from Burberry and Louis Vuitton to Tiffany Co. I didn't want to know how much she spent, but I was sure it was more than my annual salary.

We were now enjoying a coffee at a quirky little place nearby. She looked exhausted after all that excitement, but she still managed to look stunning. Her curly brown hair was tied in a high, messy bun, decorated with a bandana-type bow.

I took a deep breath, unable to keep the words to myself. "Seen much of Sebastian lately?" Then, I took a sip of my cappuccino.

She peered up from her latte. "He's away on business, isn't he?" She threw the question back at me.

"Oh, yeah. I just didn't know if you'd heard from him." I tried to smooth it out the best I could.

"He doesn't tend to make contact at all on those trips." She shrugged it off.

Maybe I was thinking too much into it.

A small, playful smile suddenly appeared on her face, and she leaned forward.

"Why are you so interested in Sebastian all of a sudden?" she teased.

I could feel the blood rising to my cheeks as I shifted in my seat, unsure how much to say.

"There's something you're not telling me." She smirked, then sipped her coffee. "Spill."

What did I have to lose?

"We kissed," I said quietly, taking another sip to try and hide my face with the cup.

Her gasp turned straight into a smile as she eyed me.

"I knew there was something there." She tapped my arm playfully.

Was there something there? I mean, he pulled away and had now been on a business trip for a week.

"Is that why you were asking if I had heard from him?" she questioned.

"Yes," I replied sheepishly.

"Ah, I see. Look, Sebastian is like a brother to me." She placed her hand on top of mine. "He's got issues, but he's got a good heart. I'm sure he's just had things to deal with on his trip," she reassured me.

I smiled back at her, although I still couldn't help but wonder if he was avoiding me.

We'd probably been gossiping in the coffee shop for about an hour when Hayden turned up, and of course, he went straight over to Serfina and kissed her before sitting in the chair next to hers.

"Looking better than the last time I saw you at a café," he joked.

"Safe to say I have fully recovered."

"I heard Sebastian dragged you to one of his boring work events?"

I looked up at them. "Yeah, he did. I met one of his old business associates. What was his name? Nick? Nicholas Rossi?" I said, like I was trying to remember, but I remembered it all too well. There was a history there, and I wanted the tea.

Serfina and Hayden's eyes met for a second; it was minor, but I saw it.

Then, Hayden shifted in his chair, clearing his throat. "I don't think I've met him before."

"Oh. I just thought you may have known him, as you and Sebastian have been friends for so long."

There was a short pause.

"Yeah, the name doesn't ring a bell. But then, I don't know everyone Sebastian has worked with." He shrugged it off.

"Shall we get going? I need to get all these clothes away," Serfina said, rustling her bags playfully.

I gave her a small smile, but my mind was elsewhere. They both knew exactly who I was talking about.

I just wasn't sure what they were hiding from me.

ET LUX IN TENEBRIS LUCET

18

SEBASTIAN

Seven Years Ago

"Sebastian, you don't have to cook for me. I have people for that."

I looked over at the fragile man who'd raised me—the man who took care of me when my father couldn't be bothered, which unfortunately was most of the time.

"Well, your favourite grandson is doing it. No arguments." I smiled at him.

"You're my only grandson." He chuckled.

"That's why I'm your favourite."

"Let me help," he said, getting up from the chair.

I rushed towards him, taking hold of his arms. He hadn't been well the last few months. He said it was nothing to worry about, but deep down, I knew he didn't have long. He was my entire world, the only person who'd shown me any love after my mum died.

"Have you grown? You look taller," he said, looking up at me.

"Last time I checked, I was still six foot two."

"I think you've grown."

"Sit down, Granddad. I'm looking after you," I said, helping him back down.

He slowly lowered his body back into the chair, and I sat next to him.

He leaned over, arching his brow. "What are you making, anyway?"

"Lasagne."

"Trying to butter me up with my favourite. What have you done?" he asked, suspicion running across his face.

I let out a light laugh. He didn't know anything that I got up to, and I wouldn't want him to. I couldn't bear him being disappointed in me.

I got back up and continued with the cooking. I'd helped my grandmother cook all the time when I was little. Every Sunday, we'd make the roast dinner and apple crumble. She used to tell me off for sneaking into the fridge and pinching bits of the crumble. I couldn't help it; there was something special about her crumble. It felt like warmth, a home wrapped up in it, and I couldn't get enough.

"Have you met a nice girl yet? I was married to your grandmother at your age."

"I'm nineteen. People don't get married at our age anymore."

"That's why relationships no longer last. Don't be like your father. One day, you'll meet someone special, and you need to do everything to keep her."

"You'll be the first to know if I ever find someone," I lied.

He wouldn't be the first, because he wouldn't be here to see it. A sick feeling rose in my stomach, forcing its way through my body at the thought.

Not that there would be anything to see.

"How's your friend? What's his name? Jayden?"

"Hayden."

"Ah, yes. He seems like a good lad. He grounds you."

I turned to face him, smiling. "He'll be over later to raid your rum."

He chuckled. "Well, I won't have much use for it."

I paused, pressing my lips together. That sick feeling returned to my stomach as I took a deep breath, exhaling slowly. I could feel my throat getting dry, trying to close up, so I swallowed hard a few times to push it back down.

"Don't say that, Granddad," I said, trying not to choke on my words.

"Come, sit with me for a minute."

I took a deep breath, wiping my eyes so he wouldn't see anything, then sat next to him.

He turned slightly to face me, taking my hand.

"I know you don't want it, but promise me you won't let your father ruin the business."

He was right; I didn't want it. I never wanted to run the company or be part of it. It was my dad who'd forced me into it—sent me to private school, chose my university degree, all to groom me into the company I had no interest in. Yet after all of that, he was still adamant I'd never be a good CEO. That I was just a disappointment to him.

"Your great-granddad built that company from scratch. He wanted more than just money to pass down the family. He wanted something to be proud of. If there's one thing I ask of you, please keep it something to be proud of. Promise me."

I let out a deep breath. This man meant everything to me. He showed up when my dad didn't, was there when I needed him, and looked after me when he didn't have to. He was a good man.

"I promise."

ET LUX IN TENEBRIS LUCET

19
SEBASTIAN

My granddad was buried not far from here.

Six years ago today, I'd watched him pass, a fragile old man hooked up to every machine in the hospital. I'd watched the life drain from him as I held his hand through the night, refusing to leave him.

Six months later, Aria had appeared, bringing that light with her. That hope of one day being able to become someone better.

I didn't know if my granddad would be proud of the man I'd become. I was trying to keep myself straight and do everything I could to keep my promise to him, but I was struggling every day, torn between the light and the dark.

I sat on the cool pebbles, watching the waves crash to shore, as I swigged the bottle of whisky. It was dark, and my days had blurred into one. The flame from the lighter illuminated my face as I lit a cigarette.

Folkestone Beach. A place my granddad had taken me all the time when I was younger. I had so many happy memories of our time together, finding weird-shaped pebbles to take home to show my grandmother.

I slowly pushed to my feet and swigged from the bottle before staggering down the beach. Car lights flickered in the distance, and I used my hand to shield my eyes. I knew who it was, and I didn't want to deal with that right now. I just wanted to forget everything.

I'd allowed myself to feel something with Aria, something I hadn't felt with anyone. I was terrified of ruining everything with her, of allowing myself to be loved, only for it to be taken away from me. To feel that abandonment again scared the life out of me. Could I really give myself to Aria fully, without breaking her heart again like I did four years ago?

I carried on stumbling across the beach, the moon reflecting on the sea ripples, a torturous reminder of Aria's eyes. It didn't matter how hard I tried to forget her; I just couldn't. I could hear the faint crunching of the pebbles behind me, getting louder as it grew closer.

There was only one person who would dare approach me in this state.

I paused with my back still to them.

"Go away, Hayden," I told him. "Me and my bottle are fine." I held up the whisky bottle, then downed some more.

"Thought you'd be here, having a pity party for one."

I was not having a pity party; far from it. I was just taking some time out. I deserved to have a break from that corporate world now and then and enjoy myself. I wasn't doing anything out of the ordinary.

Who was I trying to kid? He knew me better than I knew myself, and right now, I was a mess.

He'd seen what I'd been like after my granddad died, seen the darkness come out of me and take no mercy on anyone. He even saw the way I was when Aria arrived, changing little bits of me. He noticed everything.

I gave up and sat back down on the pebbles. The crunch stopped as he sat next to me, grabbed the bottle from my hands, and took a swig. His face said it all.

"When are you going to start drinking rum instead of this shit?" He looked over the bottle and gave it back.

"When you buy me a bottle," I said, patting him on the back as we let out a little laugh before falling into a comfortable silence, both of us looking out at the ocean.

"You need to sort your shit out," he said bluntly.

He was right. I couldn't keep living like this, but I didn't know how to be any other way.

"That baggage you hold on tight to … you need to let it go," he continued. "If you don't, you will drown." He nudged me. "She's worried about you, you know."

I could see his eyes flicker to me, waiting for a reaction. I took a deep breath, plucking up a pebble and throwing it into the sea.

"She doesn't need to worry about me," I replied quietly.

"She's a good woman, Sebastian. Don't lose her again because you can't be man enough to admit how you feel about her."

I looked over at him, raising an eyebrow. "Since when did you become so wise?"

"I've always been wise. You've just never listened to me. Now, are you coming home, or are you going to stay here on your 'business trip' forever?"

I slowly, reluctantly pushed myself to stand, facing him with a small smile. I knew I needed to sort these demons out, but I didn't know where to start—or if it were even possible.

In that moment, though, there was one thing I was sure of: Aria was mine, and I was going to do everything in my power to keep her.

20
ARIA

It had been over a week, and Sebastian still wasn't back.

I was sorting papers for his meeting later today, and I didn't even know if he'd turn up to it. It felt pretty grim in Sebastian's office without him.

I placed the papers neatly on his desk before spinning on my heel and walking straight into Sebastian, sending the coffee in his hand all over his suit jacket and shirt. I froze, my hand covering my mouth, eyes following his hand as he placed the half-empty cup on his desk and started to remove his suit jacket.

"Still clumsy, I see." He chuckled.

His response must have unfrozen me, because I immediately started taking tissues off his desk, trying to rub his shirt dry while not allowing myself to become flustered. He placed his hand on mine, freezing me in my tracks again, and my eyes flicked up to his.

"It's fine, Nyx. I've got other shirts in my office."

I swallowed hard, trying to compose myself. His gaze was still fixed on mine. I didn't want to look away; his eyes were always so warm, even if they were blue.

He pointed to the papers on his desk. "Are they the ones for the meeting this morning?"

"I … erm … yeah," I replied, stumbling over my words, turning to look at them.

By the time I'd turned back around, he was already over by his cabinet, removing the shirt I had spilt coffee on. My eyes widened at the sight of his bare chest. I swallowed hard, trying to stop the blood from rushing to my cheeks. Either he hadn't noticed me, or he didn't care. He was toned; you could see he worked out regularly. Full sleeves of ink covered both his arms, and there were more tattoos over his chest. One caught my eye—a crescent moon with what looked like Latin writing over his ribs.

I absentmindedly ran my finger over my undamaged wrist, the crescent moon tattoo and butterflies I'd had done four years ago. I got it when he left, a little reminder that he had been a part of my life for a little while.

As he covered his chest with a clean shirt, I glanced down at the floor. I didn't want him to know I'd been ogling him the whole time.

Once he was done, he strode over, stopping beside me as he picked up the paperwork to look through it. Flutters appeared in my stomach, my heart skipping a beat. My palms started to feel sweaty from the heat spreading through my body.

This was the first time I'd seen him since the night we'd kissed.

There was so much I wanted to say to him, but I didn't know where to start.

His eyes were fixed on the papers; he probably didn't even care that I was gazing at him. I was sure he was used to women eyeing him up.

"You ready to go?" he asked, taking a step forward.

"Yes." I picked up the rest of the paperwork and turned to see Sebastian's eyes fixed on my thigh.

"You've got a ladder in your tights."

He walked over, invading my space, and that heat rushed to the inside of my legs again.

"Take your shoes off."

I frowned at him. "What?"

He just looked at me, so I stepped out of my stilettos.

"Spread your legs."

I swallowed, my heart pounding, but I did as I was told.

He got down on one knee, his hands trailing up my leg until he reached the ladder. He gripped the tights tightly and completely ripped them off, then rested his hand on the inside of my thigh.

He looked into my eyes. "You're looking flustered there, little sis."

"Stop calling me that!" I snapped, trying to control the heat that was spreading like wildfire and clamped my thighs together.

"As you wish."

His eyes stayed fixed on mine as he glided his hand up my inner thigh until he reached my lace knickers. My body felt like it was alight as he proceeded to move the lace out of the way and slip two fingers inside. I caught my breath, unsteady on my feet, as his other hand gripped my hip to steady me.

"Look how wet you are."

I couldn't speak. My nerves were on overload. I'd never felt so much heat rush to my core all at once before.

He slowly withdrew his fingers, rising to stand again, and gazed into my eyes as he licked them clean.

"You taste as sweet as I imagined."

And then he turned on his heel and left the office.

I took a deep breath, trying to steady myself, and I placed my hand on my heart that was beating so fast I didn't know if it was going to stop. My cheeks were hot, flustered. Fuck. What the hell had just happened?

He'd just started a fire in me that I didn't want to go out. It was laced with need, want, a desperate burn of desire.

It should have felt wrong.

I was his PA, his stepsister, everything that was forbidden.

But my body needed more.

It needed him.

I sat at my desk, working through emails, occasionally glancing up at Sebastian in his office. He was currently in another meeting, his elbow on the table, his index finger pressed against his temple. Some of his hair had fallen out of place, covering his eyes. He sure was something to look at.

"Aria?"

I turned around to see Sophia from the main office standing there, holding a bouquet of red roses.

"These came for you." She held them out to me.

I took them from her, looking at her oddly.

"Got a secret admirer?" she teased.

"I have no idea," I said, trying to shrug it off.

She smiled and returned through the door she had come from. I placed the flowers down and found the note.

You will always have a place in my heart.

My heart started to race. My mind couldn't help but focus on *him*.

Jason Brown.

My eyes drifted back to Sebastian's office—his fierce gaze was on me.

Invisible hands tightened around my wrist, forcing my eyes to look at my scar. I rubbed hard, trying to remove that feeling, but it wouldn't go away.

I picked the flowers up and dropped them in the bin, hoping that would help.

It didn't.

I took a few deep breaths in and out, trying to focus on something else, but my breathing felt heavy, like I was struggling to catch it.

I unbuttoned the cuffs on my shirt, hoping that would free the phantom pain pulsing through my wrist. My vision blurred—and then Sebastian was there, cupping my cheeks. He was speaking to me, but everything was muffled.

And then there was nothing at all.

ET LUX IN TENEBRIS LUCET

21

SEBASTIAN

I stood steady as Aria fell into my arms. I wasn't quite sure what had happened, but I'd seen her hyperventilating through the window and ended my meeting immediately.

I swooped her up and carried her into my office, laying her on the sofa in there, my heart pounding.

What was going on?

I hesitated before sitting on the edge of the sofa, gently brushing her hair out of her face and tucking it behind her ears. Her skin was cold, and she looked pale. I ran my hand gently over her arm, reaching her wrist where her cuff was undone. I tilted my head slightly, studying the small, delicate crescent moon with butterflies tattooed on her wrist.

But it was the other wrist that caught my eye.

A soft-edged, almost silver in colour scar was etched into her wrist. I traced my finger over the seam, trailing up until I didn't want to lift her shirt anymore. She didn't have this before; I would have remembered. I'd known every inch of her.

She always kept her arms covered these days. Now, I knew why.

I felt her body move against mine, and my eyes drifted to her face.

She blinked a few times before focusing on me.

"Sebastian?" She pulled herself up, and I cupped her cheek. "Nyx, you're ok."

"What happened?"

I ran my hands gently down and rested them on her shoulders. "Hey, hey. Don't move too quickly." Her eyes flickered to my hands, then back up to my face. "How are you feeling?"

"I'm ok. My head hurts a little, but I'm ok." She touched her head. What happened?" she repeated.

"You fainted."

Her face was full of confusion, her eyes darting about. Then, she noticed her uncovered wrist. She pulled her sleeve down, fiddling with the cuff.

"Nyx." I lifted her face with my fingers for her eyes to meet mine. "Is there something you aren't telling me?"

She sat in silence for a moment, looking down at her hands.

"I should get back to work," she said, rushing to stand.

Her legs had other ideas, and I caught her again, helping her sit back down. I watched as she sat on the edge of the sofa, playing with those damn sleeves, as I sat down next to her, my hand finding hers to stop her.

No sooner did her eyes meet mine than she fell straight into me, hugging me tight. I placed my arms around her tightly, keeping her as close to me as I could.

I didn't want to push her, but my gut was telling me something was going on. Something she didn't want to tell me.

I'd find out, though.

I had ways she'd never know about.

I entered the bar, pausing to scan the room for Hayden. He was in the corner, sipping a drink at a table. I acknowledged him with a tight nod and made my way to the bar to get a drink. After today, I needed it. I'd dropped Aria home, and she was adamant she didn't want me coming in, so I left her to it.

"Long day?" Hayden asked, raising his brow as I fell into the chair opposite his.

"Could say that."

"Maybe you're just getting old," he teased, letting out a little laugh.

I smiled as I raised my glass. "If I'm getting old, so are you."

I rubbed my fingers over my chin, my lips parted, but I soon pressed them back together, shifting in my chair.

"I need you to do something for me."

Hayden leaned forwards, placing his arms on the table. He knew that if I asked him for something, it was serious.

"I need you to find out what Aria was up to in the last four years."

Hayden's eyes widened as he leaned back in the chair, taking a swig of his drink.

"Are you sure you want to do this?" he questioned.

I wasn't sure at all. I didn't know if I was doing the right thing or not. I wanted Aria to tell me everything, but I couldn't wait; I needed to know.

"I'm sure. Everything you can find." I hesitated. "She mentioned a Callum when she was drugged. I don't know if she was just wasted or if it means something."

Hayden let out a small breath. "She may not forgive you if she finds out, I hope you're prepared for that."

The truth was, Aria meant everything to me.

I would do anything to protect her—and if that meant going behind her back, then so be it.

22

ARIA

The TV murmured in the background, barely registering. I couldn't believe I was doing this to myself again, letting the past creep back in. I'd promised it wouldn't after that night. And yet, the feeling lingered, as if *he* were still there.

Jason Brown.

That name made me feel physically sick.

I met him not long after Sebastian left and soon moved to Leeds with him.

He was wealthy, taking me to lavish parties, buying me expensive gifts. It soon became dark when he introduced me to the world his money came from. The man who ran the county lines in Leeds, moving drugs through children and fear, leaving damage wherever he went.

That's when it started.

It was subtle at first—odd comments about what I was wearing, who I was seeing.

Then I had to give up university. Jason told me I didn't need it; I had him to look after me. It wasn't just that, though. Once, he'd come to pick me up as he always did, and a guy in my class stopped to talk to me. Jason saw red, and I felt every bit of pain after. It was safer to stay at home after that—at least, I thought it would be.

Everyone knew I was his, and if someone tried to look at me … they weren't the only one who felt his hand.

The only man I was allowed to be left alone with was his younger brother, Callum.

Which was quite ironic, in hindsight.

My phone buzzed on the table, and I fumbled for it, squinting at the screen.

Sebastian.

I declined the call. I didn't want to talk to him—not after yesterday.

The phone buzzed again

This man was persistent.

He always had been.

I smiled to myself, remembering the time I'd locked my window so he couldn't get in. It was raining hard, and it had served him right for trying to wind me up earlier in the day. I thought he'd just go back out again.

Nope.

He'd broken into the house, setting the alarm off. He'd knocked on my door, and I'd opened it to him leaning against the frame, looking all smug. I'd rolled my eyes at him, but I'd still let him in.

There was a knock at the door, and I reluctantly got up and made my way to it.

Sebastian stood there with his intoxicating smile, coffee in hand.

Why did he have this spell over me?

"I brought you a coffee." He held it out.

"Thanks." I smiled a little as I took it from him.

"Now, let's get you out of this flat."

The sun did feel warm through the window, and it looked nice out there. Maybe I could do with the fresh air.

"Fine."

I opened the door for him to fully step in. We stood there awkwardly for a few seconds, when I noticed his eyes glancing down at my uncovered wrist. I quickly grabbed my cardigan off the sofa and put it on. Glancing over at him, I could see in his face that he wanted to ask more.

"I'll go and get changed." With that, I shot into the bedroom, leaving him standing there.

Greenwich Park was stunning in mid-June with summer just around the corner. The Flower Garden was exceptionally beautiful at this time of year—which was where we ended up after getting another coffee. We sat down on the grass, our arms touching. I couldn't help but observe him. The loose bits of his hair fell over his eyes, making him look like some kind of model straight out of GQ magazine. The way he rubbed his stubble with his fingers had me right back in the office, remembering how wet they had made me. He must have seen me looking, because he met my eyes with a smile.

"Everything ok over there?"

I ducked my head, my cheeks burning, and I was pretty sure it wasn't from the sun.

"Yeah, I was just admiring the flowers."

He let out a silent laugh and tapped me with his arm. "You remember when I brought you here and you didn't realise how big it was and made me carry you up the hills?"

"We'd literally just traipsed all around the old Royal Naval College—"

Sebastian interrupted, "You said you wanted to see where *Thor* was filmed, so I took you."

"Yes, and every other place there. My feet were hurting."

"You can't go to Greenwich without seeing all its wonders. Besides, we found that little Moroccan restaurant that had the best briouats and vegetable tagine."

My mouth watered from the memory. "I could eat that right now."

He let out a small chuckle. "I'll take you later."

"You'd better, because that's all I want."

He looked over at me and met my gaze. "I promise." Then he took hold of my hand, his fingers locking between mine.

Heat rushed through me from his touch, and butterflies started to flutter in my stomach.

"Ok, I guess it wasn't that bad a day. Central London, though … that was a whole new level of busy."

"How could I forget?"

Sebastian used to take me around London to all the places I'd never been, and we always had so much fun together doing it. It was like he'd never really taken the time himself to just do normal things.

He arched his brow at me. "You went around the M&M shop eating them and wondered why the security guards were following us."

I took a sip of my coffee. "Look, if you're going to have all that chocolate on show, then it's inevitable."

"You do realise the only reason they didn't do anything was because they soon recognised my surname?"

"That famous name," I teased.

"It stopped you getting into trouble," he laughed, sipping his espresso.

"I'm sure it's stopped you on many occasions ..." My words trailed off as I grinned at him.

"Haven't a clue what you're talking about, Nyx." He smirked, winking at me.

I let out a chuckle and we sat there for a few minutes, sipping our coffee, before he broke the easy silence.

"Nyx, can I ask you a question? How did you get your scar?"

I paused for a moment. I'd hoped he'd never see it; it was something I wanted to hide from the world. From myself.

It was a reminder of a time I wanted to be free from.

I looked up at him. "I was in an accident a few years ago."

He looked unconvinced, but he didn't push any further. Instead, he turned to look at the view, his thumb grazing gently over my hand as our fingers stayed locked together. Was this how it was supposed to feel when you meant something to someone?

I never knew what was coming with Jason—only fear.

But Sebastian always made me feel … safe.

ET LUX IN
TENEBRIS
LUCET

23

SEBASTIAN

The city lights flickered across my face. I needed some time to gather my thoughts, and driving was one of those ways. Sometimes, I'd find myself driving around in the early morning hours to clear my head.

Aria had lied to me today. I could see it all over her face.

Did she not trust me enough? She used to tell me everything. It didn't sit right with me.

I gripped the steering wheel tightly, my fingers tensing. I had to focus on getting that information from Hayden. If she wouldn't tell me, then I would find out that way.

The Organisation was hidden deep in the streets of St John's Wood. From the outside, it looked like your typical manor house with iron gates, high trees, and the latest security system. Guards covered the entrance and around the building. As it was wealthy around here, no one would bat an eyelid at this.

I pulled up at the gates and was immediately waved through. I needed to see Hayden, and I knew he'd be here. As I approached the door, the guard eyed me.

"Hey, Sebastian," he said, taking my hand to pull me into a small bro hug. "I think I've seen you more these past few weeks than when you were running the place." He chuckled.

I probably had been here more than I needed to be, but these guys were more than family. They were part of a life I just couldn't give up so easily. He stepped aside, allowing me to enter.

The lights were dim as I made my way through the hall. I could hear chatter before I pushed open the door into the main area. Hayden was sitting at the table with Matt and Valon, playing poker. Matt, the youngest in the Organisation, saw me first, rising from his seat to greet me.

"All right, Sebastian, I wasn't expecting you today," he said.

"I needed to see this guy." I playfully hit Hayden on the back, forcing him to move slightly forward in his chair.

Valon stood up, putting his hand out. "Come, join us." I shook his hand.

I'd forgotten how strong a grip this guy had. Valon was a reserved man but very calculated. He came across as quiet, but it was because he was observing everything around him.

"Come on, you need to help this guy out," Valon added, referring to Hayden.

"I've got you where I want you," Hayden insisted.

Valon turned to me and said, "*Miku i mirë njihet në ditë të vështirë.*" A good friend is known in difficult times.

We knew that proverb all too well. Valon was very proud of his Albanian heritage. He even had the Albanian Eagle tattooed on his back.

"Yes, your friend Hayden needs your help." Valon let out a light laugh as he sat back down at the table.

I pulled up a chair. "Deal me in." I threw four hundred pounds on the table to start the bet.

"Look at this rich boy." Valon chuckled and tossed double down.

"He's a big CEO now," Hayden teased, patting me on the back.

Hayden had taken over when I had to step down. He'd be the logical choice, as we'd been together from day one. He knew it inside and out.

Matt shuffled the cards, dealing them out to everyone. "Fuck the corporate world; you know you belong with us."

If only it were that simple.

"I'm raising you lot," Hayden said, doubling the pot.

"Look at this guy," Valon said, matching him.

Matt and I called, and he turned over the first three cards.

"How's business?" I asked, looking up from my hand.

"It's doing good. Hassan has set up some more routes for us to get products into the country," Matt replied, adding more money onto the table.

"And Nicholas?"

The room fell silent. Matt turned the fourth card over. "I'm done." He tossed his cards on the table.

I arched my brow, looking over everyone. Was there something I was missing?

"Someone better tell me what's going on."

"You know what Nicholas is like," Valon replied, raising the pot.

I knew all too well. He was always up to something.

"Just the usual. Undermining everything. Questioning. Nothing I can't deal with." Hayden brushed it off.

My jaw tightened. He obviously hadn't learnt his lesson from the last time, when his need to cut corners had almost brought the whole operation down. It had left one of the crew hurt and far too many questions unanswered.

"Don't worry about it; Hayden has it under control." Matt turned the last card over, and I added more money.

I knew Hayden could handle it, but the thought of Nicholas starting his shit again fuelled the burning in my stomach. He was a damn liability.

Hayden laid his cards on the table, and Valon threw his down with force. "You've been counting cards again, haven't you?"

"I told you I had you where I wanted you." Hayden chuckled, taking the money. "Now I've beaten your sorry arses, can you give me and Sebastian a minute?"

Valon nodded, patting Hayden on the back. "Next time, I'm going to beat you." Then he got up, Matt following.

"Well? Did you manage to find anything?"

Hayden shifted in the chair, clearly still uncomfortable about what I'd asked of him. He reached inside his jacket, pulling out some documents, and slid them over, his hand staying on top of them.

"Are you sure you want to do this?" he pushed.

Was I? I could just slide them back over to Hayden and never look at them. I could do the right thing and wait for Aria to trust me enough to tell me herself.

But I never claimed to be a saint.

I nodded firmly, and Hayden slowly withdrew his hand.

"It's not everything yet. I'm waiting for a few more bits of information."

I scanned the documents in front of me. She'd stayed in London for a bit after I'd left and continued uni. I moved further down the page, fixing my eyes on a name.

"Jason Brown? As in, the man who runs the county lines in Leeds?"

"Yeah, but I haven't got his full file yet. It's got extra security around it."

There's only one type of file that Hayden would need time on, and that would be one related to a government agency.

What the fuck was Aria doing with that piece of shit?

"It says she moved to Leeds with him?" I questioned. "I don't remember this guy being around."

Hayden just shrugged. "What do you want me to say? You left, remember?"

I glared at him. He was right; I had left her.

"And Callum?"

He let out a heavy breath. "You won't like this." He threw the file on the table.

I opened it up, and my eyes widened.

Callum Brown.

Jason's younger brother—also part of their gang.

"Fuck."

"If Aria has been rolling with these guys ... maybe you should just tell her about you."

My jaw clenched, my body tensing.

Why the fuck wouldn't Aria tell me about any of this?

Did she already know who I was?

That wasn't the only question that was burning in my head.

Was she now working for Jason and Callum?

Was that why she was back in London?

24

ARIA

I squinted at the bottle, readying myself to refill Serfina's glass. I wasn't sure if it was her hand swaying or mine, but it was safe to say we were both tipsy. This time, only a dribble trickled out. I examined the bottle, trying to work out where the rest was, and we promptly burst out laughing.

"We need more wine." She giggled.

Two bottles down in a few hours, and I was having fun.

I couldn't remember the last time I had laughed so much. It was nice to be able to do so without worrying about any consequences. To be a normal twenty-two-year-old, to fully enjoy myself without fear of what was to come after.

"Wait." I placed my arms out, expecting everything to freeze in the room. "I have another bottle in the kitchen."

Serfina danced excitedly. I stood up, but it must have been too quickly, because my body felt like it was spinning. I paused for a second.

"Oh! Let me tell Hayden to bring some more as well," Serfina suggested, grabbing her phone and somehow managing to dial his number.

"Bring more wine!" she ordered him as soon as he answered and then hung up without another word.

I managed to make my way to the kitchen without falling over, then stumbled back to the living room, bottle of wine in hand. Without delay, I opened it and refilled our glasses. Serfina turned the music up slightly, grabbing her glass and swaying to the beat. Angel's voice singing "Wonderful" filled the room, his smooth London R&B drawing me in. There were no words to describe how talented this man was. I put down my wine and joined her.

I didn't know how long we'd been dancing and laughing. All I knew was that the bottle was empty again. Serfina squinted as she scrolled through her phone, searching again for Hayden's contact.

Just as she located it, there was a knock on the door. She squealed, tossed the phone onto the sofa, and flung the door open, proceeding to jump on Hayden and straddle him as he caught her, kissing him as he carried her back into the room.

My eyes drifted back to the door as Sebastian strolled in. Serfina soon jumped off Hayden and plucked the wine from his hands. He raised his eyebrow, smiling at her, before meeting my gaze intensely.

I felt it in my soul.

I looked away nervously. "Let me grab some more glasses."

In the kitchen, I leaned against the counter, breathing deeply, trying to get control of myself. My head spun from the alcohol and the sudden rush of heat to my core. I tried to push the feelings down, but they wouldn't go away. I jumped up on the counter, crossing my legs to extinguish the heat still lingering between them. All I wanted was to feel his fingers push into me.

"Nyx." Sebastian's low voice broke through my thoughts.

He looked more rugged this evening. Every time I saw him, he seemed more handsome. Maybe I was just noticing details now, like the faint scar above his right eyebrow. I didn't remember that from before. He stood in front of me as he brushed my hair behind my ear, his fingertips lingering on my cheek, causing my breath to hitch. I leaned in, that ache returning between my thighs. He took a step closer, my legs instinctively parting for him. My breathing quickened, heart pounded as he leaned in, his lips brushing my ear.

"You have no idea how badly I want you."

"Then take me," I whispered back.

He slowly lifted his fingers to the seam of my leggings, gently brushing my centre. My breath caught, his touch starting a fire between my legs.

"Damn, look how soaked you are."

"Sebastian, please." I could feel my breath getting heavier, my body desperate for his touch.

"There's a good girl."

I leaned back as he slid his hand under my waistband, his fingers gliding directly to my clit.

I let out a moan, and his free hand covered my mouth. "Be quiet."

I nodded, and he pushed two fingers in, causing my body to arch into his touch and whimpers to escape my mouth.

He quickened his movements, his thumb massaging my clit, and my hips started rolling to meet him. My body was on fire, my heart racing. I was ready to explode.

"Fuck those fingers for me," he whispered in my ear.

"Aria! Come on, girl!" Serfina interrupted from the living room.

Sebastian withdrew his fingers, and I whimpered against his hand, my body aching, begging for release.

"That's a shame." He brought his fingers to his mouth, licking them clean. "Fuck, Nyx. You taste so good. Shall we go back in?" He threw his smile at me, forcing the heat to my cheeks. Then he turned around, grabbed two glasses, and left.

ET LUX IN TENEBRIS LUCET

25

SEBASTIAN

"Do you think you should maybe call it a night?" I suggested once Hayden had taken a wasted Serfina home. Aria had just picked up the half-full bottle of wine again.

"No, no." She attempted to point her finger at me. "You don't get to tell me what to do." As if to demonstrate her point, she took a swig from the bottle. "No one gets to tell me what to do anymore."

I frowned. The fact that she was talking to me like that proved she didn't need any more tonight. I grabbed the bottle from her and placed it on the table as she pouted.

"Sebastian Knight, you don't get to control me." Her tone was stern this time, her eyebrows furrowed dramatically.

I let out a silent laugh. She clearly had no idea what she was saying and didn't understand that it wasn't control; it was me looking out for her. Yet, she was never one to fully listen to that when we were younger, so I didn't know why I ever thought she'd listen to me now. My eyes met hers, searching for an answer. It was probably the alcohol, but they seemed to twinkle more this time.

I shifted slightly, opening my eyes. Aria was fast asleep, her head in my lap. She looked peaceful. I flicked my wrist, looking at my watch. It was 3 a.m. I didn't know what time she fell asleep, but she was adamant she was finishing that last bottle of wine, and I'd decided not to argue with her about it.

I gently brushed the hair from her face with my fingers.

"Aria," I said softly. She shifted slightly with my voice. "Aria, we need to get you to bed."

She slowly lifted her head, and I helped her sit up. I stood, taking her hand to steady her as she swayed onto her feet, and guided her to her bed. We were a step away when she stumbled on the rug, grabbing my T-shirt to steady herself, but ending up pulling me with her onto the bed. Her heart raced against my chest as she let out a soft giggle.

She brushed my loose hair out of the way so I could meet her eyes. I ran my thumb over her lips, and she trembled beneath me. I leaned into her, taking in that sweet apple scent of hers, desperate to taste her skin. My cock hardened at the feel of her curves beneath my body.

I closed my eyes and gritted my teeth, trying to regain a semblance of control as I pushed myself off her, my dick aching in protest. There was no way I was going to sleep with her whilst she was still drunk.

"Sebastian," she whispered, her lip trembling. She held out a hand. "Can you stay with me tonight?"

I looked down at her hand and then took hold of it, squeezing it tight.

I'd stay forever, if she wanted me to.

I climbed behind her, wrapping my arm around her waist. She naturally shifted her body back, curves fitting perfectly into me. I gripped her hip, preventing her from getting any closer so she couldn't feel how hard I was. She tried to wiggle back again.

"Aria." I tried to control the desperation in my voice. "Stop." I tightened my hand on her hip to make my point. It was pure torture being this close to her and not being able to touch her like I wanted to.

What felt like a lifetime of restraint ended when I could feel she was asleep.

I couldn't take my eyes off her; she was hypnotising, beautiful—everything I wanted, and that only made me more desperate for her.

I didn't want to wake her, so I returned to the living room and sat back on the sofa, rubbing my face, trying to erase the feelings that were exploding through my body. I got up and made my way to the kitchen to try and distract myself by making coffee. Thank fuck she had a coffee machine; there was no way I'd be drinking that instant shit.

I leaned my back against the counter, waiting for the machine to warm up. My mind soon drifted back to Aria—when didn't it? Was this normal? To want someone so much to the point it was almost obsessive? I rubbed my face again, trying to wipe the thought away.

"Sebastian?" I startled. I hadn't noticed Aria standing in the doorway, confusion on her face. "What are you doing in my kitchen?"

Before I could reply, the machine pinged, telling me it was ready. Perfect timing. "Making coffee," I told her. "Do you want one?"

She stood there, staring at me for a few seconds, before she fully entered the room. She balanced on her tiptoes to try and grab a cup from the top cabinet.

"Do you want me to get that?" I reached up, and instinctively she ducked away, I stared at her as she recovered and swatted my hand away, pretending it hadn't happened.

"I'm perfectly capable." She eventually grabbed one and placed it on the counter, then turned to face me. "See?"

I took a step forward, closing the gap between us. "Perfectly capable," I whispered, brushing her hair from her face. "I'm taking that as a yes to coffee?"

I smiled, but inside my heart was aching. What had happened to my sweet girl? I carried on making the drinks and then handed her a cup before we returned to the sofa.

"You never told me what you were doing here?" she asked, breaking the silence.

"You were pretty drunk last night. You asked me to stay."

Her eyes searched my face as she took a sip of her coffee, then placed it on the table. She was about to speak but was interrupted by the post being pushed through her letterbox. She stood and flipped through the envelopes quickly, barely glancing at them, until she paused on one. Her fingers gripped it tightly.

"Is everything ok?" I asked, standing up.

"Yeah, everything's fine," she replied, a little too quickly, smiling at me.

Her eyes didn't quite meet mine, and her shoulders had stiffened. I took a step closer.

"Nyx, if something is wrong, you can tell me."

"It's fine," she snapped, slapping the letters on the table, then rubbed her forehead. "I'm just feeling the effects of too much wine." She tried to form a smile, but it looked pained.

Something wasn't sitting right with me. She was hiding something serious, and I didn't like it.

This wasn't Aria.

She wasn't a liar.

I grabbed my jacket, putting it on.

"Where are you going?"

"I have business to attend to," I lied, storming out the door.

26

ARIA

I stared at the front door, I couldn't believe Sebastian had left like that. What an asshole. My eyes flickered to the letter on the table for a split second. No, he wasn't; I was for snapping at him. I shouldn't have. Did he suspect anything? I'd never forgive myself if I dragged him into Jason's world.

I sighed as I sat down on the sofa, my focus solely on that letter, I was scared to open it. I should have done it when Sebastian was here—then I wouldn't have been trembling right now. But I didn't want him to see me like this.

I shook my hands out, trying to stop them from shaking. Maybe I should call him, ask him to come back? I grabbed my phone off the table and found his number, my finger hovering over it, hesitating. What if he didn't want to talk after what I'd just done? I couldn't bear that rejection right now—not with this letter looming over me.

I took a deep breath in and released it slowly, trying to gather my wandering thoughts. No, I wouldn't call him.

My mind wandered to Callum; he'd know for sure if it was Jason.

I found his number and dialled, tapping my foot nervously on the floor.

"Hello?" The voice was groggy, as if he'd just woken up.

"Callum …"

He cleared his throat. "Aria? What's happened?"

"I need you to be honest with me."

"Always."

"Have you heard from Jason?"

There was a pause before he spoke. "He's my brother. Of course I have."

I stood, rubbing my hand over my forehead. "Is it you?"

"Is what me?"

"The letters, Callum. Is it you?"

"What letters? Is everything ok? You don't sound right."

I let out a heavy breath. Deep down, I knew he'd never do anything like that. He was the complete opposite of his brother, even though he was pretty high up in the organisation Jason ran.

Callum dealt with anything you could imagine—guns, drugs, money, and everything else that came with that lifestyle. Everyone knew who he was, and they feared him.

Yet, with me, he was different. He was kind.

"I'm sorry for what he did to you. If I'd known what he was going to do, I would have kept you safe." His voice was a whisper. "I miss you, my little Astra."

The tears formed in my eyes, and I blinked, releasing them into the world. The name he only ever called me in private. He told me I'd always be his bright little star, no matter where I was.

Callum was five years older than me, and I considered him a brother.

"You paid me to leave."

"Yes, to protect you."

"I don't need your protection," I replied bluntly.

He let out a little laugh. "Still got that fire in you, Aria. You know how deep you were with us. If some of the men knew why Jason was on remand … well, let's just say you wouldn't be talking to me right now."

I knew he was right. Where Jason had gone, I was forced to follow. Most of the time, I'd sat there whilst they all met to talk about "business." Always quiet, always observing.

Always listening.

"I'd cross county lines for you, my little Astra. Just remember that."

Then, he hung up.

I placed my hand on my heart to try and steady my breathing. I shouldn't have called him. He was the past, and I was trying to move forward.

My eyes flickered over to the letter again. Not today. Today, I was going to go out and enjoy myself.

I straightened my tight, short black skirt and brushed over the invisible creases on my long-sleeved crop top. It had been a while since I'd worn anything like this, but I didn't care.

Tonight was about being the old me. I was determined to heal, and this was something I needed to do for myself.

The bar I'd found down some back alley in Hackney was heaving as I entered. The music was pumping loudly, and everyone looked like they were enjoying themselves. I'd ordered a shot to calm the nerves in my stomach, and I could feel it make its way through my system. I'd managed to find a quieter area near the back, and I leaned against the bar, vodka and Coke in hand. This was what I needed: some fun in my life without worrying.

"Aria, isn't it?"

I turned to the familiar voice to come face to face with Nicholas Rossi.

"That's me."

"I never forget a pretty face." He smiled, then took a sip of his drink. "By yourself?"

"Yeah, I am."

"How about I keep you company?"

I hesitated. "Sure."

He smiled, gesturing to the table in the corner. We made our way over and sat down.

"So, what brings a girl like you to a place like this?"

"I could say the same about you, with that tailored suit." I raised my brows, then took a sip of my drink.

He let out a silent laugh, taking a sip of his amber liquid. "I own the place."

"You … what?"

He nodded, then signalled the barman to bring me another drink.

"Is this how you know Sebastian?"

He leaned back in the chair, his eyes making their way from my bare legs to my eyes.

"I know Sebastian from a lot of places."

This guy wasn't going to tell me anything. I felt my phone vibrating, and I grabbed it out of my bag.

Sebastian.

I cut the call.

It started again. I watched it ring out, and then I switched it off.

"You can get that, if you need to." Nicholas gestured towards my phone.

"It's nothing important."

I took another sip of my drink, and the next thing I knew, I'd been grabbed by my wrist and pulled from my seat.

"What the fuck are you doing here?" Sebastian's voice was laced with anger, and his eyes burned into me.

My heart pounded. I ducked my head, curling in on myself, fear running through me for a split second before my body caught up that it was just him. Then it turned into something different, a fire deep in my being that set everything ablaze.

"Let go, Sebastian," I demanded, and he reluctantly released my wrist.

"I don't think she wants you here." Nicholas sat there, swirling his amber liquid, eyes on Sebastian.

"This has nothing to do with you," he hissed.

Nicholas rose, stepping from the table and straightening his suit. "Oh, but it does when you're in my establishment."

Sebastian took a step closer to Nicholas, his body tense, fire burning in his eyes.

"You wouldn't have this place if it weren't for me."

Nicholas smirked, letting out a heavy breath through his nose. "Sebastian Knight, the little rich boy who thought he could be a leader. Instead, he was just crying over his dead mum."

Sebastian swung straight for Nicholas, hitting him clean in the jaw, causing him to stumble back into the chairs. My hands flew to my mouth, and knots started tying in my stomach.

"Sebastian!" I shrieked.

Before Nicholas even had a chance, Sebastian had grabbed him by his collar, and his left fist met Nicholas's face. My body weight shifted, forcing me to take a step back as I watched in horror. Sebastian hit him again, and this time, blood splattered in all directions.

"Sebastian, stop!"

I rushed over, grabbing Sebastian's arm, trying anything to get him off Nicholas, but my efforts were in vain as the bouncers arrived.

It took four to finally pull Sebastian off Nicholas and keep him back.

Nicholas laughed as he stood, spitting blood.

"Look at her. She's terrified of you." He smirked through the blood in his mouth.

Sebastian turned to face me, and I tried my hardest to hide it, but he could always see through me.

"You're such an asshole, Sebastian."

I stormed through, pushing past them all as I went. I needed some air.

ET LUX IN TENEBRIS LUCET

27

SEBASTIAN

The bouncers released their grip. I rolled my shoulders, shaking out the tension, and dragged a hand through my hair. The rage still burned hot in my gut, feeding the fire that spread through my veins.

"Stay away from her," I snarled.

He laughed again, straightening his suit. "Get out."

The bouncers pushed me towards the door "This isn't over, Nicholas," I warned him over my shoulder.

"Oh, I'm counting on it."

Stepping out into the cool, fresh air, I took a deep breath to try and calm that anger in me.

My eyes flickered down the alley, catching Aria's silhouette.

This girl was driving me crazy.

"Nyx, what the hell were you doing back there?"

"Trying to have a good time, but once again, you ruined that," she snapped.

I backed her against the wall. "You want a good time, Nyx?" I growled in her ear.

I pinned her wrists above her head. My whole body pressed against her, consuming any space between us. I traced my fingers down her arm and rested them on her chin, tilting her head for her eyes to meet mine.

"Look at me."

Her eyes burned like the full moon laced with desire. "Sebastian, please."

I leaned into her ear, taking in her scent. "Please, what?" Her breath hitched, her heart racing against mine.

"I … I …"

My eyes dropped to her full, pink lips, and I was powerless but to give in to this unbearable need. I tightened my grip around her wrists and trailed my lips down to her neck, my cock straining against my trouser fabric. She had no idea what she was doing to me.

"Sebastian …" Her voice was lower than a whisper.

My hand trailed up her thigh, under her skirt, my fingers pushing the little lace that barely covered her to the side.

My lips made their way to her ear. "Who do you belong to?" I whispered, massaging her clit.

She caught her breath and let out a desperate whimper.

"Who do you belong to?" I asked her again, running my two fingers down and thrusting them into her dripping pussy.

She rose to her tiptoes, her body pushing harder against mine, her moan vibrating through my ear, heightening every nerve in my body.

I slowly pulled my two fingers out and started rubbing her clit again.

"Last time I'm going to ask you, Nyx. Who do you belong to?"

"You. I belong to you," she finally managed to get out.

"Good girl."

She was mine and always had been. I wasn't about to let anyone else have her.

I released her wrists, and her hands found my belt buckle, undoing it and releasing that tight coil of tension in my core. She lowered to her knees and started to stroke my long length. Any control or restraint I had left flew out the window. The tip of her tongue licked the pre-cum off that I'd already leaked from her touch, sending shivers up my spine.

"Fuck," I growled, my palm hitting the wall to steady me.

Her eyes met mine as she slowly took me into her mouth. My body was igniting, lighting everything in it, setting a blaze through me.

"That's it. Look at you, taking all of me."

My free hand took hold of her hair, and I gently started thrusting, holding off for a beat when she gagged around me.

"Fuck, Nyx. Play with yourself for me. I want to watch you come whilst you take me in your mouth."

She took her free hand and started rubbing herself, her moans vibrating on my cock, heat rushing straight thorough my body.

Her breathing became heavier, her moans intensifying. She was nearly there, and I was ready to explode, the pressure unbearable, the burn flooding through me.

"Look at me. I want to watch you come."

Her eyes fixed on mine, I could see her orgasm hit as her body trembled. All it took was that look.

"Fuck." I slammed my palm into the wall, releasing everything into her mouth. She swallowed and flicked her tongue out to clean up anything that was left before I pulled her up and pressed my lips hard onto hers, tasting myself on her tongue.

"You're so fucking beautiful," I said after pulling away.

After zipping my trousers back up, I removed my jacket and wrapped it around her, then locked my fingers with hers.

"Let's go," I said, pulling her along the alley.

"Sebastian, slow down. I can't keep up."

I stopped, picking her up and placing her over my shoulder.

"Put me down," she squealed.

No chance. Besides, I had a pretty good view of her arse.

"Not an option, little sis," I laughed, knowing full well it would wind her up.

"Stop calling me that!" She hit my back.

We reached my car, and I opened the passenger door and gently placed her in, pulling the seatbelt over her. I got in as she sat there, her arms crossed, looking out the window.

"Nyx, look at me."

She turned to face me, and I leaned over, resting my hands on her cheeks.

"Promise me you'll stay away from Nicholas."

She sighed. "You need to tell me what's going on."

It's nothing you need to worry about," I whispered, then gently kissed her forehead.

I wanted to tell her everything; I knew she wouldn't be satisfied with that brush-off. What I had been involved in until taking over the company. Yet I still had that niggling feeling about why she'd come back, and I couldn't shake it.

She turned to face me, her brows furrowing. "Where are we?"

"My place."

I stepped out of the car and made my way around, opening the door for her. She took hold of my hand as I helped her out.

She looked up at the building. "Guess you can't take the boy out of Chelsea."

I was born and raised here; nowhere else would compare. I'd bought this place a few years ago after leaving the house I grew up in, a house I was glad to leave behind. The only good thing about it was when Aria was there. For those two years, she made it liveable, managing to bring light into the place.

I opened the door and switched the light on. She released my hand, taking a few steps forward and looking around, then turned to face me.

"You live here all by yourself?"

"Yeah. Apart from Jane, my housekeeper."

I was hardly here, anyway. If I wasn't with Hayden or at the Organisation, I was at work. This house was more of a show home than anything else.

I held my hand out and she took hold of it, allowing me to lead her to the kitchen. The spotlights came on, dimly lighting the space, but it was always enough to see what you were doing.

I gripped Aria's waist and set her on the counter. She had a thing for sitting on them. She grabbed my tie, pulling me in between her legs, and brushed the loose strands of hair from my face.

I was weak for this girl.

She leaned in, her lips inches from mine, and I wanted to devour them, but instead, I kissed her forehead.

"Let me make you something to eat," I said, grabbing some bacon from the fridge.

"What makes you think I'm even hungry?"

I smiled, letting out a silent laugh. "I know you, Nyx."

She crossed her arms. "Maybe I don't want bacon."

I walked back over to her, placing my finger over her lip. "Shhhh."

She rolled her eyes at me and tapped my hand away.

About thirty minutes later, she'd eaten the whole sandwich, covered in mayonnaise, because that was her favourite thing.

She sat on the edge of the bed, legs crossed, still in my suit jacket.

"Wear this." I handed her one of my T-shirts.

I sat next to her and unbuttoned the jacket, removing it from her arms.

"I can get changed by myself."

She rose, pulling her top over her head, then wiggled her tight skirt over that curved arse. She stood there, her lace, black knickers not even covering it. My eyes trailed up her body, landing on her matching bra covering her full breasts. This girl was mesmerising.

She pulled my T-shirt over her, then tied her hair in a messy bun and made her way back, moving her body to straddle me.

She pulled my tie and unbuttoned my shirt. I placed my hands on her jaw, gazing straight into those beautiful eyes of hers. I shouldn't have been so rough with her before, but she was driving me insane.

"I'm sorry," I whispered.

Confusion ran through her face. "For what?"

"What happened in the alley."

She grinned. "I'm not." She leaned in, hesitating for a brief moment before her lips softly met mine. "If it was something I didn't want, you'd soon know about it."

Lifting her by the waist, I placed her in the middle of the bed and got up, removing my clothes. She pulled the blanket down and slid underneath, lying on her side to face me as I got in. Our eyes met as my fingers gently played with the loose bits of her hair.

"You're so special, Nyx. I don't want to hurt you."

She shifted closer and wrapped her leg over mine as our bodies naturally met each other's.

"You could never hurt me, Sebastian. I trust you with my life."

As my lips met hers, that spark spread into me, flowing through my veins, warming me from the inside out.

ET LUX IN
TENEBRIS
LUCET

28

SEBASTIAN

Turning off the engine, I sat there, staring out the window at the Organisation's HQ. As peaceful as it was having Aria wrapped up in my arms, I couldn't sleep, replaying finding her with Nicholas in the bar over and over, then circling back to the big question of whether Aria was working for Jason and Callum.

My mind was going a hundred miles an hour, and I couldn't stop it. I needed to find Hayden. I needed that information now. I didn't care if he was still working on it—nothing else mattered, only the truth.

"Sebastian." The guard nodded as I approached the door.

I just gave him a curt nod; I didn't have time for small talk.

"Is everything ok?"

"Everything's fine," I snapped.

He hesitated, his eyes lingering on my face before he nodded and opened the door. *Finally.* I marched through the building, making my way to where I knew Hayden would be. I flung open the door—there he was, sitting with Matt, laughing and drinking.

"Hayden," I called as I approached them.

Hayden's laugh trailed off as he glanced up at me, taking a sip of his drink. Did he not realise this was urgent?

"Join us for a drink, Sebastian," Matt said.

"No," I replied bluntly.

Hayden looked at me, raising his brow, as he rose from his seat. I clenched my fists as he stood there like everything was normal. His laughter pierced every part of my body, reminding me that he was not taking this seriously. The anger started to surge in my chest again as I thought about Aria, about what she might be hiding from me.

"Don't bring your issues in here," he warned.

"Is this what you've been doing instead of getting the information I need? Having a laugh?"

Hayden took a step closer to me. "I don't answer to you. I never have, and I never will. So do not come in here, making demands like you own the place. Because you don't."

That was all it took.

I saw red.

I swung for Hayden. I knew I shouldn't have, but I didn't care anymore. He stumbled back from the force of the punch, but before I could do anything else, Matt grabbed hold of my arms from behind, forcing me to give up. "Calm down, Sebastian."

I pulled my arms free as I breathed heavily, starting to pace and then running my hand through my hair. I glanced over to Hayden as he wiped the spot of blood from his lip, which forced me to stop pacing and turn to face him.

"You're falling back into bad habits, Sebastian."

"I don't have time for your shit right now," I said.

He snorted, unfazed. "And I don't have time for your issues."

He said his goodbyes to Matt and started to walk towards the door. I inhaled a deep breath, forcing myself to calm down.

"Hayden," I called after him.

He ignored me. I knew I shouldn't have hit him, but I wasn't in the mood for his games. All I had on my mind was finding out what Aria was hiding from me.

"Hayden, I'm sorry."

He paused at the door. "Don't ever bring your shit in here again, Sebastian," he warned me, then pushed through to the back, Matt quickly following.

I shook my head, running my hands through my hair.

My mind was foggy, and rage pulsed through my veins. I grabbed the bottle of whisky on the table, smashing it against the door before kicking the chair over and violently pushing the papers on the table into the air. My breath heaved, taking in as much oxygen as I could between the primal sounds I didn't recognise.

The table was next. I flipped it over, then stamped on it until the legs broke off. I picked one up, swinging for the cabinet, smashing the glasses, and raised it again, ready to smash the picture on the wall, when I caught my reflection in the mirror.

I paused. My shoulders were rapidly rising and falling, and my hair was wild, unrecognisable. My grip around the table leg loosened as it hit the floor with a thud. I looked around at the carnage I had just caused, my pulse throbbing through my knuckles from where I'd hit Hayden.

I slumped onto the floor, my shoulders hunched, chin tucked to my chest, my hands trembling.

I knew the old me was still fully in there, clawing at his cage to get out, and I'd seen glimpses of him recently, but I'd always managed not to jump over that edge again.

This felt different.

I'd lost control.

I stood at Hayden's front door, ashamed. I took a deep, steadying breath, getting ready to knock, but before I could, the door swung open, Serfina standing there with her arms crossed as her eyes burned into me.

She knew what I had done, and there was no way she'd let it slide.

"You've got some nerve coming here after the way you behaved," she said sharply.

She was right, I probably shouldn't be here, but I couldn't leave it like this with Hayden. It wasn't the first time I had lashed out, but this felt different. The thought of Aria and everything I didn't know about her had tipped me over the edge, but I needed to stay calm right now.

"Is Hayden here?"

She stood there, throwing daggers at me with her eyes. I wasn't sure how long it lasted, but eventually, Hayden pulled the door open a touch more, revealing himself. The silence was heavy between us.

"Let me talk to Sebastian alone," Hayden said to Serfina.

She looked up at him before throwing another glare my way, then storming off. Hayden took a step outside the door and placed his hands in his pockets.

"Are you done?" he asked.

"Look, Hayden, I'm sorry I took my anger out on you. I've just got this sinking feeling … I saw her with Nicholas—"

"Nicholas was with Aria?" he questioned, taking a step closer to me, confusion on his face.

"I was just as surprised. I found her in one of his bars. Something isn't sitting right," I said, trying to keep my anger down. "Something is going on, and I need that information."

Hayden hesitated. "Maybe there's a reason she's not telling you."

I crossed my arms, standing in silence as he glared at me for a moment. He soon sighed, accepting defeat, and strolled back into the house for a moment before returning with the file.

"Don't do anything stupid."

What was Aria hiding? I grabbed the file tightly as I nodded at him.

It was heavy, like it held the weight of the world.

29

ARIA

The tube was stifling. July heat clung to the packed carriage, bodies pressing in on all sides, the air thick and hard to breathe. The Jubilee line should be illegal in summer.

The carriage jolted, sending me straight into the man next to me.

"I'm so sorry," I said, gripping the rail tighter.

He pressed his lips together and looked away.

Londoners were so antisocial at times.

Finally, Canary Wharf. I apologised as I squeezed through everyone to reach the doors and get off.

Freedom.

My heels clicked along the reception floor as I hurried along.

"Aria." I stopped, turning to see Sebastian. "Why are you so late?"

"Oh, the tube was delayed."

He rose, rolling his shoulders. "You'll stay with me instead."

I narrowed my eyes at him, taking a step closer. "What? There's nothing wrong with where I live."

"I'm not arguing about it."

"Sebastian, you can't just tell me what to do," I snapped at him.

He snorted. "I can, and I just did. Are you coming, or are you working down here today?"

I screwed up my face, rolling my eyes behind his back as I followed him to his private lift. There was no way I was going to make a scene at work about it, so I'd let it slide for now.

We stepped in. He leaned against the back, and I stood a little in front as the doors closed.

"Seb—" Before I could get his name out, his arms wrapped around my waist.

"Take your knickers off," he whispered in my ear.

Butterflies started in my stomach, heat pouring from between my legs. I turned to face him.

"What?"

He leaned over, pressing the stop button on the lift, and it jolted, freezing in place.

"Don't make me ask again."

I swallowed hard, hitching my skirt up slightly and pulling my knickers down, stepping out of them, then bending to retrieve them. His hands found my arse, squeezing it as he let out a growl. I straightened, and he plucked them from my hand, inhaling my arousal.

"They're wet."

Of course they were—this man only had to look at me and I was gone for him.

He ran his hands over my waist, reaching the end of my skirt, pulling it up. He rested one hand on my lower stomach, pulling me back into him so I could feel how hard he was against my arse. His other hand found my pussy, and my knees buckled, but he held me steady against him.

He thrust two fingers in, and I rose to my tip-toes, catching my breath. I wrapped my arm around his neck, gripping the back of his hair, forcing a groan from his lips, everything on fire as he pushed his fingers in and out, circling my pulsing clit with his thumb.

"You're mine, Nyx," he growled in my ear.

"I'm yours," I managed to get out between my moans. "Please don't stop."

His lips curled against my neck. "Come all over those fingers." His fingers went faster, deeper, as my body started to reach that high.

My breathing got heavier, my moans louder, and my heart was racing against my chest. My cheeks were flushed, the heat unbearable between us until I finally let go, my orgasm hitting me.

His hand pressed hard against my stomach, keeping me steady, and a low growl vibrated through my ear. Complete bliss ran through every part of my body; it was like fireworks going off all at once. Stars clouded my eyes. I had never come this hard before.

He slowly withdrew from my body and turned me, his eyes fixed on mine as he licked up every drop of the mess I had made on his fingers. I bit my lips, so turned on by him I already wanted another.

My breathing started to steady, but he soon pushed me against the wall.

"I need more." He groaned, getting to his knees.

His tongue soon found what he wanted, my body rising again from his touch, his hands gripping my hips to hold me in place.

He teased me with the tip of his tongue, then sucked my clit, sending sparks through my body. I bit my lip, leaning my head against the wall. Stars had started to form in my eyes again.

The lift started moving.

I glanced down at Sebastian as he ran his tongue over me one last time before rising.

His hands found my skirt, pulling it back down, just as the lift pinged and the doors opened, forcing us to spring apart.

"Clearly the lift wasn't stuck." Logan smirked.

Heat rushed to my cheeks.

Sebastian straightened his cuffs, tucked my knickers into his pocket, then stepped out, patting Logan on his chest.

Fuck.

I threw my keys on the table next to the letter I had left unopened. Sebastian wanted me to stay at his, but I liked my little flat. It wasn't much, and it wasn't forever, but it was my fresh start. My new beginning. Even if I hadn't fully unpacked yet. I'd agreed to stay the night, but there was one thing I needed to face first.

I took a deep breath and opened the letter.

You will always be mine.

My fingers loosened, and the paper slowly fluttered to the floor. I'd heard those words so many times, they were burned into my mind. My heart started racing as my stomach tied itself in knots. I knew it had something to do with Jason, but I didn't know how. There should have been a restriction in place whilst he was on remand. I couldn't make sense of it all; how was this happening?

I needed to get out and give my mind space to process what was going on. I didn't know where I was going, but I needed to move. I grabbed my phone and keys and walked out of my flat.

An hour and a combination of different tubes later, I stood there looking up at Serfina and Hayden's house on Bishops Avenue. It was a vast contrast to my small flat in Woolwich. The pillars holding the house stood tall, shining as the moonlight reflected onto them. I knew Serfina was born from wealth, and she had mentioned that Hayden was in the intelligence field, but I didn't even realise a place like this existed in London.

The pebbles in the drive crunched with each step I took closer to the front door, leaving an eerie silence behind. As I reached the door, the porch light came on, forcing me to put my hand up to block some of the light out. I took a deep breath as I pressed the doorbell. Minutes later, the door opened to a slightly surprised smile on Serfina's face.

"Aria! To what do I owe this surprise?" she chirped.

"I … I just needed a change of scenery."

I stepped into a grand foyer, looking around, and she gestured for me to follow her through into the kitchen. It was vast compared to mine. The floor was covered with white tiles, and the kitchen counters … well, they were some sort of grey marble that glistened in the spotlights.

She grabbed some glasses from a cabinet. "You look like you need a drink."

I needed more than one. I sat on the stool at the kitchen counter, and Serfina placed the glasses down and retrieved a bottle of wine.

"Who was at the door?" Hayden asked, strolling into the kitchen.

Serfina finished pouring the glasses and looked over at him as his eyes met mine with a smile.

"Aria, what are you doing here?" he asked, making his way over.

"Does she need a reason?" Serfina asked playfully.

He raised his brow, then sat on the stool opposite me. Serfina grabbed a small glass and the bottle of rum for Hayden. I guessed he wasn't a wine drinker.

"Is everything ok?" Serfina asked, sitting next to him, her eyes bouncing between mine.

I ran my finger over the rim of my glass. "I just needed some air."

She leaned forward, resting her arms on the counter. "There's more to it, isn't there?"

My eyes flickered to her, then Hayden, and back to my glass as I raised it to take a gulp. I wanted to tell her everything that was happening between Sebastian and me, as well as the letters I was receiving, but I couldn't get the words out properly.

Except one.

"Sebastian," I whispered.

"What has he done now?" Frustration ran through her voice as she tapped Hayden in the stomach. "Give me my phone, Hayden. I'm going to have words with him."

Hayden rolled his eyes. Serfina frowned at him, then turned back to me with a smile.

"He hasn't done anything; I'm just so confused by it all."

"What do you mean?" Hayden asked.

I started to feel flustered, and I think Serfina realised.

"Hayden, I think I can hear your phone ringing in the other room."

Confusion covered his face. "It's in my pocket." He pulled it out.

"Get out of the kitchen," she ordered.

He looked at her, then at me, then back to her. "Oh. Yeah, that's my cue."

She rolled her eyes as he walked out.

"That man could never take a hint." She giggled. "Now, tell me."

I took a deep breath, trying to gather the right words in my head. "Things have happened between us."

"Things?" She topped up my glass, and I took another gulp, nodding.

"Ohhh." Her eyes widened, her mouth turning into a smile. "Those things."

I pressed my lips together.

"Look, Aria, if you two like each other, then go for it. What's the worst that could happen?"

Rejection? Him not feeling the same? Being another man's property again and losing my freedom? The list was endless, really.

"There's more to this, isn't there? It's not just Sebastian," she pushed.

There was more—everything with Jason, the flowers, the letter— but the words lodged in my throat. Years of being taught to stay quiet had a way of doing that. If I said it out loud, it would stop being something I could keep contained in my head. It would become real. And once it was real, I wouldn't be able to control what happened next. I took a sip of my wine, more to give my hands something to do than because I wanted it. I should tell her. Maybe not everything. Maybe just enough to breathe again.

"I've … I've had a few flowers and letters sent. It's probably nothing." I tried to brush it off.

"From who?"

"I don't know," I lied, the habit coming too easily.

Serfina reached for my hand, her grip firm. "You need to tell Sebastian."

The panic was instant. I couldn't. I didn't want to see the change in his eyes—the anger, the need to fix it, the danger that would come with that. If I told him about the flowers and the letters, I'd have to tell him everything. And if I told him everything, I wasn't sure who it would put in the line of fire.

ET LUX IN TENEBRIS LUCET

30

SEBASTIAN

It was late, and everyone had long gone home. I was meant to be collecting Aria, but everything had been swirling around in my mind all day. She was mine, there was no question about that. I had fully given in to everything I felt for her. She drove me wild, and I couldn't help but want to be with her all the time.

It was everything else that was going on with her that I wasn't quite sure of.

The way I felt about her had made me hesitate about opening that file, hoping she'd open up to me, but she hadn't. She'd told me everything when we were younger, so I wasn't quite sure what was so different now.

I glanced over at it on my desk, dread sitting heavy in my stomach. There was going to be something in that file I wouldn't like, and I wasn't sure if I was ready to know what it was.

I downed my whisky to try to numb the fear, but it didn't work; I needed more.

As I got up to pour another, the door opened, Hayden walking through it. I studied him, wondering if he already knew what was in the file. I poured myself another and grabbed a glass for Hayden. My fingers lingered on his glass for a split second as I placed it in front of him on the desk, then sat back down in my chair. Unspoken words lingered between us.

"Aria's at ours."

"What? Why?"

"Not sure, but she wanted to talk to Serfina about you." He smirked. "What have you been doing to her?"

I rolled my eyes at him.

"I never thought I'd see the day the great Sebastian Knight was weak for a woman."

He was right—I was completely and utterly weak for her. She was my kryptonite, my downfall. Everything a man like me shouldn't have, because I'd fuck over everything in my way to keep her safe, no matter what it was. I'd destroy everything for her.

His eyes flickered to the file. "Did you read it?" he asked quietly.

I picked up my glass, taking a sip, and watched his every move, as if there was something he was trying to tell me. "Not yet," I replied, trying to control my frustration.

He fixed his eyes on mine. "You need to."

I frowned at him. Why was it suddenly so important now when he hadn't wanted me to only a few days ago? I glanced over at it; the edges looked sharper than before, like it was ready to cut through what remained of my restraint.

I took a deep breath, slowly pulling it open. My eyes started to dart about the page, fixating on the picture at the top. A man with sharp jawline and cold, lifeless eyes looked back at me. *Jason Brown.* The guy Aria had moved to Leeds with. My eyes drifted under the photo, the words ringing in my head. *GBH with Intent domestic abuse case.*

I didn't understand at first; my eyes skimmed down the page, trying to piece it all together, and then it hit me: *Victim: Aria Summers.* I gripped the file tightly as my jaw clenched. Had I read that right?

The words started to sink in, and I moved further down the page to the incident report.

Victim found unconscious in a hallway … severe laceration to the wrist … multiple bruises consistent with blunt force trauma.

My eyes blurred for a second before sharpening again, every word cutting deep.

I turned the page, unprepared for what I was about to see.

I barely heard Hayden shifting in his chair. My entire focus locked upon the images in front of me.

Photos of Aria's bruised arms. The wound on her wrist trailed up her arm. Photos of the hallway. It was all there.

I felt sick, my stomach twisted in knots. My Nyx had gone through all of that, and I hadn't been there for her.

Jason had done this to her. He'd attacked her, then abandoned her.

And now he was on remand, awaiting trial.

This man didn't deserve a trial.

I stood up, my jaw clenched, and I took hold of the whisky glass and threw it, smashing it against the wall. I ran my hands through my hair, trying to get my head around it, and all the while Hayden was sitting there calmly.

He already knew.

"I told you not to do anything stupid."

"Where is he?" I demanded.

"Sebastian. No."

"I'm going to fuck him and his brother up."

"Don't start a war."

"It won't be a war when I've finished. It'll be a bloodbath."

"Sebastian, you know we'd all be behind you, but the lines are calm right now. You need to see *her*," Hayden ordered.

I glared straight at him. He was right, as usual; I did need to see Aria.

I knew now why she'd flinched when I'd reached past her, why she'd reacted the way she had when I'd attacked Nicholas and the guy in the bar. I knew now where he was from. He was one of Jason's.

She wasn't working for them; she was running from them.

31

ARIA

After talking to Serfina, I realised I needed to be honest with Sebastian. I had to tell him everything, even my involvement with Callum. If we were ever going to work, he needed to know about what had happened to me.

I didn't need to be frightened anymore.

Being around Sebastian again made me feel like I could do anything.

Stepping out of the tube station, I made my way around the corner. My phone started to ring, and I pulled it out of my pocket.

Callum's name lit up on my screen.

I frowned, pressing the side button to decline the call.

My phone rang again, Sebastian's name lighting up, and I smiled as I answered.

"Where are you?" he asked.

"I'm just walking back into my flat."

"I'll be there in ten."

The call ended and I pulled my keys out of my pocket, opening my front door.

A folded letter sat at the base of it, as if it had been slipped underneath.

We will be together again.

I froze, my breath catching—but before my mind could start racing, a sharp knock startled me into action.

I swung the door open to reveal Sebastian on the other side. He didn't look his usual sharp self; he was a mess.

He stood at the door, staring at me, the black core of his eyes consuming the blue, his hair everywhere. He looked like the weight of the world was on his shoulders. I had only ever seen him like that once before.

The night he'd left.

Was he about to leave again?

"Can I come in?"

I stepped aside, allowing him to enter, and closed the door behind him. He glanced down at the paper in my hand.

"What's wrong?" I asked, tucking it into my back jeans pocket.

He placed his hand on my shoulder. "Nyx. We need to talk."

His touch was warm, heating my body from the inside, but something felt off.

"No, don't you dare to do it to me again."

He furrowed his brows. "Do what?"

"Leave," I whispered.

He looked at me oddly. "I'm not leaving. What makes you think that?"

I let out a heavy breath of relief. "You look like you did four years ago."

He rested his hands on my cheeks. "There's no way in this lifetime I would ever leave you again. You're mine, Nyx. Always have been. I just didn't realise it soon enough. I should have stayed back then."

My heart started racing, those butterflies now stampeding around in my stomach.

"I gave you my heart a long time ago," I whispered.

His lips met mine, and the kiss was raw, desperate, like he had been deprived of oxygen. He was reminding me that I was his, claiming me again like it was the first time.

But we needed to wait.

He needed to know the truth.

I pulled away, our foreheads touching, his lips trying to reach mine again. "I need to tell you something." My breath was heavy.

"I don't care," he whispered, kissing me again.

I separated our lips again. "Please, Sebastian. You need to listen."

He let out a heavy breath, taking hold of my hands. "What is it, Nyx?"

"After you left, I met someone. His name was Jason. He was a lot older, and I moved to Leeds with him."

He placed his hands on my jaw, looking into my eyes. "We've both got history, Aria. I'm not going to look at you any differently than I do now."

"I didn't know who he really was. He was kind, took me to lavish parties, and bought me things that I never really cared for. Then he changed."

I shuddered, and Sebastian squeezed my hand.

"You don't have to tell me if you don't want to."

I took another deep breath. "He ran the county lines in Leeds. He took me into that world, drugs, illegal activities, which was when he started to get violent."

I swallowed a few times to wet my dry throat.

"Callum—his brother—did his best to protect me, but he didn't see everything. Then one night, Jason was in such a rage, I didn't think I was going to make it out alive."

I pulled my sleeve up, exposing my scar. Sebastian lifted my arm and gently kissed it.

"If I hadn't reacted when I did, I don't think I would be here."

I swallowed hard again, clearing the lump in my throat.

"Jason was arrested. He's on remand. Callum gave me enough money to leave Leeds. To protect me, because I was deep with them. Everyone knew who I was up there. The number of meetings I sat in on … I knew everything about them. I couldn't stay there anymore. So, I took the money, and I came down here to start over."

I started fiddling with my sleeves, and Sebastian soon grabbed my hands to stop me. "I should have told you sooner, but I was so scared you would look at me differently. I'm so sorry." I could feel the tears starting to form in my eyes.

He found my cheeks and tilted my head to meet his eyes.

"Nyx, don't ever apologise, you've done nothing wrong. Do you know how brave you are?"

I blinked, releasing the tears. "I don't feel brave. I allowed it to happen for so long."

He wiped my tears away. "Shhh, Nyx, none of this is your fault. You survived and broke free."

He pulled me into him, wrapping his arms around me, and my head fell into his chest. I could feel his steady heartbeat, grounding me. I inhaled deeply, breathing him all in, melting into his arms. In this moment, nothing else mattered but us.

I didn't know how long I'd been in his arms when my phone rang, cutting through the silence like a blade. I pushed away from Sebastian and picked up the phone vibrating violently on the table, my fingers hesitating before I accepted the call.

"Hello?" My voice was barely a whisper.

"Is this Aria Summers?"

"Yes, who's this?"

"This is Sally Reeves, your family liaison officer from Leeds District Police Headquarters." Her tone was steady and professional. "I'm sorry to notify you, but following the outcome of court today, CPS has decided to discontinue the case due to insufficient evidence. Jason Brown has been released, all charges dropped."

My stomach twisted. *What?*

"If you need any support or have any concerns, please don't hesitate to—"

I hung up without a word.

My fingers went numb as the weight of the news sank in. I somehow found my way to the sofa and sank onto it, the words burning through me. I hadn't even noticed Sebastian had sat next to me, his lips moving, but I couldn't hear a word he was saying. I watched my hands in my lap, my fingers tightly gripping the phone, but I couldn't feel it.

Sebastian plucked the device from my hands and took hold of them again, now kneeling in front of me. I knew I should respond to his distant voice, but I seemed to have little control over my body right now. His warm hands cupped my lifeless cheeks, his eyebrows furrowed with something close to panic.

That's when the ringing started in my ears.

Alarm bells.

He's out.

My body jolted up, but my legs weren't ready. Sebastian's grip on my arms caught me, anchoring me back to the room, to the here and now.

He searched my eyes for answers. "Aria? What's happened?"

All I could do was blink, releasing the tears that had been building. He wiped them with his thumb, waiting for me to speak, but there were only so many words I could manage.

"He's out."

ET LUX IN
TENEBRIS
LUCET

32

SEBASTIAN

I didn't want Aria in her flat anymore.

After the police called her last night, I'd brought her back to my place, and this time she didn't push back about it.

She belonged with me, so I could keep her safe.

She looked peaceful, like the nightmare of last night hadn't touched her in her sleep.

I gently brushed the loose hairs off her face. How could anyone hurt someone so perfect?

I didn't tell her I already knew. I didn't want her to know what I had done.

But hearing it from her hit harder than reading it off some piece of paper. I had let that happen to her because I left. Not this time. I wasn't going anywhere. She needed me, and for the first time in my life, I wasn't afraid to admit that I felt deeply for her, that she meant so much to me and always had.

I would find Jason, and I was going to kill him. There was no way I was going to let him get away with what he'd done.

Aria's body shifted as I softly stroked her cheek, her eyes blinking as they fixed on mine.

"I should get home."

"You're not going anywhere. Let me take care of you, Nyx."

She deserved the world, and I was going to give it to her.

"Let's go get you some clothes. I'm taking you away," I said.

She sat up in bed. "Taking me away?" She started to fiddle with her sleeves.

"It would do us both some good to get away from everything for just a little bit," I said firmly. "Besides, Serfina and Hayden are going to meet us there."

She looked at me, her eyes searching for something in mine. She must have found what she was looking for, because she smiled. I sat up, got off the bed, and held my hand out for her.

"Come on, Nyx."

She screwed her face up at me and then threw the covers over her head.

"Don't make me drag you out of bed, little sis," I teased.

She threw the blanket back off her head. "Don't ever call me that again," she said, glaring at me.

She sighed, finally tossing the blanket aside, and took my hand so I could pull her up. She paused and turned to face me.

"What if he finds me?"

I pulled her into me.

"Trust me, Nyx, no one's going to find you. Not with me around." I tilted her chin so her eyes could meet mine. "I promise I won't let anything happen to you."

I felt her body relax as she let out a breath and then started to pull away from me. I didn't want to let her go, so I tightened my arms.

"If you're not going to let me go, how am I supposed to get ready?"

I chuckled, keeping her there. "You're not going anywhere." Then I leaned in, kissing those soft lips of hers.

My phone started vibrating, and I let out and little groan, pulling it out to answer.

"Hello?"

"Sebastian Knight. I heard you were looking for me."

My eyes flickered to Aria, and I gestured to her that I needed to step out. She smiled and sat back on the bed as I left the room.

"More your brother, but I guess you'll do."

He let out a little laugh. "I'm not looking for war. I'll make sure he stays away from Aria."

"He needs to pay for what he did to her," I said, trying to control the anger I could feel bubbling inside.

"You and I both know how this works. I've protected her by sending her out of Leeds. If anyone knew why Jason was in prison, they'd kill her."

"I'd do the same to anyone who tried to come for her."

"I don't doubt that. But just remember, I know where she is. One word from me, and she won't be safe anymore."

My jaw clenched, my fists tightening by my side. This fucking asshole.

"So, I'll make you a deal. You stay away, and I won't speak a word."

I gritted my teeth. I wanted Jason to pay for what he did to Aria, but I couldn't risk her getting hurt. As much as I knew if anyone came near her, I would make them bleed, I didn't want her to feel like she was constantly looking over her shoulder.

"Fine. But I'm warning you, Callum, if I get even a whiff of him sniffing around, I will fuck him up so bad, you won't be able to identify him as your brother."

I hung up.

I cracked my knuckles, trying to release the tension in my body, to calm that burning rage inside of me. Aria didn't need to see me like this.

I walked back into the room, and her eyes met mine.

"Who was that?"

"Just work," I lied.

I rested my hands on each side of her on the bed, desperately kissing her lips like they'd been taken away from me.

"Sebastian," she giggled in between.

That burning rage soon turned into burning desire. I was fucking wild for her; everything about her drove me crazy. I'd fucking claim her as mine over and over.

"Lie down. I need to taste and worship this fucking beautiful pussy of yours," I growled in her ear.

She lay back on the bed, and I grabbed a fistful of her lace knickers, ripping them off in one go. She was always ready for me. Her chest was rising and falling fast, her breathing heavy. Pulling at her hips to bring her closer, I ran the base of my tongue over her slit, making sure I got every drop she'd already made for me. All I wanted was that sweet come of hers to linger in my mouth, until I needed more, desperate for it. I was a fucking addict for her.

Her breath hitched, and her hips arched as I ran my hands under her arse, gripping it tightly as I reached her clit and started sucking. Desperate moans fell from her lips. She gripped my hair and started grinding against my face, making my body weak for her.

"Fuck, Nyx, there's a good girl. Come all over my face."

"Sebastian …" Her voice was needy, desperate for more.

I felt her body tremble, my fingers digging into her arse to steady her as her moans got louder, more desperate, reaching that orgasm with full force. Her thighs clamped against me, her body burning, as I drank every single drop.

It was fucking beautiful.

Her breathing was heavy, and her movements slowed and stopped. I carried on cleaning the mess she had made with my tongue, her legs shaking as I sucked her sensitive clit.

The traffic was ridiculous as usual for the Blackwall Tunnel as we sat waiting for the lights to change. It was only midday, and we weren't going too far out—somewhere special to Aria that she had told me about when we were younger.

"Regretting me kidnapping you?" I joked.

She turned to face me. "I'd never regret anything with you."

She pressed the side button of her phone on and off, so I took hold of her hand, bringing it to my lap and squeezing it gently.

"I've got you, Aria. Always."

"I know." She smiled, locking her fingers in between mine tightly, then turned to look back out the window.

Eventually, we arrived at the house I owned in Margate, Kent. I'd bought it a few years ago, telling myself it was an investment, but deep down, it was because of Aria. She had spent most of her childhood here—days out with her mum when she was little and then days out with friends when she was old enough.

"I can't believe you own a house here."

"I own a lot of houses."

She rolled her eyes at me. I retrieved our bags from the boot and then made my way up the path to the front door. Realising she wasn't next to me, I turned to see her still leaning on the car.

She bit her lip. "Are you sure you want to do this?" she asked.

I wasn't entirely sure what she was referring to, but I knew there was nothing I was more sure of than being with her.

"I couldn't be more certain."

33

ARIA

It had been about an hour since we arrived. I was putting things away in the bedroom, the sun warming through the sash window. It was nice to be away from the busy city, but I couldn't help but keep checking my phone, waiting for … something. I wasn't sure what. I sighed. I still couldn't believe they'd just dropped the case like that.

I caught my reflection in the mirror.

I wasn't the same girl I was before. Just like the butterfly had to go through metamorphosis, I'd changed, transformed into someone else. This was me now. I needed to start looking forward and be strong.

I pushed the side button on my phone, switching it off and placing it into the drawer.

There was a knock at the door, and Sebastian opened it, standing there in the doorway.

"You ready to go?"

"Yeah, I am." I smiled.

We made our way downstairs, and Serfina soon hugged me.

"Aria, girl." She pulled away. "Sebastian's normally no fun; what did you do to him?" she teased.

"I am fun," he protested.

"No, you're intense." She patted him on the chest.

"Serfina, why have you got so many bags for one night?" Hayden held up three travel bags.

"A girl's got to look good. Besides, I never hear you complaining." She smirked, then kissed him on the lips.

He rolled his eyes, then proceeded to take the bags upstairs.

I loved these two together. There was never a dull moment with them. She was the sharp salt to his smooth caramel.

"Hayden, hurry up. I'm starving," Serfina shouted.

"Well, if you hadn't brought so much stuff, you could have eaten by now," he shouted back from upstairs.

"Hayden, Serfina is getting hangry." Sebastian laughed.

"Shut up." She hit him in the stomach, and he doubled over, pretending it hurt.

"You're such a child." She rolled her eyes at him.

"I'm done," Hayden said, appearing in the room.

"There's a really nice fish and chip shop down the road," I suggested.

There's no way you could come to the seaside and not have fish and chips. Me and my mum used to get it every time we came. It was one of my favourite memories as a child.

We were there within ten minutes and didn't have to wait long for the food to arrive. It smelled amazing, and the batter on the fish was golden, crispy, ready to be crunched.

I watched as Serfina picked up some haddock on her fork, putting it near Hayden's mouth, telling him to try it, much to his protestation, so she moved it further to his mouth and told him he had to. He soon gave in and took it off the fork. I quietly chucked to myself. These two would be comical to watch when they were an old married couple.

Sebastian's hand rested on my thigh, bringing that instant heat to it. He then ran it down between my legs. My body jolted from his touch, knees banging the table.

"Aria, you ok?" Serfina asked, arching her brow.

I cleared my throat. "Yeah. Pins and needles."

The heat rushed to my cheeks, and my eyes flickered to Sebastian, who was scrubbing his stubble with his other hand.

"You should eat up. It'll get cold," he said.

I pushed my lips together, frowning at him, as he started to trail his fingers up again. I took a deep breath, putting a chip in my mouth.

He then leaned into my ear and whispered, "You're soaking."

The chip went down hard as I swallowed to clear my throat.

The warm, salty summer breeze hit me, carrying the smell of freshly baked doughnuts as we walked down the road towards Dreamland, the neon lights flickering in the distance and the sound of the arcades growing louder. I hadn't been here since I was a teenager.

Sebastian's hand brushed against my own as we walked through the entrance, his fingers naturally intertwining with mine, holding on tight enough for me to know he was there.

"Would you look at you two, holding hands and all," Serfina teased, linking her arm through Hayden's.

"Took you long enough," Hayden said, nudging Sebastian.

Sebastian rolled his eyes. I could feel my cheeks starting to burn, but I didn't care; I was happy.

"Don't make me get rid of you two," Sebastian joked.

Serfina patted him on the back. "You wouldn't dare."

"Try me."

I looked up at Sebastian, who smiled back at me. Today, I was going to enjoy myself like I used to when I was younger. I was going to be the girl from before I'd ever met Jason Brown.

Sebastian leaned into me as we reached the Waltzers. "You smell delicious."

A flush hit my cheeks. I was completely obsessed with him, and I couldn't stop it. I thought I always had been. Then he leaned in, gently kissing my forehead and we got onto the ride. Serfina and Hayden were in the cart next to us. I hadn't been on these in years, and I'd forgotten how much they spun around. Laughter fell out of my mouth. Sebastian took hold of my waist, sliding me to him so I stopped moving about with the speed. Serfina screamed with excitement in between the spins as they got faster.

We'd spent a few hours in the amusement park. Serfina and Hayden had gone off to find the roller skate room. Sebastian wrapped his arm around my shoulders and pulled me in as we sat on the beach together, watching the waves. Everything about today had been wonderful, and being with him made it perfect. He always knew how to brighten my day and stop me from falling into the darkness. It was he who did it. Those bright blue eyes that smiled when he looked at me. Everything about him made me feel safe and warm. He felt like home and always had.

I looked up at him. "Thank you."

"What for?"

"Today. For knowing this was what I needed."

He kissed my forehead. "You never need to thank me, Nyx. Everything I do for you is because I care about you. I always have."

Being like this with him was what I always wanted, but never imagined it would happen. It felt right that everything we'd been through had led us to be back together and like this.

"I know what you need," he said, smiling at me.

"Oh yeah?" I arched my brow at him. "What's that?"

"Fresh doughnuts."

He stood, holding his hand out. I took it, and he pulled me up. He wrapped his arm around my shoulders, and mine naturally slid around his back as we made our way to go and get some.

The sun started setting across the beach as I glanced over to Serfina and Hayden sitting on the sand, cuddling. The sea splashed over my feet as the tide came in and out. Sebastian stood next to me, his hands in his pockets, looking out at the ocean. I took the last freshly baked doughnut out of the bag and was about to take a bite when Sebastian snatched it from my hand.

"Give it back." I giggled, reaching for it.

It was no use; he started to jog backwards, his eyes locked onto mine, giving me a cheeky smile as if he were daring me to chase him. I rolled my eyes and picked up my pace, the water splashing with my footsteps. As I reached out to grab his T-shirt, he jumped back, laughing, and took a huge bite.

That was it.

I bent down, cupping the seawater in my hand before splashing it all over him.

He stood there with his mouth slightly open and burst out laughing as I splashed him some more, grabbing my waist to stop me and pulling me into him.

I gazed up into his eyes as our laughter died down.

He tucked the loose bits of my hair behind my ear, resting his fingers on my chin, then slowly leaned in and kissed me as the sun came down around us.

I hadn't had this much fun in a long time.

ET LUX IN
TENEBRIS
LUCET

34

SEBASTIAN

It was late now, but we were all sitting on the floor in the living room, laughing, drinking, and having a good night. I couldn't help but keep stealing glances at Aria—the way her eyes sparkled when she laughed. The way her face lit up. She looked happy.

After everything she had been through, she still managed to look forward in life, and I wanted to be with her every step of the way. I knew the time was coming that I needed to share my own past. She had been brave in telling me about Leeds; I just hoped I'd have a portion of her strength when the time came, and that she'd not look at me differently.

Hayden nudged me. "Has the great Sebastian finally found someone?" he joked in a low voice.

I raised my brow, taking a sip of my whisky. I guess I did have someone. I had Aria.

"Right, you. I think it's time for bed," Hayden said, taking Serfina's hand and pulling her up.

Her laughter faded as her eyes flickered to Hayden, then to me and Aria, and back to Hayden. "Oh, I see." She giggled.

Hayden rolled his eyes as he led her upstairs.

The room was silent, full of unspoken words between us. Aria was everything I wanted, and I wished I'd never left her all those years ago because we'd missed out on that time together. She was more than beautiful; she was phenomenal—everything to make a grown man fall to his knees. Every look, every touch, drove me completely insane. I felt like I couldn't breathe without her next to me, as if she were my oxygen.

That spark of hers ignited my heart, forcing a surge through my veins. I took a deep breath, and just as I spoke, she did too.

"Nyx," I whispered.

"Sebastian."

We both looked at each other, smiling, as I moved closer to her.

"You go."

"Today was perfect."

"Nyx, I want the best for you, I always have," I said, taking her hand.

I paused for a moment, swallowing hard as I gently brushed my thumb back and forth over it. This was hard, allowing myself to fully feel. To fully open up. It was something I never thought I'd have with a woman. This time, I wasn't going to walk away from it. I was going to fully embrace everything with her.

"You mean everything to me. You always have," I said, barely a whisper.

The silence between us returned for what felt like a lifetime before her hand brushed the loose bits of my hair from my forehead, causing me to look up and meet her eyes. She lightly placed her hand on my cheek, smiling at me.

And in that moment, I knew.

She didn't need to say a word; those sparkling eyes told me everything.

She was my Nyx, that goddess of the night who brought the moon to light the darkness.

I brushed her soft blonde hair behind her ear, my finger lightly tracing down her cheek before skimming over her lips and resting them on her chin, her chest rising and falling with every touch. My gaze dropped to those full pink lips of hers, and I slowly leaned in.

They were warm, inviting, and I claimed them as mine. Her hands slipped under my T-shirt before she pulled it over my head, our lips desperately making their way back to each other, unable to bear even a second apart. My lips brushed against her neck, and the heat from her delicate, smooth skin hit me like wildfire—slow but inevitable. Her breathing became heavy as I slid her straps down, kissing every sweet, delicious inch of her. Her apple scent infused into mine, becoming part of me. She gripped my hair, sending a spark down my spine that set every nerve on fire. I could feel her heart pounding against my chest, and mine soon synced with hers. My hands skimmed up her sides, removing her top, then unclipping her bra. I gazed at her perfect body for a second; it was the kind that could make a man feel weak at the knees.

Her hand found the inside of my joggers, and she started stroking my length back and forth. My lips found hers as my breathing became shallow, her touch sending me wild and desperate for her. I rose and she pulled my joggers down, my cock springing free. She looked up at me, biting her lip, then shifted to her knees. Her fingers wrapped around my cock, and as she gently starting stroking, pre-cum glistened on the tip. My senses were on overdrive; her touch was fucking magical. Fuck. This girl had me fighting every urge in my body to stop myself from coming.

I tilted my head back, letting out a low groan. "Fuck." I felt her tongue tease the tip, and my hands rested on the back of her head. Her mouth slid over it.

My cock was pulsing, aching, my whole body ready to detonate. I didn't think I could get any harder for this woman, but she somehow managed it. I took her hands, bringing her to her feet. My lips crashed onto hers, and she playfully bit my lip.

Her jean shorts came off, and I soon squeezed that curved arse of hers and gently laid her down on the floor, then got to my knees between her legs. The heat between us was intoxicating. I slid my fingers over her pussy, watching her back arch, her chest rising high, moaning breaking through as I teased her with my fingers, then licked them dry.

I leaned over, taking a condom out of my wallet. She bit her lip, watching me rip it open and slide it over my cock. She ran her hands over my chest as I positioned myself, pressing into her slowly. I wanted her to feel every inch of me.

She gasped.

"You take me so well," I groaned, desperate for her. "You're so fucking tight around me."

Her hips arched, drawing me deeper as a whimper came from her. Fuck me, she felt so good. It was driving me crazy, and I could feel myself on the edge. She wrapped her arms around my neck as I pounded harder, faster, claiming every bit of her as mine.

"I'm going to enjoy fucking you all the time."

Her kiss was deep, full of passion. Her nails pressed into my back, pushing me deeper into her.

"Fuck, Nyx, you're going to make me come." My words were a desperate, low growl in her ear, as every nerve heightened with the tension building.

"Say my fucking name."

Her moans intensified, the heat burning between us.

"Sebastian." Her voice was low, needy, as she completely gave herself to me.

Her pussy tightened around me, and with one last, deep thrust, she completely let go, her beautiful orgasm touching every part of me as if it were telling me I didn't have to control myself anymore. I pushed my lips onto hers. "Fuck." My body jerked, releasing everything into her.

My movements slowed. They stopped. I could feel her heart pounding against mine as we tried to steady our breathing, and I brushed back her hair that was sticking to her forehead. I kissed her, slowly pulling out and shifting beside her. I wrapped my arm around her, her head resting on my chest. This was what I had been craving, what my body had been begging for. Her.

Our breathing started to steady as her fingers lightly traced over my tattooed skin.

"When did you get this?" she asked.

"About four years ago."

"What does it say?"

I lay there silent for a moment before I responded. "And the light shines in the darkness."

She pulled me closer to her.

"What about this?" I turned her wrist over, tracing the small grey crescent moon with butterflies.

I felt her take a deep breath, and her heart raced against my chest. "When you left me," she whispered.

I pressed my lips to her head. "I'm sorry, Nyx. I won't ever leave you again."

Her eyes flicked open, her body moving slightly. She looked different from before, like she'd finally let go of everything she'd been holding on to. Like she was free from it all.

She looked happy.

That sass in her smile had returned.

Her eyes looked brighter.

She looked more like the old Nyx again.

I tilted her head, leaning in to kiss her and tracing my fingers slowly down her body, causing her to giggle.

"Oh, ticklish, are you?"

"No, I'm not," she protested, trying to suppress her laughter.

I started to tickle her playfully, her giggling growing less restrained, until she shifted her body to straddle me, linking her fingers in mine, and our eyes locked onto each other.

I couldn't believe how lucky I was to have her, to be able to hold her.

She was finally mine.

35

ARIA

The smell of bacon floated up the stairs, and I held tightly to Sebastian's hand as we reached the bottom.

I paused, causing him to stop and look back.

I couldn't help but smile at him; we were finally together after all these years. I guessed fate had plans for us, after all.

I just wished I hadn't gone through what I had to get here.

I grabbed his T-shirt, pulled him in, and kissed him.

He gently rubbed his hands up and down my arms. "Are you ok?"

"Yes. I promise."

He smiled at me, took hold of my hand, and led me through the hall.

Serfina was slumped on the kitchen island, letting out little mumbles as Hayden stood at the stove, cooking.

"Good morning, lovebirds," he teased.

Serfina jolted her head up, looking over at us and playfully pointing. "Oh, look at you two, all cosy and that. How cute."

I could feel my cheeks burning slightly, but I couldn't help but smile, because for once, I was happy.

"Stop it, you two. Anyone would think you'd never seen a couple before." Sebastian squeezed my hand gently.

"It's like Romeo and Juliet—two star-crossed lovers," Hayden joked.

Sebastian playfully hit Hayden's arm. "You do realise they die in the end, right?"

Hayden grabbed hold of him as they started to play-fight with each other.

"Can you two not act like children for once?" Serfina said, rolling her eyes. "My head hurts."

Hayden pushed Sebastian, and Sebastian playfully hit him one more time before they stopped, looking sheepish.

"Your head wouldn't be hurting if you hadn't drunk so much," Hayden helpfully pointed out.

She shot daggers at him and then laid her head back on the table.

"Just be quiet and make me breakfast."

Sebastian made a "whipped" motion with his hand, grinning at him. In response, Hayden gave him one final hit.

Sebastian joined him in cooking breakfast, and I sat next to Serfina—who looked like she was dying—and handed her a glass of water and some tablets. She lifted her head to take them, grinning at me.

"So, you and Sebastian," she whispered, raising her brows. "Tell me all. Are you officially together now?"

My eyes flickered to Sebastian and back to her. We were together, weren't we? He said we were a couple.

"I think so."

"Stop gossiping, you two. Breakfast is ready," Hayden said, turning to face us.

I was about to sit at the dining table when Sebastian grabbed my hand, pulling me to sit on his lap instead, wrapping his arms around my waist.

"Get a room, you two," Hayden joked as he joined us.

"I think it's cute." Serfina shrugged, grabbing some bacon.

I did the same, placing it in a roll with some mayonnaise. I lifted it, and Sebastian took it out of my hands and bit into it.

"I will never understand this, or how I weirdly like it," he said, with a mouthful.

"Is there something wrong with you?" I asked, swatting at him. "Who eats bacon with anything else?"

"There are many things wrong with him," Hayden chimed in.

Sebastian threw a roll at him—it promptly hit his head and bounced off, and we all burst out laughing.

Serfina and Hayden had become like family to me. And Sebastian? Well, he had become everything I'd ever wanted and more.

A few hours later, Serfina and Hayden had already left to head back to London, and we were finishing packing up to do the same.

"Sebastian, did you mean what you said?" I asked, turning to face him.

He walked over, placing his hands around my waist. "What did I say?"

I hesitated before asking. "That we were a couple."

He smiled at me, kissing my lips gently. "Every word." His voice was lower than a whisper. He stroked my cheek. "You don't have to worry. I'm not going anywhere, Nyx."

I looked into his eyes, and I knew he meant every word.

ET LUX IN
TENEBRIS
LUCET

36

SEBASTIAN

The view I had of Aria from my office was the only good thing about it.

She hadn't noticed me admiring her, but I couldn't help it.

Damn, that woman had stolen my heart.

After everything she'd been through, she'd still managed to come out the other side. I admired her for it. She was strong, even if she didn't believe it herself. She was so beautiful—and she was all mine.

A knock on the office door interrupted my thoughts. "Come in," I said, glancing over.

Aria walked in, papers in hand. "You need to sign these."

I leaned back in the chair, my eyes making their way over her shirt, the buttons whispering to me to rip them open. My gaze trailed down, and I arched my brow. I rose from my chair and leaned into her ear.

"I don't ever want to see you in trousers again."

She screwed up her face at me. "What are you talking about?"

"You'll wear pencil skirts in this office."

"Sebastian, you can't tell me what to wear," she snapped.

"You will wear pencil skirts so when I take you—and I will take you, Nyx—I'll know your thighs will be rubbing together, sticky with my cum."

I grabbed her arms, pulling her back against my chest, her breathing heavy. Her apple scent flooded me all at once as I traced my lips over her neck. I ran my hand over her stomach, reaching her pussy, the fabric of her trousers denying me easy access to that sweet drug.

"Fuck, Sebastian," she whispered, her head tilting back into me.

I could still feel she'd dripped through as I rubbed back and forth.

"I don't think we should be doing this in here," she said breathlessly.

"I'm the boss; I can do anything I want, anywhere I want."

I pulled her round to face me, resting my hands on her jaw. "I fucking need you now."

My lips crashed into hers. The kiss was raw, almost primal, as I devoured her, sparks flying around my veins, trying to find any way to escape my body.

Someone cleared their throat, and I opened my eyes to see Serfina standing there with her arms crossed, a massive grin on her face.

"In the office, Sebastian, really?" Serfina teased.

I hadn't even noticed her come through the door, I was so focused on Aria. I smirked at her, releasing Aria's lips, and she turned to face Serfina.

"Can you blame me?" I asked her.

"Anyway, I've come to take Aria to lunch, if you can bear to be apart that long."

I couldn't, but I wasn't going to stop her from doing anything she wanted.

"Let me get my things," Aria said.

She placed her hands on my chest and kissed my cheek before joining Serfina.

"Nyx," I called, stepping closer. "Take my card." I pulled it out of my suit jacket.

"I can buy my own lunch."

I rubbed my fingers over my chin, eyeing her up and down. "Get a pencil skirt."

She rolled her eyes at me but plucked the card from my hand.

"Bye, lover-boy," Serfina said before strolling out of the office with Aria.

I let out a little laugh as I sat back down in my chair.

I gathered all the paperwork together and placed it back in the file. My mind may have wandered a few times, but I couldn't help it. I'd never felt this way before, and wasn't sure if I was doing it right, but I didn't want to stop.

I found myself scrolling through my phone, my fingers lingering over texting Aria or not. She hadn't long left to go back to mine, but I already missed her. She'd offered to stay and help, but I'd told her she didn't need to and had Logan come and collect her.

It was my fault; I hadn't finished it, so I didn't want her waiting longer than she had to.

I looked up at the sound of the door opening. Hayden walked in and sat in the chair in front of me, forcing me to place my phone down.

"You look different," he said, eyeing me. "Happy."

"Did I not look happy before?" I joked, leaning back in my chair.

"No, you looked like a brooding mess."

I rolled my eyes. I wasn't a brooding mess before; there was just never much happiness in my life. Aria had brought something out of me I never knew I could feel. Something I never thought I wanted until she came back into my life.

"You've gone soft. Guess love will do that to a man," Hayden teased.

I rubbed my chin. Love? I hadn't a clue what that felt like or if I was even capable of it.

"It's nothing to be ashamed of. It happens to us all, eventually," he continued.

"Just because you're under the thumb …"

"You think that, but that's how you keep women happy. You let them believe they're the boss," he said.

"You keep telling yourself that."

He shook his head at me, but he knew I was right; he just wouldn't admit it.

Then again, what did I know about love? I'd never had a relationship in my life, so who was I to know what was wrong or right? It felt strange, knowing that I had someone who was mine.

"Look," Hayden said, leaning forward in the chair. "I get you're scared with all of this, but don't ruin it by overthinking like you always do. What you have with Aria is special."

He was right, as always. I did overthink everything, and if I let that take over, I would spoil it. Something I didn't want to do. I wanted this. I wanted all of it. For once in my life, I was happy with where I was, and nothing would stop me from being with her.

"Besides, if you do fuck it up, Serfina will kill you, and I don't feel like covering up a murder anytime soon."

I let out a small laugh.

"You coming?" Hayden got up from the chair.

"I've got some things I need to do before I leave."

Hayden nodded and made his way to the door. He paused, turning, and said, "She's not your past, Sebastian. Don't let that get in the way of her being your future."

37
ARIA

I leaned against the kitchen counter, wine glass in hand, as I took a sip. Sebastian's place really needed a woman's touch. It reminded me of an old, sterile asylum, where nothing had been touched in years, kept pristine as if preserved for history.

His room had been the same when we were younger. Everything had its rightful place. I used to go in there sometimes and move things slightly to see if he noticed, and sure enough, he always did.

"I hope you haven't eaten," Sebastian said, one-handedly unpacking the bags of Chinese on the kitchen counter. It looked like he was hiding something behind his back.

"What else have you got?" I asked, trying to peer around.

"These."

He pulled his hand out to reveal grey roses, and my eyes widened. I placed my hand over my mouth. I had never seen this colour before; were they even real? I took hold of the bouquet, admiring its beauty. They smelt sweet and fresh. They were real.

"Grey?" I questioned, looking up at him.

"They're rare, just like you." He kissed my forehead.

I tilted my head, gazing into his eyes, leaning in to kiss him. "Thank you. They're beautiful."

"Not as beautiful as you in my T-shirt."

"Have you got a vase?"

"I'm not sure. You'll have to ask Jane."

I placed the roses on the counter, leaning back against it. "How do you not know what you have in your house?"

He bit his lip, then grabbed me by the waist, placing me on the counter. "All I need to know is I've got you in this house, and that's all I want."

His hands soon found my jaw, his lips grazing mine, becoming needy and raw as he kissed me. I wanted him just as much. My body ached for him when he wasn't touching me. It craved every inch of him, trembling every time he was near. And when he did touch me, it was earth-shattering, his mark burning into my soul, taking it as his.

Sebastian had dished up the food, and we were now finishing the last bit as I picked up the controller, pressing play to start the movie I was surprising Sebastian with. I knew he'd have something to say about it, but before it started, he stole the last chicken ball off my plate.

"Can you not steal my food for once?" I chuckled, playfully hitting him.

"I've come to realise yours always tastes better," he said, taking a bite. "What are you making me watch, anyway?"

"You'll see."

He looked at me suspiciously as I planted a kiss on his lips, then smiled back at him. As the movie started, he shook his head, rolling his eyes. I'd forced him to watch this many times before.

"Out of all the movies you could have picked, you decided to go with something portrayed as a tragedy, but in reality, it's pure madness?"

"*Romeo + Juliet* is a classic. It's devotion in its purest form," I said, finishing my noodles and then placing my plate on the table.

He arched his brow at me. "At least they've got guns in this one." He placed his plate down.

I rolled my eyes, then leaned into him as he put his arm around me, pulling me closer to snuggle on the sofa.

"If it were me, I'd have taken the whole Capulet family out for you. Then you wouldn't have to die," he told me.

"You'd have taken out my whole family?!"

"I'd take out anyone in my way if it meant keeping you safe," he whispered, kissing my head.

I supposed that was romantic, in its own kind of way.

"Nyx, it's your favourite bit. When he declares his undying love in the pool after only knowing her a few hours," he said through the kiss I had just landed on him.

It was my favourite bit, and Sebastian had seen it so many times with me to know that. But I didn't believe in sex after marriage, so they could wait; I, however, could not.

"You're not really watching this, are you?" he murmured through the kisses.

My lips curled into a playful smirk as I ran my hands under his T-shirt, lifting it off in one go.

"You drive me crazy; you know that?" he whispered in my ear.

He stood from the sofa effortlessly, holding onto my thighs as I wrapped my arms around his neck, kissing him as he pushed me against the wall.

His kisses were raw, desperate, devouring me like he was starving. He ripped my lace knickers with one rough pull. He thrusted two fingers into me. My lips parted from his, trying to catch my breath as the heat between my legs caught alight.

"You'll always be mine. No one else will ever be able to have you but me," he growled in my ear.

His words and the rough-edged tone of his voice set me on fire. It was different with Sebastian. Jason always made me feel dirty with his words, like I'd done something wrong, but all I saw with Sebastian was adoration and pure desire. What he said was true: I would always be his. There would never be anyone but him.

My hips started rolling. His fingers got faster as he pushed them in and out, massaging my clit with his thumb, those lips of his consuming mine. Moans were trying to break free, my breathing getting heavier. The fire in me was unbearable.

"Sebastian," I breathed out. "I want to feel you."

He slowed his fingers and met my eyes with his, pure, primal desire running through those bright blues.

"Nyx, I've never …" he whispered.

"I trust you."

He pushed his fingers deep, my breath catching. Then he slowly withdrew them, bringing them between our lips. I sucked his fingers, his eyes on me.

"How do you taste?" he whispered.

"Like I belong to you."

"Good girl," he growled.

I freed his length and started stroking, a raw groan falling from his lips. Then, I ran my finger over the tip, wiping the pre-cum off and licking it off my finger.

"Fuck, Nyx."

He shifted my body and rammed his cock straight into me. Pain turned into pure pleasure as I gasped. He thrusted in and out, hard and fast, primal.

"Fuck. You feel so fucking good around me like this."

I tightened my arms around his neck, desperate to keep him close, to feel that heat from his body as it lit a fire beneath my skin. My eyes rolled back as constellations started forming, sending my orgasm into meltdown.

"Don't stop," I begged, wanting to feel it again. "Fuck me harder."

He bit my bottom lip, then started to kiss my neck. Every inch of him bare against me felt intense and raw. I could feel everything start to build up again as he pounded into me, each thrust pushing me harder into the wall.

"Do you like me fucking you raw?" he growled against my neck.

"Yes," I breathed out heavily. "I don't ever want to feel anything else."

My whole body was on fire again. I'd never felt so wanted before. Every thrust, kiss, and look was filled with pure need and want mixed as one, causing my body to react in ways I never knew it could. That spark ignited as my orgasm came in hot and fast. "Fuck, Sebastian," I panted, letting everything go, my body shaking.

It sent a spark straight into him as he growled, his body jerking against mine as he released everything into me.

"Shit, Nyx. Look what you fucking do to me."

His lips took mine again as he gently lowered me to the floor, my knees shaking, but he soon grabbed my hips to steady me. He got on his knees and started cleaning up that beautiful mess we made together with his tongue. My breathing was shallow, my heart pounding as my nerves started sparking again.

He rose, placing his hands on my cheeks, and looked into my eyes. "We taste fucking beautiful together. I never want to taste anything else," he whispered.

Then he claimed my mouth as his, his tongue sharing that taste with me. It felt like he worshipped every part of me, that he knew what I wanted and needed.

"Where are you taking me tomorrow?" I asked, between kisses.

"I'm not telling you."

"You know I hate surprises."

Sebastian had wanted to surprise me for my seventeenth birthday. It was my first in London, so he wanted it to be special. He'd booked a table at the Shard. That was when he found out I was scared of heights. I'd managed to get to the top because I didn't want him to feel bad, but the minute he'd been trying to get me to look out the window, I'd completely freaked out. I'd never seen him get me out of somewhere so fast.

"You'll love this one."

I bit my lip, unsure, but I trusted that after that disaster, he wouldn't take me anywhere unless it was somewhere he knew I'd like.

He let out a deep breath, kissing me one last time before pulling away. "Do you know how lucky I am to have you?"

I smiled at him. I didn't quite understand how he was the lucky one. I wasn't anything special. If anything, I should be lucky to have him in my life. He made me feel complete, like I wasn't damaged anymore. He showed me how a man should treat a woman. To make me feel like I was the only one he saw. Every time he looked at me, it took my breath away.

ET LUX IN TENEBRIS LUCET

38

SEBASTIAN

It was such a beautiful July day, and I couldn't wait to see Aria's face when she realised where I was taking her. Every moment with her was precious. She was looking out of the window as I pulled up into the car park.

Confusion ran through her face. "Hall Place and Gardens?"

"You'll see." I smiled, then stepped out of the car, making my way around and helping Aria out. "You ready?" I asked.

She looked at me sceptically. "I don't know if I should trust a man who can't tell me what this place is."

"I wouldn't trust a man like that either," I said.

She let out a small laugh. I took hold of her hand, kissing it, then led her through the entrance.

She looked up at the sign to the Butterfly Gardens and back to me with the biggest smile on her face. "Is that what I think it is?" she asked, excitement in her voice.

I couldn't help but smile back at her. She soon opened the door, the heat hitting us as we walked deeper into the space, embraced by the sound of water steadily trickling from the fountain up ahead. The butterflies were flying around freely, landing on everything and anyone that was there. She let go of my hand and stood there, taking everything in for a few minutes. She soon turned back to face me and wrapped her arms around my neck, kissing me quickly.

"This is beautiful. How did you know I loved butterflies?"

I wrapped my arms around her waist. "Sometimes I think you forget how long I've known you." It may have only been two years we'd spent together, but I remembered everything about her. "What is it about butterflies, anyway?" I asked.

"They're a symbol of hope, of new beginnings. This beautiful creature that's not afraid to be free," she explained, gesturing to one fluttering on a leaf. She pushed away from me and laughed. "Like that one on your head."

We sat on a bench in the gardens, watching all the people go by, sipping on coffee. It wouldn't be long before summer ended and autumn started to kick in, turning the leaves brown. I never thought I'd be seeing the end of summer with Aria, but I wouldn't want it any other way. I was looking forward to everything we had to come together.

"This place is so beautiful. Why did you never take me here before?"

"I didn't even know it existed; otherwise, I would have taken you as many times as you wanted."

She smiled, taking a sip of her coffee. "Didn't get the grey roses from here, then?"

"No, they're special." I kissed the tip of her nose. "They have to be imported." I'd have them shipped regularly for her—anything to see that smile.

"I still can't believe you remembered all these things after so many years."

"Why? Did you forget everything about me?" I chuckled.

Her eyes met mine. "You're hard to forget. All the times you were there for me when I needed you. I wasn't there when you were growing up, but seeing what I saw in those two years … you still had so much love to give."

My body tensed slightly at the thought of my childhood.

She must have felt it. "I'm sorry, I didn't—"

"It's fine, Nyx." I pulled her in, kissing her forehead.

An easy silence fell around us as I held her. There was a lot she didn't know about my upbringing, a lot she'd never know.

"Do you remember when your dad arranged that family cruise from Jamaica, and you knew I didn't want to be stuck on the boat, so you made sure we missed it?"

"His face was a picture when I waved him off." I laughed, even though when we got back to England, he gave me a smack around the head and made me pay every penny back. As if that asshole needed any money from me.

"That was a really good holiday."

I arched my brow at her. "You do remember all the guys I had to keep away from you? It wasn't that great for me." The laughter started to die down, leaving silence between us until she spoke.

"Why did you leave, Sebastian?"

My body tensed, emptiness in the pit of my stomach. I'd hoped she'd never ask.

"Because you deserved someone better."

39

ARIA

Summer had drawn to an end, and autumn had crept in with the rain.

I hung up my black duffle coat, sat at my desk, and watched the water droplets fall off it. I sighed, missing the warmth already.

I opened my laptop, ready to see what today would hold. Sebastian was due back after a few days away on business. I was so used to having him around that it felt weird waking up without him.

The first morning felt like it did four years ago when he left, but he soon called me when he landed. It didn't stop me from missing him—he was like a drug, and I was addicted to him.

I took a deep breath in, closing my eyes briefly. I could faintly smell his cologne, which seemed to get stronger with each breath. Before I could open my eyes, a pair of hands covered them.

"Guess who?" Sebastian whispered in my ear.

I paused for a moment. "Hmmm, is it that really hot guy that works in the finance department?"

The hands soon removed themselves as my chair spun around to face Sebastian, who narrowed his eyes at me. "What hot guy in finance?"

I covered my mouth, trying to stop the laughter from escaping as Sebastian just looked at me, shaking his head.

"You're not even funny, do you know that?" He chuckled, pulling me into his chest and squeezing me tight.

"How was the trip?" I asked.

"Usual shit I had to sort out because of Dad."

I didn't know too much, but I knew Sebastian's dad, Stephen, had left the company near financial collapse. Sebastian had pushed him out to take over and keep his granddad's name intact. The board members had given him six months to turn the business around. He'd worked hard and managed to get it back on track, but some of them still kept a close eye on him.

"Ok, I've got work to do," I told him, resting my hands on his chest for a few seconds and then pulling away to sit down.

"Do you really, though?"

"Yes, I do," I said, playfully swatting his chest.

"Well, as my PA, you need to come with me to get breakfast."

"What, you need me to hold your hand now?" I teased.

"That's exactly what I need."

I heard the door open from the main office and turned to see Mr Kingsley walk through.

He was the oldest board member and owned the second-highest shares in the company, after Sebastian's dad.

"We need to talk," he said to Sebastian.

"Then book an appointment with my PA."

Mr Kingsley tensed, the wrinkles on his forehead stretching in frustration.

"It doesn't work like that."

Sebastian chuckled softly, straightening his cuffs. "Oh, but it does. No one, not even you, gets to demand to see me."

Mr Kingsley pointed at Sebastian. "You need to remember it's not you, but your dad who has the shares."

Sebastian took a step closer. "And you, Mr Kingsley, need to remember that if it wasn't for me, you wouldn't have any shares at all."

"Don't push me, boy."

Sebastian smiled and dusted off Mr Kingsley's shoulder. "You can see yourself out. Don't come back until you have an appointment."

Mr Kingsley snorted, storming back out into the main office.

I watched as Sebastian straightened his suit jacket, then ran his fingers through his hair.

"Sebastian, don't you think you were a bit of an asshole? You need him on side."

He raised his brows at me. "That's not me being an asshole. This is me being an asshole."

Blue flames ran through his eyes as he gently took hold of my wrist, pulling me into his office.

"Sebastian, what the fuck are you doing?" I said, trying to pull myself free.

In one sweep, he pushed the contents of his desk to the floor. My heart was pounding, heat spreading over my body.

"Hands on the desk," he ordered.

"What? No." I snapped back, swallowing hard, although my breathing was heavy, the heat between my thighs betraying me.

"Don't be a bad girl, Nyx. Do as you're told."

I turned, placing my hands on the desk, trying to steady my breathing.

"Good girl," he growled, as I heard him unclip his belt buckle.

His hands ran over my arse, then down my thighs as he grabbed my skirt, hitching it up.

"This is why you wear skirts for me."

He grabbed my arse, then spanked me hard, causing my body to move, a moan escaping my lips. My skin was burning, ready for him to fully enter me. He ripped my knickers down and thrusted hard into me. My body jolted, pleasure running through me.

He pushed harder, faster, pounding into me as he ran his hand over my back, reaching my neck and tightly gripping. Every nerve in my body was sparking, lighting everything up at once. I was so hot for him right now. My moans were intense, begging him to make me come.

"You're all mine," he growled, pushing deeper into me. "I'll never have enough of you."

"Sebastian ..."

"That's my girl. Now come for me."

He didn't have to ask twice. I screamed, my legs shaking, everything inside falling apart all at once.

"Oh, fuck, Nyx," he groaned.

I felt his body jerk, his cum flowing into me as he thrusted deep, letting out a growl. He slowly withdrew his cock, then ran his fingers over my pussy, causing me to flinch with how sensitive I was.

"Look at me."

I turned, trying to catch my breath. He sucked his fingers, tasting both of us, before pulling my knickers up and hitching my skirt back down.

"Every time you walk, you'll feel me dripping out of you."

My body was tingling, goose bumps rising at his words. I wrapped my arms around his neck, crashing my lips to his. I was so fucking aroused by him.

I lay on the sofa at my place, half watching some rom-com film I'd put on to waste the time waiting for Sebastian to finish up work. I'd been spending more time at his recently, and I needed some fresh clothes and other items to take over. He told me he'd buy me new ones, but he didn't need to waste money like that when I already had them. He said he'd pick me up when he finished in the office. My phone buzzed with a message.

Sebastian: *I'm leaving now. I won't be long.*

Aria: *See you soon x*

I pressed the side button, locking the phone, and looked back at the TV, when there was a knock at the door.

I sat up, alert, and noticed an envelope poking underneath.

I paused for a moment before retrieving it and opening it slowly, a few red rose petals falling out in the process.

I will see you soon, my love.

ET LUX IN TENEBRIS LUCET

40

SEBASTIAN

I picked up my phone and keys, pushing them into my tracksuit trouser pockets. I looked up as Hayden entered the living room, hands in his pockets. Jane must have let him in.

"Ignoring my calls now?" he said.

"No, It's not like that. I've been busy with Aria." For once, I could see a future for myself filled with happiness, and I was excited for everything we had to come. I wanted to give her the world. "What's up?"

"We need to talk," he said.

I nodded and settled on the sofa as he sat in the chair opposite, leaning forward. He didn't seem his usual relaxed self, his body tense. I waited for him to speak, but the silence seemed to grow more intense the longer it stretched on.

"It's Nicholas." His voice was low.

Nicholas?

"I don't want to know, Hayden, because if I do, you may not be able to stop me this time." I tried to keep my voice calm, but I could feel the anger in it.

The last time Hayden had come to me about Nicholas was when he was trying to throw his weight around the organisation. Bad enough he's nearly screwed us over, he'd had the audacity to think he could displace Hayden. That's how we ended up fighting it out between us, and if it wasn't for Hayden that night, I would have killed him.

"Everyone's meeting in a few days about him. They asked for you to be there," he told me.

I wasn't part of that world anymore, yet they still tried to involve me in some way or another. In some ways, I wanted to be there still, away from this corporate world of dishonesty, back to the people who knew loyalty, the people I called brothers.

Aria's face ran through my mind.

How would she react to it all? Would she understand? Would she want to be with me, knowing everything?

I'd left her once because of it all; I wasn't about to give up everything I had found with her to go back into that world.

"You don't need me there." I ran my hand through my hair and stood up.

He nodded, his face showing every sign of him not being happy with my decision, but I didn't care. He made his way out.

I glanced at the photo on the mantel, my granddad staring back at me.

ET LUX IN TENEBRIS LUCET

41

SEBASTIAN

I stepped outside the house, my fingers interlocked with Aria's, the rain falling hard to the ground. This was what she liked to call the grey season, where it only ever rained, and the sky always looked grey. This would be us for the foreseeable future until spring hit us again. I opened the car door for Aria before getting in. Leaning over, I put her seatbelt on for her.

"You know I can do that myself?"

"Just let me look after you. Besides …" I started kissing her neck. "It gives me an excuse to do this."

"You don't need an excuse. You can do it whenever you want."

"I think we should stay at home today." I grazed my thumb over her lips, looking into her eyes.

"Yeah, because the CEO and his PA both being absent at the same time wouldn't look suspicious. I swear, people in there already think something is going on."

"So what? Fuck them, Nyx. Not one person would say a thing to me in there."

"No, they may not say anything to you, but they'd look at me differently."

I rested my hands on her cheeks and looked into her eyes. "If anyone ever says anything or looks at you in a way you don't like, I will completely ruin them."

I'd fucking destroy anyone who did that to her. I don't care if it was at the office. I wouldn't allow it.

She kissed my lips and nudged me. "You need to drive or we'll be late."

We were making our way through the office when I noticed the boardroom was full and stopped in my tracks, Aria turning to look at me.

"Was there a meeting booked this morning?"

She furrowed her brows. "No, there wasn't."

What were these stuffy suits up to?

I stormed over, forcefully pushing the doors open to find them all sitting there. They soon quietened down when they noticed me.

"Nice of you to join us," Mr Kingsley said.

"There was no meeting booked."

"Sit down, Sebastian." He gestured to the chair.

I did so reluctantly. Who were they to decide this meeting without telling me? "We need to discuss your position."

I leaned forward, resting my arms on the table.

"My position?"

"Yes. I did try to speak to you the other day, but—"

I interrupted him. "Let me get this straight." I rose from my chair, my body tensing as I felt a burning in my stomach. "I double your capital within six months of running the place. Bring in a higher, exclusive clientele. And you want to discuss my *position*?"

"Some of us have been … *reflecting* after the incident with the Langleys."

I looked around at the table, the previous generation that had worked with my father. That remained loyal to him.

"Mr Kingsley, just because you see women as something beneath you and spend most of your time at those seedy clubs instead of at home with your wife, doesn't mean we're all like that."

Heat spread across his face, his wrinkles starting to capture tiny sweat droplets. He tugged at his tie, probably trying to catch his breath. His eyes darted over everyone in the room. Half were in shock; the others looked like they already knew.

"You need to watch yourself," he warned.

I let out a light laugh. "A man of your age should be careful in those places. You may end up having a heart attack. And we wouldn't want that now, would we?" I flashed my smile at him.

Without another word, he stormed out.

"Anyone else want to question my position?"

Silence fell, a few looking around at each other uneasily, the air thick in the room.

"That's settled, then. Now, fuck off."

Once they had finally disappeared, I sank back down in my chair, scrubbing my hands over my face. Sometimes, I wondered why I'd agreed to my grandfather's request. I should have let it fail, the way my dad failed me.

Aria made her way in as I sat there. I studied her every move until she reached me—and I pulled her into my lap.

"Are you ok?" she asked.

"Yeah, I'm fine. I'm sure they got the message."

She brushed my hair back, and I wrapped my arms tightly around her waist.

"Do you know how beautiful you are?"

"I don't think I've heard you say that before," she teased.

I ran my hand through her hair, leaning in to kiss her.

"I don't think we should be doing this in the boardroom," she said in between kisses, trying to hide the smile on her face.

"They might learn something new."

She pulled her lips away from mine as I felt her phone vibrate in my lap. She pulled it out of her pocket and looked at the screen. I felt her body stiffen.

Unknown caller

She clicked the side button, cutting it off. Her eyes lingered on the screen a little longer than normal, and sure enough, it started vibrating again.

"You can get that," I told her, watching her face.

"No, it's just a cold caller." She pressed the side button, powering it off, and placed it back in her pocket. "I'd better get back to work," she said, standing up.

"What's the rush?"

"I've just got a lot to do," she explained, bustling out of the room.

It felt like there was more to the phone call than she was telling me, but this time, I trusted she'd open up when she was ready.

I stood in my gym in front of the heavy bag, wrapping my hands quickly. I bounced on the balls of my feet and then threw the first punches. I went in fast and heavy, throwing all my weight into each one. My knuckles were burning as sweat dripped down my face, onto my bare chest.

I caught Hayden out of the corner of my eye and stepped back, my chest rising and falling heavily, resting my hands on my thighs, steadying my breathing.

Hayden leaned against the door-frame. "You good?"

I turned to face him, taking one last deep breath and unwrapping my hands.

"Yeah, I'm good," I told him, stretching out my fists a few times.

"Where's Aria?" he asked, raising his brow.

"She's at hers," I said, picking up the towel and flinging it over my shoulder. "Fancy a drink?"

After the ambush today, I needed some time to clear my head. There was a fog clouding my mind, unease creeping into it.

I sat with Hayden in a shisha bar on Edgware Road. The lights were dim, tones of red and yellow covering the garden,

Arabic music floating through in the background. The orange from the heaters burned bright. I brought the hose from the shisha up, the tip touching my lips, and I inhaled deeply. The watermelon hit my lungs before I exhaled, the cloud of smoke surrounding us. I took another hit, noticing the women on the table next to us looking over. I slowly exhaled again, watching them. The old me would have been inviting them over, but things had changed.

"Are you going to tell me what's wrong?" Hayden asked, taking the hose from me.

I sipped on my drink, sitting back in the chair. "Those fucking board members thought it would be a good idea to ambush me at work today," I told him.

I downed my drink, looking over at the bartender and lifting the glass. He acknowledged me with a salute.

"Shit, that kind of day," Hayden said, exhaling the smoke. "What did they want?"

I ran my hand through my hair, pushing the loose bits back in place.

"They wanted to talk about my position, as if I hadn't been making them more money since I pushed my dad out."

He leaned back in the chair as the server brought my drink over, taking another toke of the shisha, the cloud escaping his mouth as he spoke. "What you going to do about them?"

"Not much I can do. You know the promise I made to my granddad. I can't let the company fall apart."

He passed the hose back, and I inhaled again.

"You're better than that place. You know you're wasted as a CEO. Just come back."

I arched my brow at him, taking a hit of the shisha. I wanted to be there more than anything. My heart was torn—torn between the company, Aria, and the life I should be living. That place was my life before; everything about it ran through my blood. My body itched to be back in it, in the dark chaos calling to me, trying to lead me back home.

"You don't need me, Hayden."

I took another drag, exhaling the smoke as it clouded around us. Aria flickered through my mind. I needed to be better for her. She'd suffered enough with her life in Leeds. She didn't need to be dragged into that world again.

But the darkness still called, and the devil still whispered, pulling me back to purgatory where the man I'd once been waited.

Waited to be set free.

42

ARIA

My beautiful, sweet Aria. I miss you, my love.

My pulse quickened, those words playing over in my mind. Why couldn't he leave me alone? He had been let off for what he'd done to me, yet he was still controlling me from behind the scenes, acting like he hadn't done anything wrong.

I stormed into my bedroom and stuffed the note in my dressing table drawer, with the others. The shower turned off, and I knew Sebastain would be out soon, so I hurried to the kitchen to make coffee. Sebastian's phone started to vibrate on the counter as the machine was heating up, and I glanced down at it. It was his dad, Stephen, calling.

I watched as it turned into a missed call notification before starting to vibrate again.

"Who's that?" Sebastian asked, pulling his T-shirt on as he walked into the kitchen.

"It's your dad."

"Just ignore it," he said, wrapping his arms around my waist from behind. "Nothing good ever came from talking to that man."

Sebastian and his dad had never had a great relationship. He had told me that when his mum died, Stephen was too busy with women to raise him like a dad should. Even though I knew there was more, Sebastian never told me. I'd seen the way Stephen treated him when we lived together, and most of the time, he only acknowledged Sebastian when it involved the business. Even then, he seemed reluctant about it.

"Surely if he's called that many times, it might be important?" I suggested, passing him his coffee.

He raised his brow at me, taking a sip, then leaned over and picked up his phone. I watched as he cleared the notifications and placed it back on the counter.

He could be stubborn at times, and when it came to his dad, he didn't want to know.

"Fuck him. I'm more concerned about you." He placed his hands on my waist again, pulling me flush to him, his lips meeting mine.

"Sebastian, please," I said sternly, removing myself from his grip.

Confusion shone in his eyes. "If this is about me not calling my dad, then I suggest you stop. You know how that man was with me growing up."

"It's not about that. It's not always about you and what you want," I snapped.

His eyebrows rose, a flicker of a blue flame trying to ignite in his eyes. "Are you fucking kidding me right now?"

I exhaled slowly and cupped his cheek with my palm. "I'm sorry. It's just been a long day." Those damn letters. They were etching their way beneath my skin, trying to poison everything it came into contact with.

I didn't want to argue with him. It wasn't his fault I was allowing them to affect me the way they were. I needed to push it away, forget about it all. I wouldn't allow Jason to ruin what I had with Sebastian. He'd destroyed my heart, and Sebastian had helped put it back together. I wouldn't allow it to break again.

His eyes brightened, that flame extinguished with my touch. He took my hand, planting a kiss in my palm.

"I'll drop you off at Serfina's."

I spent the day with Serfina, enjoying myself, and taking my mind off those letters, doing things I could never do before. Friends were something I wasn't allowed with Jason.

We'd ended up back at Serfina's, sipping glasses of wine in front of the fire, waiting for Sebastian and Hayden.

"Aria girl, surely you don't want to stay as Sebastian's PA forever? I remember you wanted to be a social worker. What happened?"

I brought the glass to my lips and took a gulp. I'd given up everything for Jason because I was scared to do anything wrong. Not that it made a difference; I'd only have to look at him in a certain way and I'd feel pain.

"I was at university, but with everything that happened ..." I trailed off, taking another sip.

I'd opened up to her about it all after I told Sebastian. It felt right, and I had been ready to tell her. Serfina took hold of my hand. "Girl, you don't have to worry about any of that anymore. You survived and came out stronger. Sebastian may be many things, but he'd never hold you down. That's one thing I always loved about him. Even when we were younger, the way he was with you ... I saw him encouraging you to follow your dreams. If it's something you still dream of, then do it for yourself."

That was true. Sebastian was always behind me with everything I did.

"You should look into going back and doing what you dream of doing."

I smiled at her. "I'll think about it."

I supposed it could be something I looked into once I was fully settled with work and finding somewhere decent to live.

"Omg." Serfina giggled. "I've just remembered this time I keyed Sebastian's brand-new Audi. You should have seen his face. Served him right for pushing me into that bush on the way home from school. Now, that's the annoying Sebastian."

"I would never be able to do that." I chuckled.

"Please, girl, I see a fire burning deep in you. I bet you would have smashed the windows as well."

Wine came dripping out of my mouth as I tried to hold my laughter in. Serfina pointed, bursting into tears.

There was never a dull moment with the two of us. She was this fiery energy that lit up any room.

"You ready to get going?" Sebastian asked me, walking in.

"Why are you always trying to take my girl away from me?" Serfina teased.

"Because you always take my man away from me," he joked, grabbing Hayden to pull him in.

"Keep him." Serfina laughed.

"He's too high maintenance. I can't afford his lifestyle."

Hayden pushed him, chuckling to himself as he made his way to Serfina to kiss her.

"That's our cue," Sebastian said, taking my hand, and I stood.

Serfina got up, giving me the biggest hug. "I'll see you soon," she said, pulling away.

As we stepped out of the front door, I could see my breath in the crisp night air. Sebastian opened the car door for me, and I got in. He sat in the driver's seat, started the car, and turned the heating on. I looked over at him. The letter from this morning ran through my head again.

Should I tell him about it? I was so happy, I didn't want to ruin anything between us. I didn't want him to think I was still affected by Jason. I wouldn't be the one to get him involved in the darkness again.

He didn't need to know.

I'd deal with it myself.

ET LUX IN TENEBRIS LUCET

43

SEBASTIAN

My dad called me a few more times over the week, but I let them ring out. He'd never had any time for me growing up, so why should I give him any now?

Sometimes I wondered why my mum ever married him. She was a warm presence in my life growing up, and then my world went cold after she died. My granddad was there as much as he could be, and I loved him for it.

Then, Aria had appeared. This bright, warm, shining light in my dark, cold world. I looked over at the beautiful woman lying next to me in bed. How did I get so lucky?

I'd never wanted anything like this before her, and now, I wanted everything with her.

I gently moved her hair out of her face with my fingers. She always looked so peaceful when she slept, like nothing bad had ever happened to her.

But it had, and I should have been there to protect her. I should have been there to kill the man who had laid his hands on her.

If I were still part of the Organisation, I wouldn't have thought twice. But Hayden didn't want a war, and I wasn't about to let Aria suffer because of me. And after the other morning, I didn't think the board members would take kindly to their CEO being involved in nefarious business.

It wasn't just Hayden who had been on my case about this meeting. Soran had said he wanted me there as well. I thought I owed it to everyone to attend and deep down, I missed the place more then I cared to admit to myself.

Aria shifted, bringing me out of those thoughts. She blinked a few times at me, a smile curling on her lips. She looked tired, as if she hadn't slept.

"Morning, Nyx." I kissed her warm lips.

"Hey," she replied, her voice a little raspy.

"Did you not sleep well?" I asked her, stroking her hair.

"Not great." She laid her head on my chest. "Do you have to go out later?"

"Yeah, I've got something to sort with Hayden," I said.

It was only bending the truth slightly.

~

The table fell silent as I entered the main room with Hayden. Valon sat there, rubbing his hand over his chin, sitting next to Soran, whose body was tense. Matt walked in from the back office with Hassan, joining us. Hassan hadn't long returned from Morocco after dealing with some transport issues. I hadn't seen this guy for over a year now, and he'd changed a lot. His once-short curly black hair was long, slicked back into a ponytail.

The air was thick with tension, everyone on edge. Before Hayden could speak, Sean came through the door with Connor—those two always worked closely together.

Connor straightened his tailored suit.

"Sebastian—I thought you'd traded us for that stuffy corporate world," Hassan joked.

"If you need some help getting out, I'll draw you up a death certificate." Sean laughed, lighting a cigarette.

"I'm sure he'll come back when he's finished playing dress-up." Hassan leaned back in his chair, hands in his jacket pockets.

"Yes, yes, as much as this family reunion is great, we've got a serious issue to deal with," Soran said, and the table fell silent.

"Nicholas has been selling our routes to Nico," Matt told me.

"He fucked up my shipment last night. He won't be breathing if I get my hands on him," Valon gritted out.

"Unless I can find the proof, we can't touch him," Hayden said calmly.

Valon slammed his hands on the table. "Come on, Hayden." His voice was laced with frustration. "We all know it was him."

"Get that proof." Soran's voice was stern as he looked over at Hayden. "We all know the rules. Unless there's solid evidence, no one touches him."

Valon rose, cracking his knuckles, the fire burning through his eyes.

The rules were in place for a reason, but a man like Nicholas?

Well, he didn't play by the rules, so why should I?

44

ARIA

My dresser drawer was mocking me.

I should get rid of those letters piling up in it, but I couldn't bring myself to do it.

Jason was a dark cloud looming over me that I couldn't shake.

I felt Sebastian's arm around my waist, pulling me close. My eyes lingered on the drawer a few more seconds before I turned, half smiling at him.

"I don't know why you still have this place when I want you at mine all the time."

"It's where I live."

"Come on, Nyx. It'll be just like old times." He started kissing my neck. "Well, apart from the fact I'll be fucking you all the time."

I playfully hit his chest. "So that's why you want me there."

"You can't blame a man for trying." He kissed my lips. "But no, that's not the only reason. I want you there because I want you fully in my life, all the time. However, I respect that you want to do things on your own, and if you don't want to give up this place just yet, I understand." He kissed the tip of my nose and then my forehead.

I did want to be with him all the time, but I couldn't rely on him like that. I wouldn't lose myself to a man again. I needed to be able to stand on my own two feet, no matter what happened. This was my new beginning, a chance to start over from everything that happened to me. I never expected to find someone, let alone Sebastian, and I was glad he understood that.

He rested his hands on my cheeks as he looked into my eyes. "Right now, though … I just want to hear how good I make you feel."

His lips met mine, full of desperation, like an addict who had been waiting for their fix. He backed me onto the bed and positioned himself between my legs. He'd barely touched me, and I was already dripping, aching to feel him inside. He ripped my leggings down like he couldn't wait to get inside of them, then started teasing lazy circles with his tongue over my inner thigh, causing my body to shiver as I gripped the bed sheet.

"Beg me for it," he whispered as he carried on kissing me, knowing full well I was desperate for him.

"Please, Sebastian." My voice shook with every word as my body ached. "I need you."

"That's my girl," he growled.

As soon as his tongue hit me, I could feel that electricity dancing under my skin, setting that fire ablaze. Desperate whimpers fell from my mouth as he started enjoying his favourite meal.

"Oh, fuck, Sebastian. Please don't stop."

My body arched as he gripped my hips, pulling me further to him and burying his face between my thighs. I fisted the blanket tighter as I felt the heat coil around me.

"Don't you dare come. I want to enjoy you," he growled.

My breathing got heavier, and my body quivered as I tried to stop myself from fully letting go. He slid two fingers into me, causing an intense moan from my lips.

"That's a good girl."

He teasingly sucked my clit, his fingers pushing deep to bring me to the precipice, then slowly withdrew them, edging me to the point that I wanted to self-destruct, and I knew it wouldn't be long before my body betrayed me.

"Sebastian, please," I begged, my voice quivering, desperate to let go.

"How badly do you want it?"

I couldn't hold back any longer. My body was begging to be filled by him.

I rose to my knees. He looked at me, but I didn't give him a chance to say a word as I pulled his top off in frustration and ran my hands up his bare chest, our lips crashing together. Then I pushed him to the bed, climbing on top, and started grinding against his hard cock, soaking his trouser fabric.

"Fuck, Nyx." He groaned.

I unclicked his buckle, and those trousers soon came off. I slowly eased my way down, taking every inch of him as I felt the heat rising in my core.

"You're always so fucking tight around me."

His hands pressed into my back, his body rising, to pull us together. I wrapped my arms around his neck, rolling my hips hard. I was on fire, ready to jump over the edge. His hands found my arse and squeezed it tightly, bouncing me on him, as he bit my bottom lip.

"You're a bad girl," he growled in my ear, then started kissing my neck.

"I'm your bad girl," I whispered back.

He bit my neck as I felt his lips curl into a smile. "Come for me, Nyx."

My motions got faster as he pounded into me, the heat between us burning every part of me as my orgasm hit. Moans fell from my lips, that pure euphoric feeling rushing over me, forcing my body to shake.

His motions got harder as he slammed me up and down against him, picking up speed. My pussy clenched around him.

"Oh fuck," he moaned, his body trembling against mine, releasing all of him into me.

His lips met mine. The kiss was raw, primal, claiming.

My breathing was heavy, but I didn't need oxygen when I had him.

I could hear Sebastian in the kitchen as I sat down at my dressing table, the drawer tormenting me.

I needed to deal with this.

Taking my phone out, I looked over at the door, then shot off a text.

Aria: *I need your help. Can you find out if Jason has been sending me letters?*

The bubbles came up fast.

Callum: *I'll do what I can.*

Taking a deep breath, I threw some clothes on and made my way to the living room, where Sebastian was sitting on the sofa, his elbows on his legs and fingers together, his chin resting on them. He'd made coffee and breakfast muffins covered in butter, just how I liked them, so I grabbed one.

"Do you want to tell me why someone is sending you red roses?" he asked calmly.

"What?"

Sebastian picked up a bouquet from next to the sofa and held it out to me.

"Are these from you?" I asked, trying to figure out if this was a joke.

"Aria, I know you hate red roses, so why would it be me?" He raised his brow at me, his jaw clenched.

I put the muffin down and fiddled with my sleeve. "I don't know who they're from." I tried to stop my voice from shaking, a sick feeling forming in my stomach.

I swallowed hard, trying to clear the lump in my throat.

"Serfina. Serfina said she was sending me flowers," I blurted out, my voice going up a notch.

"Aria," he said quietly, "if there's something you need to tell me, now's the time." It felt like his eyes were piercing my soul.

I couldn't. Jason wasn't someone Sebastian needed to involve himself with. He had already been walking a fine line when we were younger, and now that he was on the straight and narrow, I wouldn't be the one to draw him back there.

"There's nothing. It was Serfina."

He searched my eyes for more, but I wasn't going to let him see it.

He sighed, placing his hand on my cheek, kissing my forehead.

"I need to go deal with something. I'll pick you up later," he said, grabbing his coat.

"Sebastian, please don't go," I called.

His chest rose high as he turned to face me. "You're fucking lying to me, Aria."

"I'm not. Please."

He let out a breath through his nose and tucked the loose hair behind my ears, resting his hands on my jaw.

"You know where to find me when you want to tell me the truth. If not, I'll pick you up at six for dinner."

He pressed a kiss to my forehead and left.

45

SEBASTIAN

"Just say it," I told Hayden, my eyes flicking over to him.

"Say what?"

I shook my head. I wasn't in the mood for games. This guy always did this to me; he'd pretend he had nothing to say, so I'd tell him, and then he'd add his wise words.

"Fine," I said, placing the glass on the table. "Did Serfina send Aria roses today?"

"I haven't a clue what Serfina does half the time." He chuckled. "Serfina!"

"Why are you shouting?" she questioned as she entered the room.

"Did you send Aria roses?"

"I did. Why?"

Shit.

I could feel a sinking feeling creep into my stomach; my heart started to race as I swallowed hard. I had accused Aria of lying to me, and she hadn't. I was such an idiot. What the fuck was wrong with me?

"She doesn't like red roses," I blurted out.

"What?"

"Don't send her red roses again. She doesn't like them."

"Ok, Mr Stroppy Pants." She stuck her tongue out at me.

Ever since I had known her, she'd hated red roses. She hadn't long moved in with us, and we were in the kitchen. I remembered her touching the petals of the red roses in a vase. The housekeeper had cut them from the garden. Aria had told me that behind each red petal that represented passion, desire, and romance, there was always something dark and sinister waiting to come out.

"I'd better go and get her for dinner."

Surprisingly for London, it hadn't taken me long to get back to Aria's, and we were now both in the car on our way for dinner. She seemed a bit quieter than she normally was.

My eyes flickered between her and the road. "Nyx, can we talk?"

"Hmm," she replied, not turning to face me.

"I'm sorry about earlier. I shouldn't have been that way with you." I took her hand and squeezed it.

"It's fine." She pulled her hand away and started playing with her sleeves.

"Aria." I took her hand again and pulled it to my lap. "Look at me."

I heard her take a breath and exhale deeply as she finally turned to me.

"I'm so sorry I accused you of lying. I trust you, and I regret everything I said."

"Ok," she said simply.

It wasn't long before I arrived back at Hayden's with Aria for dinner. I walked into the kitchen, holding her hand.

"Aria," Serfina sang, making her way over to hug her. "How are you?" she asked, pulling away.

"I'm good," she replied, quickly letting go of my hand as if she didn't want to be in contact with me any longer than she needed to be.

Maybe I was just seeing things that weren't there.

"I hope you didn't cook, Serfina." I chuckled, remembering the last time.

It was before Aria had come back into my life. I'd felt like I was going to die from food poisoning. Serfina was not a cook in any way, shape, or form. If any cooking was going on in the house, it would be Hayden.

"Don't start." She narrowed her brows at me. "Hayden will be back in a minute. He's gone to get Chinese."

Good. I didn't feel like dying tonight.

Hayden soon walked through into the kitchen, holding bags of takeaway.

"About time," Serfina said, grabbing the bags and bouncing out of the kitchen.

I went to grab Aria's hand, but she had already started moving.

Hayden raised his brow at me. "What did you do?" he asked.

"I didn't do anything," I said, shrugging.

When we got to the dining room, Serfina had already opened everything.

"You two are so slow," she complained as Aria sat down next to her.

I sat next to Hayden, as all I could feel radiating from Aria was cold.

"Hayden, can you pass me the noodles, please?" Aria asked him.

The fire in my stomach started burning, slowly making its way through my veins.

"Take this." I passed her a can of Strawberry Miranda, her favourite.

"I don't want it." She pushed it back.

"Chicken balls?" I asked her, holding out the bag.

She flicked noodles onto her plate, eyes fixed on it. "No."

She loved chicken balls. It was something I'd bring home for her when we were younger, after I'd be fighting, when she couldn't sleep. We'd sit in her room watching movies and eating them.

My jaw tightened.

"I'll take them." Serfina took the bag from me and placed it on the table, taking one.

Seconds after, Aria took two and placed them on her plate.

What the fuck was happening?

I slammed my fist on the table, fire raging through me. I pushed my body to stand and stormed out of the house.

"Fuck." I ran my hands through my hair, gripping it for a few seconds before letting go.

The rage was festering, waiting to escape my body, but I needed to push it back down. Leaning against the pillar, I lit a cigarette, exhaling the smoke.

"Well, that was awkward." Hayden appeared from behind. "Did you not sort everything out with her earlier?"

"She seemed fine. A little quiet in the car, but not like this."

"When I piss Serfina off, she can go days without talking to me. It's quite peaceful." He chuckled, placing his hands in his pockets.

"This is different."

It took about an hour to get back to Aria's flat, where she insisted on going. She didn't say a lot, and when she did, it was short and sharp. I placed my keys on the table, then slowly took my jacket off, hanging it up.

"Aria." She turned to look at me. That was something, I guessed. "What's going on?"

"Nothing, I'm just tired."

"You know you can talk to me."

"I know," she replied, smiling. "Honestly. Just tired." She squeezed my hand.

Maybe that was the truth. There had been a lot going on at work recently, so perhaps it was getting on top of her. Maybe it was just all my insecurities pushing through, making me second-guess our relationship. I wanted to be with her completely, but this was all new to me.

"Let's get you to bed."

She half smiled and made her way to the bedroom, leaving me standing there.

I was scared I was going to lose her. Maybe I was being overbearing, and she felt like she couldn't breathe. But I couldn't help it; she was everything to me, the only one who would have my heart. I wanted her around me all the time, and I couldn't bear the feeling of her being distant. I wanted to feel her warm touch on my body. I felt like I couldn't breathe without her next to me, like my heart was suffocating, ready to stop beating if she left.

It wasn't much longer until I followed her and got into bed. Aria shifted. She'd fallen asleep straight away. I brushed her hair out of her face and just watched her. She looked like she was dreaming, mumbling words I couldn't make out. She used to talk in her sleep when she was younger, so it wasn't anything I hadn't seen before. I placed my hand on her arm, hoping that would settle her, but it didn't.

"Please," she whispered. "I don't want to." Her voice was low, pleading.

Was she having a nightmare?

All of a sudden, she jolted awake, her feet kicking, pushing her body against the headboard. She gasped for air, scrabbling at her neck.

"Hey, hey." I quickly took hold of her hands to ground her. "Look at me," I told her, and her eyes met mine, panic running through them. "Deep breath in," I said, trying to keep her calm, but she was still struggling to catch her breath. "Nyx." I placed my hands on her cheeks. "Breathe with me."

Her eyes were fixed on mine as her breathing started to steady. I pushed her hair out of her face, then ran my hands down her arms, taking hold of her hands. She felt cold.

"Are you ok?" I asked, concern in my voice.

"Yeah, I'm fine," she replied, placing her hand on her heart.

"You're clearly not fine. You're shaken up," I said, feeling her body trembling.

"I'm fine, Sebastian, it was just a dream," she snapped, getting out of bed. "I just need some space. Let me breathe."

46

ARIA

I grabbed a water from the fridge, taking a few sips as my hand trembled. Leaning back on the counter, I inhaled deeply, exhaling slowly as I touched my neck. I could still feel his hands around it. I shivered and wrapped my arms around myself.

It was a nightmare, Aria. It wasn't real. You're safe. He can't hurt you.

But it felt real.

He was in my dreams now. I couldn't escape him; he wouldn't let me. All those letters and roses and now this? Should I tell someone? The police? I sighed. What could they do, let me down again?

Was he watching me? The thought of it made me sick. What if he attacked Sebastian, and I couldn't stop him?

My heart started to race at the thought. Maybe I should just go.

Run.

Start again somewhere.

I grabbed my phone off the table and sat on the sofa.

Aria: *Please tell me you have something.*

A few minutes passed as I stared at the screen, then the bubbles came.

Callum: *He promised me he was leaving you alone.*

Aria: *It has to be him. There's no one else.*

Callum: *I'm sorry. I'm limited in what I can do.*

Locking the phone, I lay down on the sofa, my eyes fixed on the butterflies in the bell jar.

It had to be him.

Everything started to swirl around, and my eyes soon closed, drifting back to sleep.

The sun was rising through the window, speckles of warmth kissing my skin. I shifted my body, opening my eyes slowly.

I must have fallen asleep on the sofa last night after my nightmare. I couldn't face seeing Sebastian after; I wasn't ready to face what was happening. I made my way to the kitchen, making a coffee to take to Sebastian, then walked through into the bedroom. I paused. My bed was empty, and Sebastian wasn't there. I threw the cup against the wall, tears flooding my eyes as I sat on the edge of the bed. His citrus smell flooded my system, but that sick feeling in my stomach rose, clawing its way up into my throat. I swallowed hard to try and push it back down, but it was no use. It lingered, forcing me back to four years ago. I grabbed my phone, trying to push past It, when I noticed the message from Sebastian.

> **Sebastian:** *Hey. I needed to get to work and didn't want to wake you. Take the day off and get some rest. I'll see you later.*

My stomach turned. I put my phone back on the side table and climbed into bed, pulling the cover to my nose and taking a deep breath, sighing as I exhaled. I could feel his warmth around me. I wanted so much to feel his arm around my waist, holding me tight. Tears filled my eyes. I blinked and they ran down my cheeks, hitting the pillow. I hugged the blanket tight, closing my eyes, and drifted off into a fitful sleep.

I shifted in my bed, spreading my arm out to feel for Sebastian, but nobody was there. I opened my eyes, my room now covered in darkness. Had I slept all day? I grabbed my phone, pressing the side button. I squinted at the bright light, looking at the time. 2:45 a.m.

Sebastian had said he'd see me later. I pressed my phone's button again, lighting the screen. No notifications. What if Jason had got to him?

My heart raced as I dialled.

"Hello?" His voice cracked, half asleep. "Aria, are you ok?" he asked, a little more alert.

"I … I thought you were coming over," I said.

"It was late when I finished; I didn't want to disturb you."

"Oh. Ok," I whispered.

"Get some rest. I'll speak to you tomorrow," he said softly.

"Yeah. Goodnight," I said, trying to ignore the sinking feeling in my stomach.

He'd promised he wouldn't leave me again, but it was feeling more and more like he had.

ET LUX IN TENEBRIS LUCET

47

SEBASTIAN

I flicked the pen in my hand as I sat at my desk. I couldn't concentrate on anything. I glanced at Aria's desk outside; she hadn't been in all week.

I'd texted her a few times to check she was ok, but I never got much back. I found myself driving to hers most nights, but I always ended up turning back. She clearly didn't want to be with me anymore, or she'd have told me what was going on. Why else would she be so distant?

I should never have started this. She should have stayed as my PA, my former stepsister, everything I shouldn't have touched. I was spiralling with it all, and I didn't know what to do. I would not beg her to love me. So why did my heart hurt so much? The thought churned something deep inside of me. Who was I kidding? She could bring me to my knees in a heartbeat if it meant she'd stay; I'd fucking crawl to her. I'd give up everything I ever owned. Fuck, I'd give my life for hers. I'd burn down these streets and beg her not to leave me. She was the only one, and it would only ever be her.

I glanced down at the file in front of me. I needed to focus; I couldn't sit here staring at Aria's empty desk all day.

I soon looked up again as I heard my office door open. Hayden strolled in, sitting back in the chair opposite me. Another fucking interruption I didn't need.

"I know that look," he said.

"What look?" I asked, abandoning the file.

"Like you want to fight someone. Which, for your sake, I'd advise against," he said.

It wasn't the worst idea. I probably could go a few rounds. It would help clear my mind of everything.

"Don't do it. You're not about that life anymore."

I looked up at him. "I didn't ask for a running commentary." My voice was calm, but I was trying to hide how frustrated I was.

He just let out a heavy sigh. "What are you doing here, anyway?" I asked.

"I might have something on Nicholas."

My jaw clenched at the name. "Go on."

"I've been told he's been hanging around at the docks with Nico the last few days."

Nico. Some guy who worked the streets of East London. He wasn't anything major, but if Nicholas was around him, something was going on.

"Well, keep me updated," I said, looking back down at the file.

"Don't you dare go fighting tonight," he said, getting up from the chair.

I didn't look back up, but I heard the door open and close as he left. I threw the pen on my desk and leaned back in the chair, rubbing my face.

I should have tried to get her to talk to me about what was happening with her.

I couldn't leave things like this between the two of us. I needed to know why she was being so distant. Maybe it was me, and she couldn't see a future anymore.

After finishing up for the day, I drove to her place on autopilot. I sat outside her flat for what felt like a lifetime before I could get my body to move.

I had a key to get in, but I wasn't sure if she'd want that, so I lifted my hand, pausing mid-air for a second before I knocked. A minute later, there she was, standing in front of me. Her long, blonde hair was tied up in a messy bun, and her eyes looked red, tired, like she hadn't slept for weeks.

She wrapped her long cardigan around her body as if she were trying to protect herself.

I'd seen every inch of her; I knew every part of it. She didn't need to hide herself from me.

She moved to the side, allowing me to step in, and I closed the gap between us, tucking the loose bits of hair behind her ear. She wrapped her arms tightly around my waist and rested her head on my chest. I could smell that green apple shampoo that I loved so much. My hands hesitated for a second before I put my arms around her, pulling her close.

"I'm sorry, Nyx," I whispered.

She tilted her head up to look at me, furrowing her brows. "For what?"

"For not being here for you."

I kissed her forehead, and she rested her head back on my chest as we stood there in each other's arms.

The silence was broken by the sound of her phone ringing from the bedroom.

"I'll get it. Go and sit down," I said, and she smiled at me.

I walked through the hall and made my way into the bedroom as it stopped ringing. It was sitting on the dressing table. As I retrieved it, the corner of my eye caught her drawer slightly open. I tilted my head so I could see better. I was about to close it, but I saw what looked like a pile of letters stuffed into it. My chest tightened, my mouth went dry, and I could feel my palms begin to get clammy. My eyes flickered back to the door, whispers in my ear telling me to look.

No. She'd tell me when she was ready.

But the voices got louder as I struggled to remove the invisible rope pulling me back.

That drawer was screaming my name.

And I opened it.

It won't be long until we're together again. I miss you.

My heart sank. She was seeing someone else. I unfolded another.

I'll make you pay for what you did to me.

And the next.

Soon, my love. I'll see you soon.

No, she wasn't seeing someone else.

This was worse; she'd been getting letters from Jason, and she had kept them from me.

"Sebastian, did you find it?" Aria called from the living room.

I looked back at the door. "Yeah, I'm coming," I called back, trying to hide the rage in my voice.

I shoved the letters back in her drawer, slamming it closed. My jaw clenched at the thought of her keeping this from me.

"Who was it?" she asked as I rejoined her.

"Serfina," I said, holding her phone out.

"I'll call her back later." She smiled, wrapping her arms around my waist.

I pulled them off me, stepping closer to the front door. I couldn't be here. I needed to get out. My fists clenched tight, forcing the blood from them. I ground my teeth to push that fire back down, lighting the dynamite in my stomach that was about to explode.

"I've had an urgent call about work. I need to go sort it out."

I lied to her.

Like she had lied to me.

"Oh, ok. Are you coming back?" she asked, fiddling with her sleeves.

"If it's not too late," I said, trying to stop the explosion from happening.

I wasn't coming back.

I was going to fight.

If I didn't, I would find that man and make him pay for everything he had done.

48

ARIA

I stared at the date in big letters screaming at me.
5th November.

Had it really been a year already? I took a deep breath in, releasing it slowly, logging into the system. It was time I got back to normality and forgot about those stupid letters and my past. I needed to get rid of them.

It had been five months since they'd released Jason, and he wasn't one to sit around and wait. If he was going to do something, he would have done it straight away.

Seeing Sebastian last night made me realise I couldn't lose him over my past; he meant so much to me. It felt like we had never been apart. I was stronger now, and I wouldn't allow that man to control me anymore.

I glanced up, looking through the window at Sebastian in his office. He'd been in there since I got here. He hadn't come back to mine last night, either.

Sebastian hadn't left the office at all, and it was now lunchtime. He had back-to-back meetings booked in his diary, and I could see he was on video calls all morning. But he would normally make time to step out and see me for lunch.

I brought up his diary. Sure enough, there was a meeting booked over lunch. I glanced over into his office, and I could see him talking to his laptop. I closed my laptop and stood up, grabbing my bag. I glanced over at him once more, but he didn't notice me, so I turned, making my way to the door. I pushed it open and walked into the main office that was attached to mine. One of the good things about the office building was that it had its in-house cafeterias, so I didn't need to go far—just down from my thirty-eighth floor to the sixteenth.

I reached the lift, pressing the button to call for it as a few other people stood waiting. They were talking about how they couldn't wait for the fireworks tonight. I gripped my sleeve, pulling it down, making sure my scar was covered even though I knew it was.

Just before I could sit back down at my desk after lunch, Jessica came out of Sebastian's office, smiling as she reached me.

"Hey Jessica, everything ok?" I asked. Why had she been in there?

"Yeah, Mrs Rogers asked me to grab him something from the cafeteria for lunch. I think she knew you'd be on your break," she said.

Jessica was Mrs Rogers's PA, who was an executive in the company. They were based two floors below this one. I'd been down there a few times to get paperwork for Sebastian, or Jessica brought it up to me.

"Oh, ok, makes sense." I smiled, trying to hide the fact that I thought it was odd.

Was he avoiding me? I didn't think I'd ever known Jessica to bring lunch up for him in the whole seven months I had been here.

It was nearly the end of the day, and I had yet to see Sebastian.

I'd thought after last night, everything was going to be fine between us. That the distance I had put between us was broken. I didn't want to stay away from him; I couldn't stay away from him.

I pulled Sebastian's diary up to check that there wasn't a meeting going on. Once I was confident I wouldn't be interrupting anything, I took a deep breath, making my way to the door and knocking.

"Come in," he called.

I pushed the door open, looking at him as I walked in. He didn't look up; he was fixed on the paperwork in front of him.

"I just need to put this file back," I explained.

He glanced up to look at me, and as he did, I noticed a small cut above his left eyebrow.

"Sebastian, what happened?" I asked, moving closer.

He pulled his hand up and touched it. He knew what I was referring to. "It's nothing."

"Have you been fighting again?"

His voice stopped me in my tracks. "Can you just grab me the Johnson file out of that cabinet?" He pointed at one I'd not been in before and then looked back down at the paperwork on his desk.

I pulled the drawer open, flicking through the files to find it. As I read the names in my head, my hands paused at one that was burned deep into it.

Jason Brown.

Why did Sebastian have a file on Jason?

I swallowed hard, pushing the sick feeling down. My hands trembled, slowly opening the file, to see a photo of Jason staring back at me.

My eyes darted all over the page, trying to grasp what it was.

Then I saw it.

It was a police report from the night he'd attacked me. I flicked the page over, photos of my injuries on display.

What the hell was this?

Had Sebastian known all along?

ET LUX IN
TENEBRIS
LUCET

49

SEBASTIAN

I had been trying to avoid Aria all day, and now she was in the office. I wanted her to hurry up and go home.

I couldn't face seeing her right now—not after the letters I found last night.

What was taking her so fucking long?

"Aria? The file?" I snapped, causing her to jump.

She slowly turned, file in hand, shuffling over to the desk.

Her eyes were filled with something I hadn't seen before. She reached my desk, tossing the file on it. She looked pale, like she'd seen something she hadn't wanted to. My eyes flicked down to the file.

Fuck.

That was never meant for her eyes.

"How long have you had this?" she asked calmly, but I could hear the cracks trying to break through.

"It doesn't matter," I told her, resting my fingers on my lips.

"Of course it matters, Sebastian. You have a whole police file on my ex and you didn't tell me?" she said, her voice breaking. "Did you know all of this before I told you?" she whispered.

"Nyx." My voice was low as I walked around to her, reaching for her hand.

"Don't touch me," she snapped, wrapping her arms around her body.

"Let me explain."

"You've violated every part of me I never wanted you to see." Her voice was shaking, the tears rolling down her cheeks.

Did she really think I'd done this to hurt her? I needed to know what was going on with her, because she wouldn't tell me. The letters were evidence enough of that.

"You've kept things from me," I said, trying to stay calm.

"I've not kept anything from you!"

"The letters, Aria. I found them," I said coldly.

"You went through my things?" She thought *that* was the pressing issue?

"Were you ever going to tell me?" I asked, trying not to let the anger consume me.

"I don't need you to protect me, Sebastian. I'm not a little girl anymore. I was going to handle it," she said.

I couldn't control the burning rage anymore. She'd lied to me. She didn't trust me.

"You fucking lied to me, Aria," I said, through gritted teeth.

"Are you kidding me right now?"

"You should have told me," I hissed, taking a step closer.

"You don't know what you've done."

"What *I've* done?" I roared.

She shoved my chest, forcing me to take a step back from her. "Fuck you, Sebastian."

And with that, she spun on her heel and stormed out of the door.

The silence felt louder than the shouting.

I watched as she yanked her things from her desk, not caring what else fell from it. She picked up the laptop and hurled it at my door.

"Asshole," she shouted. "You have no idea about anything." She stormed back into the office, throwing my door key at my feet. "You don't get to tell me what's right and what's wrong."

Then, like a force of nature, she flipped the finger at me, shouting some more swear words before disappearing from my view, the main office door echoing as it slammed shut.

Fuck. What was wrong with me?

I made my way over to the cabinet and poured some whisky into a glass, downing it in one. And another.

Fuck this.

I picked up the bottle and slumped back down in my chair.

50
ARIA

How I managed to make it home without breaking down or killing someone on the tube, I will never know. I threw my bag on the living room floor, the contents spilling everywhere. What a complete fucking asshole. How dare he speak to me like that? I sat on the sofa, curling up in the corner of it. That burning soon turned cold, numbing my body from the inside out. I could feel my heart breaking all over again. I blinked, letting the tears flow down my cheeks. I was reminded daily of what he did to me from my scar; I didn't need to see everything else again.

I jumped at the fireworks being set off outside, people shouting. It was a year ago today that I'd survived. A year of struggling to find myself again. I thought I had. I thought my life was going well.

Jason told me he would change every time he raised his hand to me. And I believed every word, until that night a year ago.

I didn't remember much. Maybe it was my mind blocking it out. The pure rage in his eyes as he pinned me up against the wall by my throat. I swallowed, touching my neck, trying not to feel his hand around me again. The knife coming at me. Then a burning, sharp pain along the inside of my arm. I pulled my sleeve up, feeling the pain on my scar. I stood up, starting to pace, shaking my arm to remove that feeling.

If Callum hadn't arrived when he did, I didn't think I would have survived that night.

Don't do this to yourself, Aria.

I thought Sebastian was different. I never thought he'd be so cruel. I thought he cared about me like when we were younger. Maybe he just felt sorry for me, after looking in that file.

I picked my phone up and started pacing, wondering if I should call Sebastian as my palms felt sweaty.

We'd lied to each other. It was both our fault. I loved him more than I had ever loved anyone in my life. He was the only one I ever wanted and would ever want.

We just needed to get past this.

I placed my phone on the table and curled back up on the sofa. I should leave him for a bit to calm down, then I'd call him. I lay my head down on the pillow, staring at the phone in silence as tears fell from my eyes again. The fireworks banged outside the window now and then, causing me to jump.

There was a faint knock at the door.

Sebastian.

I got up, wiping my eyes, making my way over and opening it.

No—not Sebastian.

Jason.

His dark, forest-green eyes stared straight at me. They weren't the kind of green that grew, but poison ivy that killed everything it touched. I pushed the door with all my strength, but he grabbed it, forcefully pushing it back at me, causing me to stumble. I gasped, trying to catch my breath. My eyes darted to my phone, and I made a dash for it. I grabbed it, bringing up Sebastian's number and pressing dial. I didn't know if it rang, but Jason soon snatched it from my hands, flinging it across the room.

"That was stupid," he said in a low voice.

He grabbed me by my neck, slamming me back against the wall. I gasped, trying to breathe, as I pulled at his hand around my neck. He smirked, letting out a venomous laugh, eventually releasing his grip on me. I took a deep breath to try and fill my lungs with the air he had removed.

"Did you really think I'd let you get away with this?" He tilted his head, stepping closer. "I'm going to make you bleed," he whispered in my ear.

My body froze. I couldn't move. I blinked, releasing the tears that had formed in my eyes, warm against my cold cheeks.

He was going to kill me, and there was nothing I could do.

"Don't kill her here. Sebastian could turn up." A familiar voice came from the doorway.

Nicholas.

What was he doing here?

He pulled a cigarette out of his packet and lit it, taking a drag and exhaling a cloud of smoke. He strolled towards us, two other men following, stopping next to Jason.

"Trash it," he told the men.

The two men did as they were told and started breaking anything they could see. The photo of me and my mum was thrown to the floor, and one of the men stamped on it, the screeching of the glass grinding together piercing my ears. They kicked over the table, coffee spilling to the floor. Then the crystal butterflies in the bell jar that my dad had sent me on my sixteenth birthday. The last thing he sent me before I never heard from him again was broken, shattered into a million pieces against the wall in one fell swoop.

"I really thought she'd put up more of a fight," Nicholas said, running his finger down my face.

I felt sick from his touch as I pulled my head away as best I could.

"She never was one to fight back."

ET LUX IN
TENEBRIS
LUCET

51

SEBASTIAN

I couldn't recall how I got to the bar or how much I had drunk, but I was completely wasted—and I didn't even care.

I had ruined the best thing in my life, completely destroyed it like I destroyed everything.

I picked up the bottle of whisky, swigging on it. The bartender wasn't happy, but he knew me, so he left me to it—it didn't hurt that he knew he'd get a great tip.

I felt a hand squeeze my shoulder and turned my head to see a blonde sitting on the stool next to me, smiling.

"You look like you could do with some company," she said, sipping on her wine.

I looked down at her hand on my shoulder. It felt wrong of her to touch me.

"You look like you need another drink," I told her, signalling to the bartender.

"I'm Chanel," she said, holding her glass out as the bartender returned with another glass of wine.

"Sebastian," I said, holding the bottle up and downing some more.

She leaned in, closer to my ear. "Should we go somewhere more private?"

Before I could answer, someone else spoke. "He won't be going anywhere with you," Hayden said. "Run along, now." He smiled at her.

She looked at me, then back to Hayden, screwing her face in disgust as she huffed, pushing past him.

"What are you playing at?" he asked me, narrowing his eyes.

"I don't even fucking know anymore. I fucked up big time," I told him. "How did you even know I was here?"

"You didn't answer any of my calls, and neither did Aria, so I called the bar." He nodded towards the bartender.

What a snake.

I pulled my phone out of my pocket, trying to focus on the missed calls. Five from Hayden and one from Aria.

"I need to see her," I told him, trying not to sway as I got off the stool.

"No, you need to sober up," he firmly told me.

I guess I did need to sober up before I saw her. I doubted she'd see me like this. I pulled a load of money out of my back pocket, giving it to the bartender. I nodded at Hayden as we made our way to the door.

I stumbled through Hayden's front door, staggering through the hall and into the living room. I stood at the door-frame, holding my arms out.

Serfina looked up from the sofa, screwing her face up. "Jeez, Hayden, why did you bring him back here like this?"

Hayden pushed past me in the doorway. "I couldn't leave him." He shrugged, sitting on the sofa next to her.

I stumbled further into the living room, slumping down on the sofa, right next to Serfina. She was easy to wind up, and right now I needed some entertainment.

"Urgh, you stink of whisky." She pushed me away, getting up and sitting in the chair opposite.

I pulled my phone out of my pocket, trying to focus my eyes on the screen as I scrolled to find Aria's number. There it was. I pressed the call button, putting it to my ear. It went straight to voicemail. Aria never had her phone go to voicemail. No matter what, she would always answer my calls.

I said as much to Hayden and Serfina.

"I mean, I wouldn't want to talk to you in this state," she said, waving her hands at me.

"It's late; maybe she's just asleep," Hayden said.

"No, she never has her voicemail on," I said, unsure why it wasn't even ringing. "I need to see her." I stood up, trying not to fall back down with how drunk I was.

"Ok, sit down. I'll get you some coffee," Serfina said, standing up and making her way out of the living room.

"What did you do?" Hayden asked me.

I sat back down on the sofa, rubbing my face with my hand. "She found the file on Jason. We argued, and I said things

I shouldn't have," I tried to explain. "I need to see her. I need to make it right."

"We will. You just need to sober up first," Hayden told me, placing his hand on my back.

"I love her. I can't lose her."

I hadn't even told Aria I loved her yet, but the words felt natural as they rolled off my tongue. I needed to fix this, make her see I was sorry and how much I was in love with her.

I sat in the passenger seat of Hayden's car outside Aria's. The fireworks were still randomly going off at 1 a.m. I dialled her number one last time. Voicemail again.

The air was cold, crisp, my warm breaths making clouds when I breathed out. My eyes flickered to a bang in the sky, golds and blues sparkling in the dark.

"Are you sure you want to go up?" Hayden asked.

I was. I wasn't going to lose her—not long after finding her again. I wasn't going to give up on us. I nodded at Hayden, and he followed me to the main entrance. I let us in with my set of keys and slowly walked up the stairs, Hayden behind, making our way to the first floor.

As we got closer to her door, something didn't look right.

It was slightly open.

My heart started to race. What if something had happened to her? I looked back at Hayden once more before I pushed the door fully open and walked in cautiously, turning the light on.

Her flat was completely trashed.

I charged through the hall to the bedroom. She wasn't there.

"Sebastian," Hayden called from the living room.

I bolted back in. He was holding her smashed phone in his hand.

52

ARIA

The car was waved through an iron gate to a rural estate, with a guard standing there peering through the window as it drove through and slowly came to a halt. My eyes flicked down to Jason's hand on my thigh, which had sat there the whole journey, making my stomach churn.

He looked over at me. "I'm taking you back to Leeds."

I opened my mouth to protest, but he interrupted.

"That wasn't a question. That was an order."

"I'd rather die."

He dug his fingers into my skin. "That can be arranged."

I sucked air through my teeth at the sting, and my fingers found my sleeve. I couldn't go back.

I wouldn't go back.

He moved my hair and leaned into my ear. "You used to like it rough."

My whole body shivered, goose bumps forming on my skin as I tried to hold the sickness down.

I didn't like it rough; I'd let him do what he wanted because the alternative would have been far worse.

"I've missed you." He leaned in, kissing my lifeless lips, forcing me to heave. He pulled away, smirking. "Don't worry, I'll make sure there's no trace of Sebastian left on you."

My eyes widened as I started to retch again, forcing my hand over my mouth to stop it, but my body was shaking. He grabbed my other hand, dragging me out of the car.

Nicholas got out of the passenger side, and Jason turned to talk to him. My eyes darted around, taking in my surroundings. Men patrolled the perimeter, but there were woods not far in the distance.

This was my opportunity.

My heart pounded, my palms were sweaty, but the adrenaline ran through me.

I ran.

I'd rather be lost in the woods than be with him.

There was shouting, and I glanced over my shoulder to see Jason barrelling straight for me. My heart was racing, my breathing fast, and the cold air burned my cheeks with every movement.

Freedom—

A full force of hands gripped my arm, yanking me back to my fate. Jason's palm met my face, and I pressed my hand onto my cheek as it started to sting against the cold, setting my face on fire. Jason's hand rose again, hitting me across the other side of my face.

My body shook, forcing me to bend over, the pain finally releasing the sick feeling in my stomach, blood from my mouth mixing with it. I gasped as I heaved, spitting out anything left as tears ran down my face, burning my cheeks as they fell to the floor.

"Try that again, and I'll post every part of you to your mum," he hissed.

He grabbed my arm, pulling me fast, my feet stumbling as I tried to keep up with him. The corner of my lips throbbed and I touched it, looking down at my fingers stained with blood.

Jason dragged me back toward the car, where Nicholas was. I still didn't understand where he fit in with all this. But instead of being pushed back into the seat, Jason grabbed my hair, pulling me and continuing. The stones in the drive crunched under my feet as I hurried to stay close to him.

When we reached an outbuilding, he opened the door, shoved me in, and closed it behind me.

"Jason, please don't do this," I begged, slamming my fists against the door.

All I heard was the lock engaging and footsteps crunching along those stones, getting quieter until I couldn't hear them anymore. I banged the door a few more times, even pulling at it, but I couldn't get it to budge. The knots in my stomach tightened. I gasped a few times to try and hold back the tears, but it was no use—they came flooding out.

I turned, resting my back against the door and sliding down it. I pulled my knees close to me, hugging them tight, resting my head on them as the tears continued. I shouldn't have walked away from Sebastian. I should have spoken to him and told him everything.

If I had, maybe I wouldn't be here, waiting to die.

I blinked a few times, trying to adjust to the winter sun seeping through the cracks of the pitch-black darkness I had been left in last night. The smell of damp mould filled my nose. I didn't know how I'd managed to fall asleep—maybe it was just my brain trying to shut everything out.

I rubbed my face, wincing at the pain in my cheek. I shivered, wrapping my arms around me to try and warm up, but I could feel the cold draft swirling around the outbuilding I had been thrown into.

I slowly pulled my body up, dusting myself off. I hadn't noticed in the dark last night that the building was bigger than I'd thought. There was an open door-frame that seemed to have a small corridor attached to it. I slowly walked towards it, avoiding the dusty boxes that were lying around.

Maybe there was another door, or a window—something to escape through.

I wasn't going to let Jason kill me here.

I crept into the corridor, looking back one last time, keeping myself close to the wall as I reached the first door-frame. I took a deep breath before I peered in. Boxes and more dust.

The next room had a dirty mattress and yet more boxes. I sighed.

I took a few more steps and reached the last room. It was a filthy bathroom, dust thick against the walls. My heart sank into the pit of my empty stomach, and I dropped to my knees as they gave way. My chest was heavy, tightening around my heart, and every part of my body felt cold. My hands trembled as I placed them over my face, tears flooding into them. My breath hitched with every intake, catching at that lump stuck in my throat with my silent cries, perched in my chest like a songless bird, begging to be heard but trapped deep inside.

I didn't know how long I had been here, but it was still light outside. The night hadn't arrived yet. I sat on the floor, my back against a box, staring at the door and praying someone would find me.

But no one knew where I was.

And after the fight with Sebastian, I wasn't even sure he'd know I was gone yet.

They probably wouldn't find my body after Jason was finished with me.

I'd just be some statistic in the system like I was before.

Faint footsteps crunched on the stones outside, drawing closer. They stopped as they reached the door. The lock clicked, and the door opened.

Jason.

Was this it? Was he going to kill me now?

He slowly closed and locked the door behind him, his lifeless eyes fixed on mine. He pulled me up by my hair, dragging me into the room with the mattress and throwing me onto it.

I scurried back into the corner of the wall it was pressed against, but it was in vain; he could still reach me. He crouched down, eyes still fixed on me.

"You know," he said calmly, "I thought you'd come visit me in prison."

"Are you delusional?"

He let out a silent laugh. "Aria, I know you put me there, but you were still mine. You'll always be mine."

His phone started to ring, and I peered over at the screen.

Callum.

He let out a heavy breath and put it on speaker.

"What do you want?"

"Jason, you need to get back up here. You'll start a war."

My heart started racing, my mind working overtime.

"It's fine. Aria has agreed to come back. Tell him." He shoved the phone in my face.

"Callum," I said, my voice shaky.

"I'm sorry, my little Astra." His voice was strained. "Do you know who she belongs to now? Fucking let her go."

"I don't fucking care who she thinks she belongs to. She's mine."

With that, he hung up.

"You can't replace me, Aria. I won't let you." He tilted his head, his eyes burning with rage. "You will always be mine." He reached out to touch my face.

I whacked his hand away. "Don't touch me," I shouted. "I love Sebastian. I always have and I always will."

He gripped my arms, and my skin crawled from his touch. I didn't want him anywhere near me. I kicked him in the chest, freeing myself from his hands, and bolted up—but he was quick, grabbing my waist and throwing me back on the mattress.

"I hate you! I HATE YOU! I hate EVERYTHING about you!"

He let out a laugh. "I don't care." I trembled as he tried to pull my lips to his.

"Get the fuck off me," I shrieked, hitting him away.

His fist met my eye socket, the pain unbearable, and I dry heaved. He grabbed my face and slammed the back of my head against the wall.

ET LUX IN TENEBRIS LUCET

53

SEBASTIAN

I stood in Hayden's study, pacing the room. The night had turned into day, and I still didn't have a clue where Aria was. Hayden was doing all he could, and he'd put the word out within the Organisation, but I felt completely useless. I didn't know where she was or if she was safe.

I had put her in that situation, and I would never forgive myself if something happened to her.

"Please tell me you have something," I whispered, looking at him.

"The system is still searching through the CCTV for facial recognition," he said, eyes fixed on the multiple screens in front of him.

With or without the facial recognition, it was Jason. I knew it in my bones.

"Thought you guys could do with some coffee." Serfina handed me a cup, then placed one on the desk next to Hayden.

I needed something stronger than coffee, but I had to keep a clear head to find Aria. She was all that I was focused on right now.

"Any news?" Serfina asked.

"Not yet," I replied quietly.

"Hayden will find her," she said, looking up at me.

I just hoped by the time he did, it wasn't too late.

"Wait," he said, eyes still fixed on the screens. "I think I've got something."

I rushed around to see the screens, Serfina behind me. My eyes darted around, trying to figure out where to look.

"This one." Hayden pointed at the left screen.

He played the CCTV. It was a camera I hadn't noticed before, across the street from Aria's flat. A black BMW pulled in and a man got out. Hayden paused it, zooming in on the face.

Sure enough, it was Jason.

I was going to burn everything in my way to get to her.

I'd make him bleed slowly, so he could feel every single little bit of pain he had put Aria through.

"Is … is that who I think it is?" Hayden said, pausing the footage.

I leaned over so I could see the screen better. Hayden slowly rewound it, then played it again slowly to show the man getting out of the passenger side.

Nicholas.

What the hell was he doing with Jason?

Fire raged through my veins, my fists clenching as my jaw clicked. I'd kill him for this.

"Run that number-plate. I need to make a call," I told Hayden, rushing from the study.

I found the number and dialled.

"Sebastian. To what do I owe the pleasure?" Soran asked.

"I need your services," I blurted, running my hand through my hair.

"Ah, is the house a mess?"

"It will be after they've finished partying," I told him.

"Let me know where they need to go, and I'll make sure they arrive on time," he replied. "Oh, and Sebastian? You know the price."

"Understood," I replied, cutting the call.

Nothing was for free in the Organisation. I knew I would owe Soran, but I didn't care; all that mattered was finding Aria and making the people who took her pay.

"Sebastian," Hayden called from his study. "We've got a location."

The forty-minute drive out of the city led us to an old stone manor house, situated next to Epping Woods. Hayden pulled up near the trees, concealing the vehicle as Logan and the men slowed behind. Stepping out to meet Logan, I grabbed my Glock from the holster, pulling back the slide slightly, checking the bullets in the chamber before allowing it to snap back.

"Is everyone ready?"

"Harry's getting into position. We'll have visuals in a minute, and he'll take out anyone we can't see. The rest are ready to go in the car, waiting for your signal."

"Nicholas isn't there. I've just hacked the CCTV. He left by himself about an hour ago." Hayden said, walking over to us.

"Fuck." My palm met the tinted window, though it did nothing to calm the anger I was forcing back down.

"Don't worry, I'll get Valon to pick him up. I'll be in the car, sorting the security system. Oh, and I've had word that Callum is on his way down."

I narrowed my brows at him. If Callum wanted to meet the grave like his brother, then so be it.

"Harry's confirmed he's ready with visuals." Logan held out an earpiece.

"I don't want it. I can't have anyone in my ear right now."

My mind was solely focused on Aria. I couldn't have any distractions, and these guys were my brothers; they knew me and how I operated.

Logan banged his hand on the car, alerting the other four men that we were ready. Kai, Zane, Rhys, and Luca stepped out, kitted up.

"We're with you, Sebastian," Rhys said.

I gave them a curt nod, a silent thank you. I owed them, but then I owed them for so much before. These were the type of men you wanted in a situation like this. Ones who knew how you operated, inside and out. Men who'd follow you to the end.

"We've got two guards on the gate. Four wandering the grounds. Two at the back and two at the front, and Harry can only see six in the house."

I tapped the car window to let Hayden know we were making our way out.

I melted into the darkness, the men falling behind as each step was silent, ready for impact. The rage shimmered beneath my skin, waiting to explode at the right moment. We approached the gate, the guards falling, pink mist bursting from their heads as Harry took down anyone in our way.

My movements were smooth, continuous. I never paused, curling my fingers around the gate and over with one push. All I could think about was getting to Aria. The men weren't far behind, scoping the place. My heart was racing, pumping adrenaline around my body. My warm breath hit the cold air, clouds forming.

They knew I had no fear of going out on my own.

I pulled my Glock from my holster, preparing to take down anyone in my way. I prowled along the stone drive, my footsteps placed with care.

Crunch.

I turned, pulling the trigger, the silencer blocking any sound as the guard fell to the ground.

Logan gestured for me to follow him into the house, and the rest continued securing the outside. He slowly opened the door as I stepped in, blending into the shadows, scanning around, my Glock ready to be used again.

Chatter came from the room, laughter following. Logan peered around. His fingers stated two, his hand gesturing where. We crept through, my arm tightening around one's neck from behind. The barrel landed on his temple. Logan was already taking out the second one.

"Where's Aria?" I hissed in his ear.

Another guard walked into the room.

He pulled his gun as I pushed Joey, sprinting for the counter, gunshots going off, bits flying everywhere. I slid down behind the counter, my heart pounding as I met Logan, who was already there. I gestured with my head, and he nodded. I made a run for it, bullets flying my way, inches from hitting my body. They stopped, bodies thudding to the floor. Logan had taken them both out.

"Harry said there are four more on the way, but he can't get a clean shot."

Gunshots echoed from outside, and we rushed out to see Kai and Luca taking two more out.

I didn't have time for this. I needed to find Aria. That burning rage fuelled my entire body as I faded from their view, back into the house.

I crept up the stairs, hiding in the shadows, checking the rooms, but no one was there.

"Sebastian, Harry took the last two out. Rhys and Zane have swept the perimeter, and there's no more."

My fist hit the wall, dynamite exploding through my body.

"Where the fuck is Aria?"

Logan pointed out the window.

An outbuilding.

I shot out of the room, bolting through the house, racing through the grounds as I charged at the door, breaking it down with all my force.

Jason stood there, his forearm tightly around Aria's neck, gun to her temple. I raised my Glock, pointing at him, eyes solely fixed on his. I couldn't look at her right now. If I did, I would break.

He smirked at me. "I've fucked her in ways you couldn't imagine." He ran his tongue up her cheek.

I gripped the Glock tighter, my finger twitching at the trigger, ready for him to move so I could blow his brains across the wall.

"She tastes like me; she smells like me. I've claimed her in the ways a woman should be claimed."

My eyes flickered to Aria's. Her moon eyes were eclipsed by darkness.

"I'll get you out of here. Just focus on me," I told her.

"I'll kill her before I let you have her," he growled.

I tilted my head, taking a small step closer. "Do you really think there is anywhere on this earth where I wouldn't find you? Every crack, every corner you try to hide … I will fucking hunt you down, and I will destroy you."

He pressed the barrel harder to her temple.

"Sebastian, I love you, no matter what happens. I always have and I always will," she said, her voice low and shaky, tears spilling down her face.

Jason covered her mouth with his hand, and I could hear her heavy breath against it. "Shut the fuck up," he roared.

She slammed her heel down on his instep, his hand jolting away from her mouth as she bit him. But before she could move, he grabbed her, smacking her across the face with such force that she fell to the boxes.

I didn't even see him charge at me, I was so fixed on her. My Glock slid across the floor as he pinned me down. I grabbed the barrel of his gun with my hands, pushing it to the side. Adrenaline surged through my veins like a storm breaking through my chest. With one full movement, I hit him clean in the head with mine, causing him to stumble back. I rose, smashing my left fist straight into his nose, and blood started to pour from it. I swung with my right, and the sound of cracking echoed from his jaw.

My eyes flicked over to Aria as I heard moans coming from her, her body shifting to sit up. Then, I felt the cold metal of a barrel pressing against my heart. My eyes locked onto Jason's, fire burning in his.

BANG!

Blood dripped from Jason's mouth, and he coughed, more splattering out. He fell to his knees, looking at his hand covered in crimson from the wound, before turning his head, eyes fixed in one spot. I glanced over.

Aria.

Her hand trembled, metal clacking, the gun still pointed. Her blonde hair was thick with dirt and wild, her grey eyes melting like silver burning in a furnace. Dust, mud, and dried blood were glued to her torn leggings. Her top barely covered her. And her face was covered in cuts, her lip swollen, her eyes red, sore, puffy. Bruises painted her cheeks.

It felt like I had been stabbed in my heart, unbearable pain wanting me to keel over as if the knife had broken, cutting me from the inside out as knots formed in my stomach, guilt seeping through my skin like I'd just downed a vial of poison. I may not have done this to her, but it was my fault she was here.

I held my hands up, slowly stepping towards her. "Nyx. It's me. Can you put the gun down?" My voice was calm, soft.

I reached her just as the gun began to dip, my hand closing over hers to steady it. She didn't resist when I took it from her; she barely seemed to register it at all. I secured it and turned back to her as her legs finally gave way.

I caught her before she hit the ground. Her body was trembling violently now, weight sagging into mine as the adrenaline drained out of her. She pressed her face into my chest, a broken sound tearing from her throat as the reality of it all crashed in.

I held her, one arm tight around her shoulders, the other bracing her as she shook. Her breathing was shallow and uneven, her whole body locked in shock. I didn't say a word. I just stayed there with her, keeping her upright, keeping her anchored, until the worst of it passed.

Then I blinked, and my own tears fell.

54
ARIA

“Nyx?” Sebastian said gently, looking at me from the driver seat. I slowly met his eyes. “Shall we go in?”

We’d been parked outside Sebastian’s house for a while now.

I hadn’t wanted to go back to my flat, to where Jason had taken me.

I looked back at the house, staring at it for a few more seconds, then forced myself to move.

Sebastian opened the front door, and I stepped through into the hall. The door clicked shut, and I jumped at the sound.

“I’m sorry,” Sebastian whispered, looking at me. “Let’s get you upstairs.”

I was tired, exhausted.

Numb.

Once we were in Sebastian’s bedroom, I sank down on the edge of his bed, fingers fiddling with the sleeve of the zip hoodie I had on.

"Why don't I run you a bath?" Sebastian offered.

I watched as he made his way into the en suite, disappearing from view.

I didn't know how I was meant to feel right now. I thought I'd be screaming, crying, but I wasn't. My mind was just … blank.

"Nyx, it's ready," Sebastian said, placing his warm hand on mine.

I hadn't noticed him reappear.

"Go get in. I'll bring you some clothes and a towel."

I slowly stood up, making my way into the en suite. It felt like it took forever, but I eventually managed to remove my clothes. My eyes caught my reflection in the mirror.

My thighs looked as if a violent storm of purples and midnight blues had raged over them, leaving devastation behind. Patches of dried blood from cuts and scratches trailed down my legs. My stomach swirled, a mixture of acid and bile trying to rise as I retched, images burning deep behind my eyes as if they were a projector playing out a film.

I reached for the corner of my lip, wincing at the sharp sting. Crimson red now turned to flakes of rust, as if oxidation had taken place. The deep plum and blues covered my cheeks like bruised fruit.

My body shuddered, goose bumps pricking my skin, as if I were being stabbed with needles.

I needed it gone.

All of it.

I climbed into the bath, fully submerging myself, hoping it would all end—

And then gasped for air as I pulled myself back up. My skin felt like he was crawling beneath it, suffocating me from the inside, torturing my soul with his shadow, consuming any light that tried to escape.

I scrubbed.

It wasn't working; I could still feel his touch on me.

My nails dug into my arm, scraping, drawing blood to bleed him out.

"Nyx, what are you doing?" I heard Sebastian's voice as he grabbed my hand.

He climbed into the bath, fully clothed.

"I need to get him off me," I said frantically, scratching at my other arm, breaking the skin there, too.

"Nyx." He gently took my hand, stopping me.

I felt dirty.

"Nyx, look at me."

My eyes met his, and he wrapped his arms around my body, pulling me in.

I hit his chest with my hands, trying to push him away. "Sebastian, please," I begged.

"Shh, Nyx," he whispered.

I carried on hitting his chest, kicking my legs, trying to free myself. The water splashed over the tub, like waves crashing in the ocean.

"Please," I cried, my hands slowly stopping.

Then his fresh citrus aftershave hit me.

My beacon through the darkness. For an instant, I was seventeen, back in Harrods Salon de Parfums whilst they designed it, helping him to choose the very scent that anchored me back into his reality.

My head crashed into his chest, my arms wrapping around him as he pulled me tighter into him, his heart beating fast against my ear.

I broke.

Tears flooded my eyes like a dam shattering, unable to stop the destruction flowing through. My body shook with each breath, my lungs trying to keep up. My cries were raw, filled with pain, memories, hurt, shame, everything I had kept down to survive.

Sebastian stroked my hair, resting his head on mine. "I'm here, Nyx."

Of course he was.

He had always been there.

ET LUX IN TENEBRIS LUCET

55

SEBASTIAN

I leaned against the house wall, sheltered from the rain, and pulled a cigarette packet and lighter out of my pocket. I didn't smoke a lot anymore, but today, I needed to.

I took a drag and exhaled the smoke, watching it float away in the rain. I rubbed my face with my hand, running it through my hair.

Aria hadn't slept much last night, which was to be expected after everything that had happened.

I didn't sleep, either. I'd just held her, watching over her, trying to keep her safe from everything she was feeling. I felt useless, like I wasn't doing enough for her. I didn't know how to fix it.

All I knew was that she needed time to heal—and I'd be there through it all with her, every step of the way.

"Hey."

I turned to face Aria, standing by the open patio door.

"Haven't seen you smoke in a while," she said.

"You caught me." I smiled, looking up at her.

She pulled her hood up as she walked over to me, even though the rain couldn't reach us here. Maybe she was just trying to hide the bruise on her cheek that I already knew was there. I stubbed the cigarette out in the ashtray on the table, then wrapped her up in my arms.

"How did you know where I was? Who were all those people with you?"

She looked like she had a hundred questions rolling around her mind.

"I'll explain everything, I promise, but I just want you to heal first."

She nodded, resting her head into my chest.

"I need to head out for a bit," I finally said.

Her arms tightened around me. I knew I shouldn't leave her, but I had to deal with Nicholas.

"How long will you be?" Her voice was barely a whisper against my shirt.

"Not long, I promise," I replied. "Serfina is going to come and stay with you whilst I'm gone."

Nicholas was going to pay for everything he had done. He'd be begging me to kill him by the end of it, but I wasn't going to make it quick.

I'd been in this particular warehouse many times before, but this time was different, the air thick. I paused at the door the man who betrayed me was behind. I heard footsteps and turned to face Hayden.

"Everything's ready for you," Hayden said.

"And Soran?"

"He's ready to send his men in when you've finished."

I took a deep breath, opening the door and walking through into the dimly lit space. A small table was set at the side, a few instruments scattered on it, and some other items. The room wasn't big; it didn't need to be. You didn't need much space to hurt a man.

To *kill* a man.

Nicholas was rigged up on a chain-through-hoop system. His wrists were bound high above his head, his feet inches from the floor. The chain was attached to a fixture on the wall to raise or lower him at any moment. His face was calm, as if he'd never seen me destroy a man before.

"Well, if it isn't the great Sebastian Knight. Thought you didn't get your hands dirty anymore?"

It had been a while since I'd tortured a man. I was sure it was just like riding a bike, something you never forgot. Either way, the end would be the same.

"How's Aria? I heard she got into a bit of bother." His laugh was laced with venom.

My fist was tightly clenched, my teeth digging into my bottom lip, as I tried to control that fire burning beneath my skin.

"Don't fucking speak her name," I hissed.

"Someone's touchy today."

I cracked my knuckles, preparing to fully unleash the man who had been clawing to get out. I lowered the chain, then dragged him by his tied wrists over to the water barrel.

"Oh, please, Sebastian, you think that's going to bother me?"

I grabbed his collar and punched him in his lower abdomen. He let out a cough mixed with a laugh. No, it probably wasn't going to bother him, but I'd enjoy watching him suffer.

I grabbed the back of his neck, shoving his face deep in the water, holding it tight. It didn't take long before his hands were scrabbling at the rim of the barrel. Muffled sounds came from under the water, air bubbles coming fast from his mouth.

"Sorry, Nicholas. I can't hear you."

A few more muffled sounds came, almost a scream.

"What? Deeper?" I pushed his head in further.

His hands started banging the barrel, so I pulled him back up. He gasped, trying to take in as much oxygen as possible.

"You want to go again?"

I dunked him straight back in, applying more pressure to his neck this time.

"Fuck you, Sebastian," he shouted, coughing up water after I pulled him back up again.

I chuckled.

"You know this is all your fault?"

I punched his nose, blood spilling, causing him to stumble back slightly.

He spat out blood. "If she weren't with you that night at the business event, I wouldn't have even known about her." He laughed, poison running through every word. "It was the perfect opportunity to destroy you. Fucking stupid rich boy."

He'd just lit the match and thrown it on petrol, engulfing everything within me.

I grabbed the chain, pulling him over to the chair and wrapping it around him, tightening it around his thighs to pin his hands against them, palms up.

Two scalpels in hand, I approached Nicholas again. Anger boiled beneath my skin as a smirk crawled across his face.

"I heard she begged him for it."

I drove one straight into his left palm, pushing it deep and down into his thigh. He jumped, nostrils flaring as he tried to breathe through the pain.

He let out another small laugh between his breaths. "Even when you touch her, she'll still feel him all over her."

I pressed the second scalpel gently into his other palm. He looked down at it and then back at me. He was trying to hide it, but I could see in his eyes he was scared of what I was going to do. I fixed my eyes on his and started to slowly push it through his palm. He panted through the pain, trying not to cry out. Sweat fell from his forehead, and his cheeks flushed with the struggle.

When I was done, I walked back over to the table, picked up a glass, and made my way back to him. I placed it on the ground and stamped on it, glass crunching under my shoe. I twisted my foot, grinding it into smaller pieces, before crouching and carefully picking up a small handful, watching it glisten in the palm of my hand like the sun hitting ice.

"Open your mouth."

"Fuck you."

I rammed my palm against his mouth, forcing the shards into it and holding my hands over his mouth and nose. "Swallow."

His head jolted from side to side, trying to remove my hands, but it was no use. I felt him gulp as I released my hands.

He gasped, coughing up blood onto the floor. I grabbed some more shards, forcing them again to his mouth.

"It's been a while since I've done this to a man, but I'm glad it's you," I hissed in his ear.

I made my way back to the table and poured myself a whisky before dragging the chair across the floor and sitting in front of him. I rested my ankle on my knee, my eyes fixed on his as I took a sip of that amber liquid.

Nicholas started to gag, sputtering blood out of his mouth, I watched it run down his chin and drip to the floor.

"That's just the glass that's sliced the insides of your mouth, cutting up your tonsils as you swallowed it down. There are probably some bits lodged in there, too."

I watched his Adam's apple move as his tried to swallow again.

I let out a silent laugh. "I wouldn't do that if I were you. It might make it worse." I took another sip of my whisky.

More blood poured out of his mouth as his body started to tremble, gurgling wet sounds trying to escape his throat as he took in shallow, raspy breaths.

"This is for everything you did to Aria. The last thought you'll have is that this 'little rich boy' won."

56

ARIA

It had been thirteen days.

With each one that passed, the bruises faded a little more—but I could still feel the scars inside.

Sebastian had taken time out of the business to stay and look after me. I hadn't left his house since that first day, but Serfina and Hayden had been over a lot.

I still couldn't face going back to my flat. Sebastian and Hayden had gone there for me and got all my things, then had someone clear it out to give back to the landlord. Sebastian had paid all the rent up on it and refused to let me pay him back.

I needed to find somewhere to live, but at the moment, I felt safer here. I didn't think he minded too much.

"Do we have to stay in this room much longer? I'm starving," Sebastian whined.

Today was 18th November—Sebastian's birthday.

He was never one to celebrate. The two years we lived together, I always made sure we did something, even if he didn't want to.

"Stop moaning." I chuckled. "I guess I could give you a distraction."

I leaned over to the bedside drawer, opening it and taking out a small gift box.

"What's that?" he asked, sitting up and taking it from my hand.

He slowly lifted the lid off, and his eyes lit up.

It wasn't much—a simple, silver crescent moon keyring.

He pulled it out by the ring, and it swayed slightly in the open air.

"Nyx," he said, looking at me. "It's the best gift I've ever been given." He leaned forward and kissed my lips softly.

"Happy birthday," I said, smiling at him. "It's like having a piece of me wherever you go."

"I've always got you with me. In my heart."

I loved this man with every part of me. He truly was everything I wanted and needed. He'd saved me and protected me and stayed with me after it all. He didn't look at me any differently because of what had happened; he looked at me the way he always did, with those piercing blue eyes filled with love.

My phone buzzed with a message. It was Serfina, telling me they were ready downstairs.

"Right," I said, climbing off the bed.

I walked to his drawer where he kept his ties and pulled one out. I turned around and held it up to him.

"You need to use this," I said, smiling.

He raised a brow. "Nyx, if you wanted to start using my ties, you only had to ask."

I playfully hit him with it. "Not like that. I need to cover your eyes."

"I don't like to walk into things I can't see."

"Hush, and do as you're told."

"Anything for you," he said, getting off the bed and kissing my forehead, then turning around.

I covered his eyes, guiding him out of the room and down the stairs, meeting Serfina and Hayden, who were trying to stay quiet.

"Can I take this off now?" he asked, squeezing my hand.

"Yes," I replied, rolling my eyes.

He slowly pulled the tie off.

"Surprise!" Serfina squealed, doing jazz hands.

He chuckled, and Hayden pulled him into a bro hug.

"Happy birthday, mate. You're officially old," he said, pulling away.

"If I'm old, so are you," Sebastian shot back.

Serfina kissed him on the cheek. "Happy birthday."

He turned to face me, wrapping his arms around my waist. "You didn't have to do all of this."

I glanced over at the table filled with the food Hayden had been cooking all day, with the help of Jane, whilst I kept Sebastian upstairs. It smelt amazing, and I couldn't wait to eat some of that mac and cheese. In fact, I couldn't wait to eat all of it.

Luckily, Serfina had been in charge of the decorations and not the food. She'd done an amazing job putting it all together. Thin, glass bottles containing blue fairy lights were scattered over the table. A silver, white and midnight-blue backdrop with "happy birthday" written on it sat neatly behind everything, and balloons elegantly decorated the room, which were also filled with blue fairy lights. It reminded me of a night sky filled with stars.

"I know you don't like to celebrate your birthday, but every year we're together, we're doing something, whether you like it or not," I said, kissing his lips.

"Is that carrot cake?" he asked.

I smiled at him. "Yes, I made it when you were out yesterday."

"Thank you," he whispered.

Carrot cake was Sebastian's favourite—but without the sultanas. He hated them. It was something I'd make when we lived together before.

"Ok, stop with soppy stuff." Hayden laughed. "I'm starving."

"Me too," Sebastian said, joining him at the table.

Serfina walked over to me, wrapping her arm around my waist and pulling me in. "We've got some pretty special men there."

I looked over to them. Hayden was pushing Sebastian out of the way to get food. I shook my head, laughing. Yes, they were pretty special. They were the complete opposite in every way, but it worked. Hayden helped ground Sebastian. He was family to him and had been since they met all those years ago.

I let my gaze linger on Sebastian. He had been my rock through these last thirteen days, and I didn't think I would have got through them without him.

I had a long way to go, but with him by my side, I knew I would make it.

ET LUX IN TENEBRIS LUCET

57

SEBASTIAN

It was the middle of December, and the board thought it would be a good idea to meet before Christmas. Sometimes I wondered how these stuffy old suits managed to get out of bed in the morning and make it here. I sat there, trying to look interested—until Mr Kingsley mentioned something that caught my attention.

"What's this?" I asked, sitting forward in my chair.

He turned to face me. "We've appointed a new COO to work under you."

"Why? You haven't needed one before."

"What with your recent time off—"

I cut him off before he could finish.

"That was due to personal reasons."

"Yes, well, personal or not, we have made the decision," he told me firmly. "And the majority shareholder has put it in place."

I blinked. The majority shareholder was my dad, and he'd fucked off to Europe. This couldn't be right.

"Mr Kingsley, I think you are mistaken. There's not a fucking chance the majority shareholder has agreed this."

"Oh, but he has, and you would do well to fall into line."

The side of my fist met the table, drawing everyone's eyes to me.

"Now, Mr Caspian Whitmore will be starting with us next month," he said. "Jessica, please can you show him in?"

I leaned back in my chair, glaring at the man who walked through the door. His dark brown hair was neatly styled back, his blue eyes staring straight at me as he strutted into the boardroom like he owned the place. He looked a few years older than me. He straightened his suit, then greeted everyone. Who did this guy think he was?

"Sebastian, Caspian will be working under you. I expect you to show him the ropes," Mr Kingsley said, looking at me.

"Sure," I replied stiffly.

"Now, let's show you around so you can get familiar with everything before you start."

Everyone got up, and I soon followed. I started shaking everyone's hands, my smile fake, as they filed out.

"I'll see you around, Sebastian." Caspian flashed me a smile, then let go of my hand.

After work, I found myself back at the place I felt most at home. The Organisation was running smoothly again, and they had already found someone to replace Nicholas. A guy called Micah. He had a chain of barber shops around London, some legit and some that ran the money through. Hayden had made sure he didn't work for anyone else before inviting him in.

I walked through into the main room of the Organisation, where Soran sat at the table alone, sipping his Kurdish tea.

"Ah, Sebastian. Come sit." It wasn't a request.

I did as asked, the tea and sugar already laid out for me.

"Has everything been sorted?" I asked.

"Yes, everything is clean. Nothing can be traced," he replied, sipping his tea. "Don't forget the price, Sebastian."

I nodded. "Soon. I have a couple of loose ends to tie up first."

I stopped in the doorway, leaning against the door-frame. Aria was decorating the Christmas tree I'd told her I didn't want, but she'd still managed to make us go and get one. The lights were already on, twinkling around it. She was adding silver and blue baubles, pausing frequently and tilting her head, considering where to place each one.

It was nice seeing her like this, being up and about, doing things.

I knew she'd still need time, but it was the small things. It made me confident she'd get through this.

She turned around, jumping slightly when she clocked me standing there. I pushed myself off the frame and walked into the living room.

"Sorry, Nyx. I didn't mean to scare you."

"No, it's fine." She smiled at me.

"I've got a surprise for you."

"A surprise?" she replied, raising her brow at me. "What kind of surprise?"

"I know you don't get to see your mum much, since she moved to New York. So I bought us tickets to spend a couple of weeks with her for Christmas," I said, smiling at her.

"You bought tickets for us to fly to New York, to spend Christmas with my mum?" she repeated, trying to grasp what I had just said.

"Yes," I replied, putting my arms around her waist.

"Does she know we're coming?" she asked.

"I spoke to her the other day to arrange it. Everything is sorted," I reassured her.

"Sebastian, I don't know what to say ..."

"Well, you don't need to finish decorating that tree." I chuckled.

She playfully hit my chest and leaned in, kissing me softly.

"You're the best." She smiled. "Hold on, wait ... my mum knows about us?"

"Yeah, kind of had to tell her when I called her."

"Was she ok about it?"

"Absolute fine. She said she was waiting for it. Go and get packed. We're leaving tonight."

"Tonight? I don't even know where my passport is," she replied, pulling away from me.

"It's all under control," I said. "All you need to do is pack a suitcase."

Aria's stepdad, James, had arranged for one of his private cars to collect us from the airport and bring us to the house. He was a successful lawyer who worked with high-end clients. Aria always spoke highly of him and said he made her mum happy, so he was certainly a step up from my dad.

I helped Aria out of the car as she stood there excitedly, watching the snow falling. The driver placed our suitcases by the front door before driving off.

The house must have been about four storeys high. The exterior walls were a reddish-brown stone colour, and the front door was decorated with a Christmas wreath.

She took a deep breath before ringing the bell.

It had been a good few years since she'd seen her mum, and she probably felt a little overwhelmed. Maria didn't know what Jason had done to her, and she wanted to keep it that way.

The door opened to a man with a wide smile on his face. His light brown eyes lit up as he saw us. He ran his hand through his dark brown hair, a few grey strands showing through.

"Aria, it's so wonderful to finally meet you in person," he said, hugging her.

"And you, James," she replied, pulling away.

"You must be Sebastian," he said, holding his hand out. I took hold of it and shook it.

"Let me help you with those," he said, taking one of the suitcases. "Come in, it's cold outside." He gestured for us to follow him.

Aria walked in first, and I followed, shutting the door. We walked into a grand entryway that felt warm and inviting, filled with Christmas decorations and the smell of something baking.

"Just leave the suitcases by the stairs. I'll have Martin take them up for you," James said.

He then led us to the kitchen out the back, where Maria was cooking. Her dark blonde hair was tied back in a bun, and her blue eyes filled with joy at seeing our faces. She stopped doing what she was doing and ran straight over to Aria.

"Aria, I missed you," she said, hugging her tight.

"Missed you too, Mum," she replied, pulling away, smiling.

Maria turned to face me. "Sebastian, it's always so good to see you," she said, pulling me into a hug.

Maria was a good mum to Aria. She was also good to me when she was married to my dad. She'd never tried to be my mum. I was twenty when she'd first met me, so she knew that wasn't what I wanted, but she was always warm. Kind.

"What are you making?" Aria asked, walking around the counter to take a peek.

"Just some cookies," Maria replied. "You two must be knackered after your flight. Why don't you go and get some rest?"

Aria hugged her one last time, and James gestured for us to follow him to our room on the top floor.

He opened the door to a big room with a cosy bed and a window nook. Everything felt warm and homely, as expected from Aria's mum. James said his goodbyes and closed the door, and I wrapped my arms around Aria's waist, pulling her close and kissing her.

58

ARIA

"There's no way you're getting me in those."

I stood in the bedroom, holding up a pair of matching Grinch pyjamas, as Sebastian shook his head. It was a tradition I used to do with my mum every Christmas Eve.

"They're perfect for you, Mr Grinch."

"I'm not a grinch; I just don't do Christmas," he replied, taking them from my hands and throwing them on the bed.

"Well," I said, wrapping my arms around his neck. "I think we need to change that."

"Oh, do we?" he said, leaning in to kiss me.

We were in a really good place, and it seemed to be getting better every day. We'd been together six months now, and even through the ups and downs, I wouldn't change that time with him.

"Now," I said, placing my hand on his chest. "Get them on so we can go downstairs and watch movies and drink hot chocolate."

He hung his head in disbelief that he was going to do as he was told, giving up way too easily. I already had mine on, ready to go; I was just waiting on him. I sat on the edge of the bed as he removed his T-shirt. He looked over at me, smiling, then caged me in with his arms, leaning in to softly kiss my lips. I placed my hands on the back of his neck, moving my fingers up to knot in his hair.

We hadn't been intimate since everything happened with Jason. I hadn't felt ready, and Sebastian never pushed. He allowed me the time and space I needed to heal. Being here with him made me realise how much I wanted to be with him like that again.

He pulled his lips away, resting his forehead on mine. "You have no idea how much I love you, Nyx," he whispered.

My heart skipped a beat, butterflies flying around in my stomach.

"I love you, too, Sebastian," I replied softly, pushing my lips back onto his.

"You'd better stop kissing me, or I won't be able to get those pyjamas on."

Sebastian held my hand as we walked down the stairs, making our way into the living room. James and Mum were sitting on the sofa. The table was filled with hot chocolates and cookies. The fire crackled with burning embers, filling the room with warmth.

"I see you were forced to wear the Grinch pyjamas too, Sebastian," James chuckled, showing off his own.

"Yeah, didn't really get a choice." He laughed, squeezing my hand.

"Must be something about the Summers women."

"Stop it," Mum replied, playfully tapping him.

I sat down on the other sofa with Sebastian, getting comfortable.

"What are you up to these days, Sebastian?" Mum asked him.

"Currently, I'm CEO of my dad's company."

"I'm surprised he gave it up," Mum said, a little shocked.

"It wasn't by choice," Sebastian explained.

"You're quite young to be a CEO. How are you finding it?" James asked.

"It's not without its ups and downs, but I've managed to fix what my dad broke."

"Sebastian's dad wasn't really around when he was growing up," Mum told James.

I could feel Sebastian's body tensing, so I took hold of his hand and gently squeezed it. He hated talking about his childhood and anything to do with his dad.

"What film are we watching?" I asked, changing the subject.

"Oh, erm … *Scrooged*," Mum replied, picking up the control and pressing play.

I looked up at Sebastian, meeting his eyes and smiling at him. He leaned down, kissing my head, and pulled me closer to snuggle up on the sofa.

I woke up the next morning in Sebastian's arms in bed, the blankets snuggled around us. I shifted and watched the snow falling outside the window. It was amazing to see a white Christmas, something that rarely happened in England now.

It was the freshly laid fluffy snow I loved. I liked catching the snowflakes in my hand and looking at them to see what pattern they were.

I felt Sebastian moving next to me, his arm wrapping around my body, pulling me back to him. His lips rested on my neck, his warm breath lighting my skin on fire. I turned over to face him, lying on my side. He looked so handsome when he slept.

He looked handsome all the time.

Sometimes, I couldn't believe he was all mine; he could have anyone he wanted, but he'd chosen me.

"Are you going to stare at me all morning?" he teased, opening an eye to look at me. "Not that I'm complaining."

"How do you even know I'm looking at you?" I laughed.

"I just know," he replied, kissing my lips.

Looking into Sebastian's beautiful blue eyes, I tucked the loose bits of his hair back and then leaned in to kiss him. This was it. I finally felt free of everything I had endured over the last few months. Those dark scars deep within that were once raw had fully healed, blossoming into light. I was ready to fully be with him again after everything. I sat up, lifting my top off. He looked up at me.

"Nyx, are you sure?"

"Yes," I whispered, running my hands under his shirt and lifting it off his head.

He sat up, placing his hands on my jaw, his thumbs grazing over my cheeks, and gazed into my eyes.

"I'll be gentle, I promise," he whispered.

His words took me back to four years ago, when he should have been my first. And somehow, it felt like he was going to be this time.

"I trust you," I whispered back, then met his lips with mine.

The kiss was everything. It was intimate, desperate, and passionate all mixed into one, and my body melted for him. He gently turned me onto my back, his fingers tracing down my skin, sending my nerves into overload. He respected every inch of my body. His fingers reached my lace knickers, and his eyes flickered to mine. I nodded, giving him permission, and gasped as they glided over my wet pussy.

His other hand moved the hair from my face, and he looked into my eyes. "If you want me to stop, tell me."

"No, I don't want you to." My breathing was heavy.

He looked into my eyes a little longer, then gently met my lips. He pushed two fingers in, my back arching from the pressure. My core was burning, melting, flooding my veins with pure pleasure. Our kisses dulled my whimpers as he slowly moved his fingers in and out.

My arms were tightly wrapped around his neck as he withdrew his fingers, licking me off them.

"You'll always be my Nyx," he whispered.

I loved this man with every fibre in my body. He shifted, removing his clothes, and settled in between my legs.

He stroked his length, his eyes on mine as I nodded again, wordlessly telling him he could continue. He slowly started inching himself into me, my breath catching, my body igniting all at once. I wanted all of him.

"Are you ok?"

I nodded, wrapping my arms around his neck again, pulling his body onto mine. I wanted to feel his warmth all over me, to seep down into every part of my soul. His motions were slow and careful; he took his time, listening to my body.

My heart was racing against his. My nerves were sparking, ready to ignite, then they lit everything on fire, my orgasm hitting me like never before. My body trembled, going into full meltdown as stars covered my eyes, our kisses not allowing anything to escape. I felt his body jerk against mine.

"Fuck, Nyx." A low growl fell from his lips.

He released everything into me with one last push. His breathing was shallow against mine, and he gazed into my eyes, stroking the hair from my face.

"I love you more than anything," he whispered.

"I love you, too."

I could feel every part of him over my skin, that spark between us running through me. That deep connection we shared as one. I was all his, and he was all mine.

ET LUX IN TENEBRIS LUCET

59

SEBASTIAN

I hadn't celebrated Christmas for a long time—not since my mum had died.

The two years Maria and Aria had lived with us, they'd spent them with family in Kent because my dad wasn't about. Maria had invited me both times, but I'd never wanted to go and pretend it was a happy holiday.

In my house, it was just another day, nothing special. There wasn't even a Christmas tree.

My dad would buy me some expensive gift that I never wanted, but he wasn't ever there to give it to me. It was usually the nanny I had at the time, and when I got older and didn't need one, it was Clive, the groundsman. Even he was more of a father figure than mine ever was.

No—I didn't care about Christmas. I was doing all of this for Aria, because she did.

I leaned on the door-frame to the kitchen, smiling, watching Aria cooking with her mum. She looked so happy, laughing and joking with her.

I felt a hand on my shoulder and turned to see James smiling. "They look happy."

"Yeah, they do."

The doorbell rang. "That'll probably be my daughter," James said, then turned and walked towards the door.

Aria looked up, smiling at me. I walked further into the kitchen, kissing her on the forehead as I reached her. She was peeling potatoes, and her mum was making coffee for everyone.

"Here you go, Sebastian," Maria said, handing me a cup.

"Thank you," I replied, taking it.

"Are you ok?" Aria asked me quietly.

"Yeah, I'm fine." I smiled.

Aria knew it wasn't easy for me being around people at Christmas because of how mine was, and I was trying to get into the Christmas spirit, but I think she could tell I felt uncomfortable at times.

"Aria, Sebastian," James said, as we looked up at him. "This is my daughter, Claire, and her husband, Mason."

A little girl, around five years old with big brown curls bouncing as she ran, was being chased by a young boy, maybe a year older, through the kitchen into the back garden.

"Excuse them—they were excited to play in the snow." Claire laughed. "You must be Aria," she said, walking over and hugging her. "It's so nice to finally meet you."

She turned around to face me as I took a sip of coffee. "You must be the stepbrother turned boyfriend."

I nearly choked on my coffee.

"I can see why." She smiled at Aria. "He's quite handsome. I'd probably have done the same."

"Please excuse my wife; she has no filter," Mason said, his voice fully apologetic.

Aria's cheeks flushed, and her eyes darted off to her mum, who mouthed an apology.

"No worries at all," I told Mason, extending my hand, and he shook it.

I took hold of Aria's hand, squeezing softly so she knew I was there if she needed me. If we had never been stepsiblings, I would never have met the kindest, most beautiful woman I now called mine. I didn't feel ashamed; that was how we'd met, and I wouldn't change it for the world.

"And this is my son, Jackson," James said. "He works with me in my law firm."

Jackson was nearly as tall as me, his dark hair falling over his almost-black eyes. He was dressed sharply in a shirt and trousers.

Jackson took a step forward, extending his hand to Aria. "It's so nice to finally meet you. I've heard so much about you."

"My mum's told me a lot about you, too."

My hand slid around her waist, pulling her back to me as I glared at him, giving him the universal look of "hands off." He must have understood, because he diverted his gaze and walked away. I smiled to myself. This Christmas was going to be a day to remember.

We hadn't long finished having dinner, and Aria was in the garden, making a snowman with the kids. Jackson had joined her, playing with his niece and nephew. I rested my arms on the decking rail, looking out in the garden, my eyes fixed on her. She would make a good mum one day. Kids were never something I could imagine in my future with the way I was brought up, but seeing Aria like this … maybe I could with her.

"She seems really happy with you, Sebastian," Maria said, resting her arms on the decking rail next to me.

Was Aria truly happy with me after everything that had happened? If it weren't for me, Nicholas wouldn't have used her as a pawn in his sick power play.

"I hope you'll look after her and keep her safe for me," she added.

"I will."

I would burn the whole world if it meant keeping Aria safe. I would do everything in my power to make sure no one ever hurt her again.

Aria jogged over to me. "I'm freezing; I need to warm up."

I wrapped my arms around her. "I'll take you upstairs."

Aria sat on the bed, texting Serfina. She was probably keeping Aria updated with the latest gossip. This woman was truly amazing, after everything she had been through. She managed to have so much warmth and made time for people, even though she was still healing.

I put my hand in my jacket pocket, which lay on the chair, and pulled out a black velvet box.

I hadn't wanted to give it to her in front of everyone.

"Nyx," I said gently, sitting on the bed next to her.

"Yeah," she replied, placing her phone down.

"I got you something."

She narrowed her eyes at me, looking confused. She took the box from my hands and opened it. Her eyes lit up at the platinum chain decorated with a crescent moon pendant, dotted with moonstones that shimmered blues and greys in the light. A butterfly pendant sat next to it, encrusted with pink, purple, and clear diamonds. She was my Nyx, that moon that lit the night sky from darkness. She was that light to me. The butterfly? Well, it was beautiful and free—just like she was.

"Sebastian," she whispered, touching the necklace, then looking up at me. "This is beautiful."

I took it from the box as she held her hair up, and I softly placed it around her neck, clipping the clasp shut. Her hair slowly fell back down as I wrapped my arms around her, tracing my lips over her neck.

"You will always be my Nyx. I love you," I whispered.

"Whose idea was it to get ice cream in this weather?" Aria said as we sat on a bench at Central Park in the bitter cold.

"Yours," I replied, dabbing some on her nose.

Her mouth opened in mock outrage.

I threw the rest of mine in the bin, then placed my hands on her cheeks, kissing the ice cream from the tip of her nose.

And I knew in that moment that I needed to be honest with her about everything. I couldn't keep it a secret anymore.

About who I was and who I had always been. I swallowed hard. What if she couldn't accept it?

"Nyx, I need to tell you something."

She looked at me, confusion in her eyes.

"Sebastian, you're scaring me. What is it?" Her voice was a little shaky.

I took her hand and held it tight. "You know I was involved with underground fighting when we were younger?"

She nodded.

"Well, it was kind of a bit more than that."

She studied my eyes for a few seconds. "Ok." She squeezed my hand.

My heart was pounding, trying to break free from its cage. My palms felt sweaty, and I was surprised Aria hadn't noticed.

"Part of the reason I left four years ago was because I was involved with an underground crime ring. When my granddad died, I went to a place darker than I had been. Then you came along. This light in the darkness. You still are. I didn't want you to be involved in it. You calmed the chaos in me. I wanted to protect you from it all." I took hold of her other hand, and my eyes flickered to them. "You deserved so much more back then. Even now, Nyx, sometimes I wonder why you'd ever be with a man like me."

The silence was deafening, and it felt like an eternity before she spoke.

"Was that how you found me?"

I nodded tightly.

"And the other people?"

"Logan and the guys worked with me. They're loyal. Never left my side."

"And Nicholas?"

"I got rid of him for what he did to you. He had to pay for that."

There was more silence for a moment.

"I … I'm glad, in a way. Otherwise I think I'd always be looking over my shoulder."

"I never thought I could love anyone but you, Nyx. You have my heart. It belongs to you."

She leaned in, kissing my lips. "I love you, Sebastian Knight. I always will."

I walked into the bedroom, placing a coffee for Aria down before we started packing for our flight back to London tomorrow.

"What are you doing?" I asked, watching her look through her phone.

"Looking for somewhere to live," she replied, her eyes still on the screen.

But why?

She lived with me.

Didn't she?

I shifted on the bed, clearing my throat awkwardly. "Don't you want to live with me?"

She looked up from her phone. "I'm sure you don't want me in your space forever."

"I always want you in my space. I don't want you anywhere else. Stay."

"What, like … properly move in?"

"Yes," I told her, smiling.

"Are you sure?" she asked, excitement running through her voice.

"Of course. I thought you already had," I admitted.

She wrapped her arms around my neck, and I placed mine around her waist. I couldn't help but smile. She seemed so happy. I didn't want her anywhere else but with me. She was this bright spark running through me, setting everything alight. I never wanted it to go out.

I looked over at my phone lighting up on the bedside table.

Seven missed call notifications.

It was my dad.

The screen lit up again with his number flashing. I clicked the side button and placed it back on the table. I didn't want to talk to him. I didn't care what he wanted; he wasn't going to ruin this moment.

Aria lay asleep on my chest as I stroked her hair. The nightmares she had been having had stopped since we'd been here, and she finally looked peaceful in her sleep again.

My Nyx.

My little light in the dark.

This woman was amazing and powerful. Everything we had been through in the last seven months had led us to where we were now.

And this was only the beginning for us.

EPILOGUE
STEPHEN

I felt the warm sea breeze hit me as I walked out to the pool. I bought this place in Marbella a few years ago to get away from the city life.

I pulled my phone out of my trouser pocket, dialling Sebastian's number again. It rang before cutting out.

That ungrateful son of mine.

I'd spent years putting him through the most prestigious education, buying him expensive gifts for his birthdays. This was how he repaid me?

I made my way over to my wife, Monica, who was sunbathing on the loungers by the pool. I handed her the glass of wine and she smiled at me, taking a sip. My eyes drifted from her long, tanned legs, the bikini bottoms hardly covering that curvy bum of hers, then meeting those perfectly perky breasts that were on show, soaking up all the sun.

I watched her place the wine glass down on the table, her bright red lipstick staining the rim, and sat down on the lounger next to her.

"Did you manage to get hold of your son?" she asked, pulling her sunglasses down to meet my eyes.

"No. He's not taking my calls," I replied, trying to hide my frustration, picking up the newspaper on the table.

"I guess our next stop is London, then."

This is only the beginning for Aria and Sebastian. Find out what happens next in book 2 of The Till Forever Series.

To keep up to date with their story and all other news, you can follow me on social media

@donnarichardsauthor
www.donna-richards.com

Scan the QR code for all the links